The characters and events portrayed in this book are fictitious. Any resemblance to actual persons, living or dead, is entirely coincidental. Victoria Connelly asserts the moral right to be identified as the author of this work.

Cover design by J D Smith.

Published by Cuthland Press.

ISBN: 978-1-910522-01-1

To my lovely fellow authors at Notting Hill Press: Matt Dunn, Michelle Gorman, Belinda Jones, Chris Manby, Lucy Robinson, Talli Roland, Ruth Saberton, Nick Spalding and Sue Welfare.

I love working with you all!

ACKNOWLEDGEMENTS

Many thanks to Liz Bailey, Jane Gordon-Cumming, Catherine Czerkawska, Jan Shepherd, Sue Moorcroft, and the late Pam Cleaver for inside information on collecting, collections and collectors.

To Jennifer Rowley and Jane Birdsall at Snowshill Manor for the wonderful tour and for answering all my questions. And to my husband, Roy, for taking me there.

To Pamela Brooks, Nora Fountain and Janet Woods for historical details, and Jo Cotterill, Dafni Ma, Carol Wright, Caroline Fardell and Nic Thompson for helping me with the Richie problem!

To Jean and Kelvin for inside information!

To Catriona Robb for her assistance.

And sincere thanks to the late Charles Wade Paget for his magnificent and inspiring collection at Snowshill Manor, Gloucestershire.

CHAPTER 1

'What on *earth* do you want another pig for?' Anna asked her sister who was rummaging through a large cardboard box in the local charity shop. 'Surely there's no more room in your house for anything else!'

Libby sighed as she picked up a large ceramic pig which was a rather disturbing shade of orange. 'I don't have one like *this*,' she said.

'That doesn't surprise me,' Anna said, casting her eyes to the ceiling and sighing.

'Just look at his little face,' Libby enthused, her own face soft with adoration.

Anna shook her head in despair. She'd never been able to understand people who collected things so being dragged around Elmington High Street by her sister, Libby, in search of yet more knick-knacks wasn't her idea of fun.

'Remind me again why we're here,' Anna said, trying to remain sweet even though she felt claustrophobic and hot in the shop.

'I'm looking for Montgomery,' Libby said, pushing a long strand of chestnut hair out of her face. Anna shared the same hair but hers didn't take on a wild look when shopping was on the agenda.

'And who's Montgomery?' she dared to ask.

'He's the last one I need in the collection,' Libby explained.

Anna shook her head. Need – *indeed!* Her sister used the word as if her life depended on this inanimate object.

'What, exactly, is *Montgomery?*'

Libby tutted. 'I told you – he's a tiny blue pig. Part of the *Farmyard Cuties* collection.'

Anna grimaced. A blue pig? It sounded like just the sort of thing she despised and yet here was her sister, a mature woman of twenty-eight, willing to pay good money for it. It didn't make any sense to Anna at all.

'Oh, just look at that doll,' Libby cooed, pointing to the other side of the shop to a doll with plaited hair the colour of straw. Actually, looking at it closer, it really was made of straw.

'I simply *must* have her,' Libby said, sprinting across to the other side of the room as if in fear that somebody might beat her to the straw-haired wonder.

It took a further ten minutes before Anna finally ushered Libby out of the shop but she couldn't help smiling. Libby was never happier than when swinging a couple of carrier bags of second-hand goods up the high street. Anna was the complete opposite. What filled her with joy was taking a couple of bags of unwanted junk *to* the charity shop. There was something rather wonderful about unburdening one's rubbish and clearing space in one's home and there was nothing that delighted Anna more than an empty mantelpiece or a clear table-top. Over the years, Libby had done her very best to try and clutter up her sister's pristine home but her attempts had been in vain.

'It's not normal,' Libby would tell her. 'You need to have a few home comforts around you. This is all so – so – austere. Minimalism is a disease, you know. I read that in the paper last week.'

'Nonsense,' Anna would respond. 'It's calming and I don't have to dust.'

'I *love* dusting all my little treasures,' Libby would say in response. 'It's like taking care of a family.'

Anna smiled as she thought of her sister's endless collection of knick-knacks. She took such great pleasure in the strangest of things. There were china plates and pottery bowls. There were floral thimbles and striped egg-cups even though she didn't sew and never ate boiled eggs. But at least Anna never ran out of ideas for birthday and Christmas presents. Having a collector in a family was a great relief when it came to choosing presents for them.

How Libby's husband, Charlie, ever found any room for his own meagre belongings boggled the mind. Lucky that he wasn't a collector too, Anna thought, as Libby opened the front door into their tiny terrace. She gave a long low whistle as they walked down the narrow hallway into the living room. It was crammed to bursting with ornaments and yet Libby still insisted on more. If she wasn't shopping in the high street, she was surfing the net looking for them, or emailing other collectors for information. She'd even been known to place adverts in specialist magazines.

Anna blamed their Aunt Miriam. One Christmas, when Anna had been ten and Libby seven, she'd arrived with two rather special packages containing a porcelain doll for each of them.

'A limited edition,' their Aunt had proudly declared. 'One of a set of twelve. A collector's item. Bound to be on *The Antiques Roadshow* in the future – you mark my words.'

Libby's mouth had dropped open in wonderment as she'd clung to her doll, Matilda.

Anna, whose doll, Veronica, was quickly renamed Suzy, much to Libby and Aunt Miriam's horror, lasted about two months before falling out of the tree Anna had been attempting to climb with Suzy strapped to her back in a strange papoose made of a scarf. Libby was heartbroken and insisted on having a funeral. Anna, who was less emotional about those sorts of things, shrugged her shoulders and declared that dolls were not really for her anyway.

But that one Christmas present had started Libby collecting. She'd hounded their parents for the other dolls in the collection. Each birthday and Christmas, she'd ask for 'Collette' or 'Jemima' or a replacement for the dearly departed 'Veronica-Suzy' and, slowly but surely, she had all twelve, lining them up on a shelf which their dad had made especially to house them all. And that was meant to be the end of that. The McCall household could relax again. No more did they have to worry about completing the collection. They could walk by toy stores without Libby dragging them in to scour the shelves just in case they had a 'Dimity' or a 'Rowena'.

But it didn't stop there. After the dolls, Libby discovered a collection of teddy bears. Then there were the limited edition hats – no bigger than the palm of your hand, and the fairy grotto figurines and the miniature music boxes. On it went until her bedroom was bursting.

Looking around Libby and Charlie's terrace now, there wasn't a bare surface in sight. Ornaments jostled each other for space. There were shelves and cabinets and side-tables all crowded with knick-knacks and trinkets. It seemed to Anna that the walls were closing in on her – maybe even about to collapse on top of her. Of course, there were some fabulous treasures amongst her sister's collection like the vintage tea set she'd bought at a car boot sale which was a gorgeous creamy-white porcelain, smothered with tiny violets. It had pride of place in a cabinet in the dining room but, the trouble was, it was now almost completely hidden from view because of subsequent purchases like the hideous green glass fruit platter and the china figurines that Libby couldn't seem to stop accumulating.

It could, Anna thought, be the most beautiful home if only Libby could limit herself to just a handful of beautiful objects. Less, was always more, Anna believed but that was one maxim which her sister would never live by.

'Would you like a cup of tea?' Libby asked Anna as she put her bags down in the hallway and ushered her towards a chair.

'I'd *love* a cup of tea,' Anna said. 'But where on earth am I going to put it?'

Libby giggled. 'I know. I know. It's a bit crowded in here. We're going to have a sort out.'

When had Anna heard that before, she couldn't help wondering? Libby's idea of a sort out never actually meant getting rid of anything – it simply meant shifting things from one place to another.

'Mummy, Mummy, you're back,' a little boy with a shock of blond hair suddenly came tearing down the narrow hallway. Libby instantly dropped to her knees and picked him up, planting a pink kiss on his even pinker cheek.

'Have you been a good boy for Daddy, Toby?'

Toby nodded. 'He's been tidying and I've been helping.'

Anna saw Libby blush. Her sister was the world's worst housekeeper and had probably left a sink full of dishes and several wash bags of clothes untouched and had gone shopping without a second thought.

'Hello, Auntie Anna,' Toby said.

'Hi, gorgeous,' Anna said, ruffling his hair.

'Come and see my dragons,' Toby said.

Anna laughed. It was the best conversation opening she'd heard in a long time. 'Okay, lead on.'

Toby grabbed her hand and bounded up the stairs ahead of her.

'Here!' he said a moment later and Anna gasped at the sight that greeted her. His tiny bedroom at the back of the house was heaving with dragons. There was a ginormous dragon poster, a dragon-shaped light dangling from the ceiling, a dragon bedspread and innumerable dragons in plastic, plaster and wood positioned on every available surface around the room.

'He's just started collecting,' Libby explained from the door to a bemused Anna.

'*Just* started?'

'Yeah,' Libby nodded proudly. 'Obviously got the bug from somewhere.'

It was a blessed relief to leave the chaos of her sister's home and return to her own little haven. Whilst Libby lived in a Victorian terrace in the middle of town, Anna lived in a modern semi on the outskirts. The walls were white, the décor was cream and the furnishings were minimal. It was a place of total relaxation and minimum fuss – a place devoid of nasty fruit platters and china figurines. Space and peace, she called it. Space and peace.

The answerphone was flashing and she paused before hitting the play button, biting her lip as she anticipated the caller.

'Hey!' the man's voice said. Richie's voice. 'Annie? You there? Come on, babe – pick up!' There was a long sigh and Anna heard the distinct sound of him lighting a cigarette. His quitting hadn't lasted long then, had it?

'You know how I feel about you,' he continued as he puffed on his cigarette. 'I just wish you'd give me another chance. You owe me that at least.'

Anna's eyes widened at his false sense of entitlement and she heard him mumble something under his breath – something which sounded like a stream of curses. Maybe he'd dropped ash in his lap.

Anna deleted the message without listening to any more. If only she could delete him from her life as easily, she thought.

She made her way to her study, switched on the computer and checked her emails. It was a familiar routine which, as a freelance journalist, was as natural as breathing. She had seven messages. Three were from editors rejecting her ideas for articles, one was from an old college friend inviting her to a divorce party, and two were from Richie which she deleted without opening. The last one was more interesting.

Dear Ms McCall. Thank you for your letter enquiring if we were interested in commissioning an article from you about Elmington Museum. We usually get our staff to write such pieces so will not need your services.

'Damn!' Anna said.

However…

Anna's eyebrows rose in hope.

… we are in the process of putting together an illustrated book about local personalities and we are looking to commission several long articles. We are particularly interested in featuring Felicia Brookes, Sam Mornington and

William Kitson. If you think you'd be interested, please get in touch.

All best wishes

Hester North, Red Moon Publications

Anna smiled. A commission. A real live commission for a chapter in a book which people could buy – and *keep*. Anna was used to writing 'disposable' pieces for local and national magazines and newspapers. Pieces her friends would invariably miss because of the short shelf-life. But a *book!*

She quickly logged on to the internet, her fingers furiously tap-tapping until she had discovered all she needed to know about the three famous locals that Red Moon Publications hoped to feature.

Felicia Brookes was the well-known novelist who wrote weepy romances which were constantly being adapted for television, won oodles of awards and meant their owner could drip diamonds from every part of her body. She was in her seventies now, looked sweet and approachable from her photographs, and lived in a Georgian mansion north of Elmington.

Anna smiled. What fun it would be to meet her.

Sam Mornington was the local boy made good. A high school dropout, he'd left for London and had made an absolute killing doing something in marketing. It wasn't really a subject Anna cared for but the pictures of him on the internet showed he was Johnny Depp-handsome and – more importantly – single.

Anna smiled. What fun it would be to meet him.

There wasn't very much about William Kitson on the internet. He lived the life of a hermit in a big house in the Elm Valley. There were no pictures of him and the clincher for Anna was that his celebrity arose from his passion for collecting.

She sighed. She really didn't fancy meeting him.

Switching the computer off, she went to make tea. She'd ring Hester North in the morning and hope that Sam Mornington or Felicia Brookes still needed features written about them. Maybe she could even do both.

She smiled. Cheating, harassing ex-boyfriends aside, things were starting to look fabulous.

CHAPTER 2

It wasn't the response Anna had been hoping for. She'd rung Hester North at nine on the dot only to be told that both Felicia Brookes and Sam Mornington had both found journalists to cover their stories. How had that happened so quickly?

'Perhaps you'd be able to interview William Kitson for us?' Ms North had said. 'He's still available.'

Anna had closed her eyes, quietly thinking, *I bet he is*. When she'd opened them, she'd caught sight of a pile of unpaid bills on her desk.

'That would be great,' she'd said, thinking of the money they'd offered her for the job.

'I'll send you over the details,' Ms North had said.

Later that morning, Mr Kitson's details were emailed across to her.

His address was Fox Hill Manor.

Typing the name into a search engine, Anna hoped something would materialise. Alas, all she found was a story on the site of a local paper about a rather curious incident involving a group of school boys who had been caught trespassing in the grounds of Fox Hill Manor. They'd been throwing stones at one of the windows and, apparently, Mr Kitson had threatened to fire his canon at them. When they'd laughed at him, he'd wheeled out an enormous black canon and the boys swore to heaven that he was going to use it.

Anna giggled. Probably would have served them right, she thought, suddenly very interested in the man who kept a canon in his home.

'I'm afraid Mr Kitson is out. May I help?' a kindly voice asked Anna when she rang Fox Hill Manor later that day.

Anna explained who she was.

'About the feature?' the lady asked. 'Oh, yes. He asked me to tell you that you can come tomorrow. Do you know how to find us? It's not easy,' the lady said and then she proceeded to give some rather unusual directions involving dilapidated barns, silage heaps and a collapsed oak tree.

'Once you see the tree, you can't go wrong but make sure you're wearing Wellington boots if it's been raining, and don't walk fast along the path. It's absolutely *lethal*.'

Anna made a quick note of everything and was about to hang up when the lady continued.

'You'll be staying, of course.'

'I will?' she said in surprise.

'Oh, yes. Mr Kitson is very keen that you absorb the house properly. It's one of the conditions of his being interviewed. He doesn't want someone turning up and hastily writing that the collection's nothing but a load of old clutter.'

Anna swallowed guiltily. 'Of course not.'

'He's hoping you can stay a week.'

'A *week?*'

'Yes. That's all right, isn't it?'

'Well, I–' Anna began, a little surprised by the invitation. She looked around her office at the half-written pieces, the bills and the rejection letters and thought that it might actually be nice to get away from everything. Richie would certainly never find her at Fox Hill Manor and, if he did, perhaps she could borrow William Kitson's canon to see him off.

'That would be absolutely fine,' she said.

'Good,' the lady said. 'Well, I'm Mrs Boothby. I'll expect you at one o'clock for lunch, okay? Ring the bell when you arrive. The large wooden door at the side of the house. Up the steps. It's got two huge pots at the bottom. You can't miss it. Don't try the front door, whatever you do. Nobody's used that since the nineteenth-century and I shan't hear you if you do. And don't mistake the old servants' door for the real door. That one's sealed up.'

Anna smiled. It all sounded rather complicated but enormous fun.

'William Kitson?' Libby said, sinking back into a snug pile of cushions – a pile of nine to be exact – she'd only stopped collecting them when Charlie had insisted that his bottom wasn't large by any standards but that there wouldn't be any room for him to park it if she bought any more cushions home.

'You've heard of him, then?' Anna said, sipping tea from a "Kittens in Paradise" mug – a special limited edition – fifteen to collect.

'Of course! He's a collector extraordinaire. I'd love to see his place. You're so lucky. Could you sneak me in, do you think?'

Anna, who was the very picture of professionalism, bit her lip.

'Don't worry. I'm only joking,' Libby said with a laugh. 'Actually, now I think about it, there was a short article about him in one of my magazines. CHARLIE!' she suddenly bellowed.

'Yes?' a faint voice returned from upstairs.

'Can you find me last month's collecting magazine?'

'Which one?'

'You'd better bring all of them,' Libby shouted.

Five minutes later, Charlie appeared with four magazines: *Collecting Today*, *Collector's Times*, *Your Collection* and *The Collector*.

'Hello, Anna,' he said with a grin, handing the magazines to Libby and stuffing his hands in the pockets of a pair of baggy jeans.

'Hi, Charlie,' Anna said. 'How's the plumbing business?'

'Ah, you know – slowly building,' he said. He'd recently started up his own small business and had ploughed virtually everything into it.

'I'm sure you'll be a terrific success,' she said. 'I tell everyone I meet about you.'

He smiled at her. 'Thanks!' he said.

Anna adored her brother-in-law. He was the most hard-working man she knew and was so kind and patient with her sister no matter how crazy her collecting got. He truly was one in a million.

'Now, which one was it?' Libby said, attacking each magazine in turn. 'Ah, here. I thought so.' She handed the magazine over to Anna. It was a half-page feature entitled, 'Collector buys twelfth set of armour'.

'*Twelfth?*' Anna gasped. 'What would anyone want with twelve sets of armour?'

Charlie shrugged. 'Beats me.'

'He's a collector,' Libby said. 'Perhaps the other eleven weren't perfect or they were from different periods or different countries or something.'

Anna and Charlie stared at her in unconcealed befuddlement.

'Where on earth do you put twelve suits of armour?' Anna asked.

'I think you're going to find out,' Libby said as she scanned the article, tucking a strand of her hair behind her ear. 'Look - it says here that he's got a room called 'The Armoury'. Isn't that wonderful? Can you imagine having a whole room for just one piece of your collection?' Her eyes danced with a dangerous light as if she was contemplating adding an extension to their house so that she could have an armoury too.

Anna and Charlie exchanged amused looks.

'He also has rooms named after their contents: there's 'Orchestra' full of instruments, 'Flight' full of stuff to do with aviation and 'Civil War',' Libby announced.

'Is that where he keeps the famous canon?' Charlie asked. Everyone, it seemed, had heard of William Kitson's notorious canon.

'Just think, we could call Toby's room, 'Dragon's Lair', couldn't we?' Libby said excitedly, handing the magazine across to Anna.

'Oh. There's only one picture,' Anna said, sighing in disappointment at the photograph of a boring old suit of armour.

Libby narrowed her eyes at her sister. 'You're not hoping he's some Mr Rochester-type, are you? Some dark, brooding hero living in a romantic pile?'

'No, of *course* not,' Anna said defensively, 'but it would be nice to see who I was going to be working with, wouldn't it?'

'Well, you will.'

Anna sighed. Libby was right. It was all just a matter of being patient which, of course, Anna wasn't.

She'd been meaning to replace her old car for years but life as a freelance journalist meant that there was always some other demand for her money first, so she rattled down the narrow Cotswold lanes in her ancient Volkswagen Polo in fear that she'd break down at any moment. It now had more rust on it than paintwork but the little red car usually got her from A to B in one piece, albeit shaken and stirred.

The Elm Valley was rather isolated but very beautiful. Tiny hamlets, villages and farms threaded their way along ribbon-thin lanes which rose and fell with the landscape. It was at its most beautiful in May. The enormous hedges were hidden by lacy cow parsley and bluebells and the cheeky pink faces of campion. The cold bleakness of winter seemed a million months away now that spring was out in full force and it was impossible to believe that it could ever come around again.

Passing through the village of Fox Hill, Anna slowed down. She drove by the church with its squat, friendly tower and took a bend in the road to the right.

There was the little bridge and a track to the left, guarded by two golden stone gateposts. She turned into it, spying a wooden sign half-hidden by an enthusiastic bramble: *Fox Hill Manor*.

The driveway dipped and then rose, bumping its way into a lush green valley quite hidden from the road. There were the dilapidated barns and the silage heaps and the collapsed oak tree that Mrs Boothby had told her to look out for but, still, there was no sign of the manor. Anna frowned. She must have driven at least half a mile by now. How much land did this William Kitson own, she wondered?

Then, as she turned another bend in the track, the valley opened up to her and there, in its centre, was the glorious honey-coloured Fox Hill Manor. Anna stopped the car and wound down her window, breathing in the soft fresh air. She'd never seen such a beautiful house and yet it wasn't conventionally beautiful. Rather than standing erect and proud, it seemed to sprawl, like a sleeping dragon, across the immaculate green lawns that surrounded it, and it seemed to be all ages at once. Anna wasn't an expert when it came to architecture but she could see ancient mullioned windows, Georgian sash windows, and were those Tudor chimneys?

'So,' she said to herself, 'this is going to be home for the next week.'

She continued on down the track which sloped dramatically into the valley towards the house. There was a large sweep of driveway into what looked like a stable-block and, finding an old Morris Minor van with only two wheels, she parked her car alongside it.

Looking on her backseat, she decided to leave her suitcase and laptop until she'd made some sort of contact first. Now, the only problem was finding the right door.

There was no sign of life whatsoever in the stable-block and she couldn't resist walking across to one of the stables and peeping inside. It was cool and dark and very clean but there weren't any horses there.

She walked on, finding another small courtyard on either side of which were low buildings. Never one to resist her natural nosiness, Anna took a look inside those too. Each one was filled with – well – junk. There were tables and chairs, wardrobes and doors, mirrors and – drums. Anna grinned.

The buildings were all in immaculate condition. In fact, they were more like spare rooms in a house than outbuildings and it was obvious to her that these items were awaiting some kind of attention before finding a place as part of Fox Hill's permanent collection.

Leaving the outbuildings, she walked on through the courtyard and came out onto a small emerald lawn enclosed by a wall in the same honeyed stone as the house. Was she going the right way? It was certainly a beautiful place to explore but shouldn't she be making her way to the house? And where exactly was the house? Something that big couldn't have just disappeared. She turned around but then couldn't resist a quick walk around the walled garden.

The early afternoon sun was warm and there were flowers blooming in the beds and young fruit trees trained up the wall, their delicate blossom promising an abundance of fruit in the autumn. She could have stayed there all day but knew she had an appointment to keep so she quickly doubled back through the courtyard and, after finding another exit, there it was: the door Mrs Boothby had told her to look out for at the side of the house, up a few stone steps worn away in their middles by centuries of feet.

Anna walked up them and saw a rope attached to an enormous bell. She smiled. A *real* door bell. She pulled it, gently at first but then with slightly more vigour, its metallic music bouncing off the walls.

It wasn't long before she heard the door open and there was Mrs Boothby. Slight of stature but round of face, she beamed a welcoming smile at Anna.

'So, you found us all right?' she asked, her Gloucestershire accent soft to the ears.

'Yes, thank you for your directions,' Anna said.

'You'd be surprised how many people never actually make it to the front door – or take their time in doing so.'

Anna blushed at her own dalliances in the stable-block, courtyard and walled garden and hoped she wasn't late.

'Come on in,' Mrs Boothby said, ushering Anna into a stone hallway in which stood not one but three longcase clocks. Mrs Boothby saw Anna's mouth drop open. 'Oh, they don't live here,' she said. 'They're on their way somewhere else. Not sure where yet but they'll no doubt find a home. Everything usually does.'

The hallway opened into a corridor and Mrs Boothby walked ahead before turning right into a small room with a dining table and eight chairs. Two places were set at the end overlooking the garden.

'Mr Kitson likes to use his rooms,' she said. 'It seems a bit strange having a sandwich and a cuppa in such a sumptuous setting but it would be a shame if the rooms were just museum pieces, wouldn't it?'

Anna nodded as Mrs Boothby pulled out a chair for her.

'I'll get the lunch,' she said, disappearing.

Anna looked around the panelled walls. There were portraits of all shapes and sizes. Were they all Kitson portraits? She examined some of the pale faces which hovered menacingly from out of the dark backgrounds. They all seemed to be wearing dour expressions as if they'd been unhappy at the time the portrait was painted.

Get on with it, man, they seemed to say. *I haven't got time to sit here all day.*

How odd it must be to have your portrait painted, Anna thought. She was one of those people who couldn't sit still for ten minutes let alone the hours needed for a portrait to be completed. Even when she was watching TV, she had to be doing something else like mending a hem on a dress or flicking through a magazine.

Mrs Boothby re-entered with a large tray on which was a baguette, a bowl of crisp salad, a cheese platter, a teapot and a small fruit cake.

Anna dragged her eyes away from the portraits. 'Thank you,' she said. 'I understand I'm the first journalist to interview Mr Kitson.'

'Oh, no,' Mrs Boothby said. 'He did one – oh, ages ago – and the reporter was a nasty sort. Wrote all sorts of rubbish about him which was very upsetting. Tends to put you off, doesn't it?'

'I hope he doesn't think I'm going to–'

'My dear, we have every faith in you. We saw that wonderful article you wrote about the Reverend Sanders, and the one last month about the retired headmistress.'

Anna beamed. It was so rare that anyone remembered her work enough to praise it and so she lapped it up as she tucked into her lunch.

'You write with real compassion,' Mrs Boothby said, joining her.

'But Mr Kitson didn't choose me for the job, did he?' Anna asked feeling confused.

'No, I don't think so but I believe he asked Hester North to choose someone who wasn't going to roast him alive again and, of course, when he found out you were to write the piece, he did his research.'

Anna bit her lip. It was usually *she* who did the research and it felt funny that somebody had felt it necessary to research her.

'So, when will I be able to meet Mr Kitson?' Anna asked at last.

'Oh, not until tomorrow. He's away on one of his hunting trips.'

'Hunting trips?' Anna flinched. Surely nobody went on those anymore? Not in this day and age, even if they were collectors.

'Yes, to an auction house in Bath.'

Anna smiled in relief.

'He'll be back later tonight. Best you settle into your room. He said you're welcome to explore the grounds but that he'd be happier showing you around the house himself in the morning.'

Anna nodded and the two of them ate their lunch in affable silence.

Finally, Mrs Boothby got up, clearing away the lunch things and leading Anna out of the panelled dining room.

'I'll show you to your room. You should have everything you need. Mr Kitson's left some books out for you about the history of the house and some of the items in the collection. If you need anything, I'm in the office along the Clock Corridor. You can't miss it; it chimes practically all the time. Mr Kitson loves clocks and sets them all at different times so there's always chiming. It's like a lovely kind of birdsong.'

Anna grinned. This was the strangest house she'd ever been to.

After getting her bags from the car, Anna was shown to her room.

'This is the Mirror Room,' Mrs Boothby said, pursing her lips slightly. 'It's about the only one that's habitable at the moment. We don't often have guests.'

Anna walked in and gasped. The whole room was silver with mirrors. There was a large swing mirror by the window, an ornate gold oval one behind the door, a plaster, cupid-festooned one by the bed and, in between, dozens of tiny mirrors in every shape and size imaginable.

'It's so dazzling,' Anna said.

'We can try and find you somewhere else if you find it disturbing. I know it's not to everyone's taste.'

'Oh, no,' Anna said quickly. 'I like it. It's different.'

'Yes,' Mrs Boothby said. 'It's that alright but, then again, each room here is. We like things different here.' She took a moment to look around the room, a warm smile on her face as if she was greeting an old friend. 'Well, I'll leave you to settle in,' she said at last. 'I leave at five but there's some dinner in the kitchen. That's down the Sword Passage. If you make your way back to the entrance hall where you came in, turn right and then first left, that's the Sword Passage which will take you to the kitchen. And there's a bathroom just out on the landing to the right. That's for your own use.'

Anna nodded, privately wondering if she'd ever find her way around, especially after dark.

'And Mr Kitson will see me in the morning?'

Mrs Boothby nodded.

'And will you be here then?'

'Lordy, no,' Mrs Boothby said. 'It's Saturday. Got to get back to my own mad house, haven't I?' And, with that, she smiled and left the room.

Anna sighed. She was all alone in a strange house. Just her and a hundred reflections for company.

CHAPTER 3

Anna awoke the next morning to the most dazzling light. She blinked rapidly, wondering where she was and then she remembered – she was in the room of a hundred mirrors – and it was like waking up in the centre of an exploding star.

She yawned and stretched and got out of bed. It was her own fault for not drawing the curtains the night before but the moon had been so beautiful and she'd looked out over the shadowy garden from her bed until she'd fallen asleep.

It had been a strange evening. She'd unpacked, putting her clothes away in an enormous old oak wardrobe and chest of drawers and then she'd managed to find her way downstairs to the kitchen via the Swords Passage. Being single once again, she was used to eating alone but it didn't seem quite right at a dining table. She usually made do with dinner on her lap in front of the television and it felt terribly formal to be sitting at a table.

Mrs Boothby really was a dear, Anna thought, as she opened the fridge where she found a pasta bake awaiting her. Once she'd eaten, she went to do the washing up and noticed that there was a bowl and spoon in the sink along with a pink mug. It looked as if Mrs Boothby had had a spot of tea before leaving for the weekend. Anna washed them up along with her own things.

She'd spent the rest of the evening in a large winged chair in her room, reading some of the books and magazines which had been left out for her, absorbing facts, figures, dates and details about the strange building in which she now found herself.

Finally, her eyes sore with tiredness and her brain too full to take in any more information, she'd got into bed, worrying about the day that faced her tomorrow. Who was this man she had yet to meet? She knew so little about him and felt so ill-prepared. He was elusive and rarely gave interviews. He went on 'hunting trips'. He was obviously wealthy and, as far as Anna could make out, didn't need to work.

For a brief moment the night before, she'd thought she was going to get her first glimpse of him. It was some time after she'd gone to bed; she'd heard a car pulling up in the courtyard and had peeped out of the window but hadn't been able to see more than a shadowy figure stopping at the entrance of the walled garden she'd discovered just hours before, a couple of small dance dancing around his feet. She'd been a little afraid that he might turn around and look up and see her standing at the window but he didn't; he seemed wholly transfixed by the silvery scene before him. They'd both stood like that for some time and Anna had wondered how often he must have seen that same view. He'd lived at Fox Hill Manor for some time, hadn't he? How long did it take before you stopped seeing the beauty of a place, she wondered?

She'd watched him until he'd turned to go inside and then she'd quickly stepped back from the window. Now, it was morning and yet the mirrors gave the impression that the room was still full of moonlight but it was definitely daytime and she had a job to do.

She tidied herself up, tying her long chestnut hair into a tight ponytail, and then left her room and ventured downstairs, wondering if Mr Kitson would be waiting for her in one of the rooms. More than anything, she longed to explore the house but most of the doors were closed. Only the most functional of rooms had been left open.

She retraced her footsteps of the night before and found herself, once again, in the kitchen. It was a beautiful room with a huge wooden table in its centre with two long benches running down either side as if a hungry army was expected at any moment. The stone floor was slightly uneven and there was an enormous fireplace. Anna walked across and stood inside it, craning her neck back as she marvelled at its size. How many meals had been prepared in this kitchen? What would it have been like to cook over a fire like this?

A fine collection of copper pots hung around the room, gilding it with the warmth of their colour and, everywhere, there were cups and plates in every colour and pattern imaginable. Libby would love this, Anna couldn't help thinking.

Already, Anna could find her way around the cupboards and had poured herself a glass of fruit juice and a bowl of Muesli before she realised that somebody had beaten her to breakfast already for there was a glass and a plate in the kitchen sink.

She quickly finished her breakfast and determined to find the elusive owner but, strangely, he was nowhere to be seen. Anna sighed. She didn't feel she had the right to trespass and poke around the rooms in search of him. Still, she felt even less like returning to her bedroom and waiting for him to seek *her* out and what harm would it do to take a quick look around the house? He couldn't really blame her, could he? He had invited a journalist into his home, after all.

She wouldn't leave the ground floor, she told herself. She'd make that her rule. Everything on the ground floor was fair game – but that was all. So she set off, excitement churning in her stomach.

The Sword Passage was her first port of call. There were several doors leading off from it – all annoyingly closed. Anna bit her lip. She could feel her heartbeat accelerating as she chose the door nearest to her, her hand closing around the beautiful brass door knob. And then she stopped. It was no good. Her sense of honesty told her that it was wrong to enter uninvited. She was a guest here and it wasn't her place to intrude.

She was just about to call it quits and return to her room when something caught her eye at the end of a particularly long corridor. It was a door – like all the other doors – but this one was ajar. She could look into this one, couldn't she? She hastened towards it and, sure enough, found it open.

'Hello?' she said, half-expecting somebody to be inside but there was no reply. Gingerly, she walked inside and her mouth instantly fell open. The room was like the Mirror Room only it was filled with photographs. There were hundreds, perhaps thousands. Black and white, sepia and colour. All jostled together in one great family album: on table tops and in cabinets but mostly on the walls and each one in a beautiful frame. Anna had never seen so many together and the effect was startling.

She hadn't realised that Mr Kitson's family was so large. How strange, then, that he had chosen not to get married and have children. Or maybe he hadn't chosen that. Maybe it was what he wanted more than anything in the world.

Suddenly, Anna felt incredibly sad as she thought of the lonely man in a huge home, all alone. Did he hope to find the right woman one day and fill it with the laughter of their children? Perhaps his collection was a child-substitute, she suddenly thought, gasping as she believed she'd hit on the heart of her story.

She walked slowly around the room, gazing at the faces from both past and present. Who were they all, she wondered?

'They're not my family,' a voice suddenly said.

Anna jumped.

'I don't have any photographs of my own family in here,' the voice continued and Anna turned around to see a tall man standing in the doorway. 'In fact, I don't have many photographs of my own family at all,' he said, walking out from the shadows as if onto centre stage. 'I'm William,' he said quietly, stepping towards Anna and holding out a hand. 'Welcome to Fox Hill Manor.'

Anna shook his hand. 'Anna McCall.'

'Good,' he said. 'I was beginning to worry you might be a burglar.'

'I think I'd need slightly larger pockets to burgle this house,' she said.

'Try a fleet of removal vans,' he said.

Anna smiled up into one of the loveliest faces she'd ever seen. It was calm and gentle with grey eyes which reminded Anna of the beautiful mirrors in her bedroom. She looked at him, noting the fine, almost aristocratic features, and the round glasses he wore which made him look slightly professorish. Anna guessed him to be in his late-thirties. He was dressed smartly in what Anna thought of as 'country-wear' – a white shirt with a light check pattern, a V-neck pullover in a camel colour, chocolate brown trousers and a pair of boots which wouldn't have looked amiss in the middle of a muddy field. And his hair was thick and fair and looked as if it might benefit from a bit of attention at the hairdressers. Next to him, Anna couldn't help feeling short, dark and decidedly ordinary in her crisp white blouse and navy skirt.

She blinked, afraid that she was staring. 'Why?' she said and then cleared her throat and tried again. 'Why do you have all these pictures of strangers?'

'Other people's families are far more interesting, don't you think?' he asked, moving across the room and peering at a tiny portrait of an elderly gentleman. 'One tends to know about one's own family but, with other people's, you can make up stories – link people who may not have been linked, declare them happy or unhappy, jealous or difficult. They're like casting photos for a film and you can be the director and give them parts,' he said. There was a pause. 'Don't you think?' he added, his eyebrows rising, and Anna found herself smiling.

'I've never thought of that,' she said. 'So where have all these photographs come from?'

'Like everything else in this house – all sorts of places. I bought a few when I was young just because I liked them – the sepia ones mainly. I'd never seen those before. It began when I bought a second-hand book. As I was reading it, a photograph fell out. It was this one here,' he said, pointing to a picture of an elderly woman with startlingly white hair, wearing a pearl necklace and a light smile.

'It's lovely,' Anna said.

William nodded. 'And homeless. Quite forgotten. Drifting in a world which no longer knew her. So I bought a new home for her.'

Anna frowned.

'I framed her,' he explained.

'Oh, I see,' Anna said, 'and then you bought her a huge family.'

William nodded again. 'Something like that. You sometimes get them in job lots in auctions. I go to buy a few small items and they come in a box with all sorts of other things in it including photographs.'

'That's sad. I mean, photographs are so personal. These would have meant something to somebody once.'

Anna walked around the room and looked at the pictures again. There were beach picnics from the seventies, promenade walks from the thirties, a horse ride from what looked like the fifties and numerous portraits: happy, sad, indifferent, but all speaking of a different time and a different life. It was beautiful and so much more like history than anything she'd ever read about in any book.

'And you don't know anything about these people?' she asked.

'Not a thing,' William said. 'Although wonder what they make of being here.'

'It must be like going to a new job where you don't know anyone,' Anna said.

William nodded. 'I often wonder if they chatter away when the door is closed.'

Anna laughed, instantly embracing this notion. 'Look at this man here,' she said, pointing to a large-faced man in a bowler hat. 'Do you think he tries to chat up these ladies here?' she asked, motioning towards a group of lacy Victorian women taking tea on an immaculate lawn.

'Or this lady here,' William said, nodding towards a matriarch from the fifties. 'I always imagine her keeping everyone in order and shouting them down if they misbehave.'

Anna smiled, picturing the imaginary scene with delight. This was not at all what she'd been expecting from the owner of Fox Hill Manor but she liked it all the same. It also made her wonder what other secrets he had hidden behind the numerous doors she'd seen.

'Do you remember what's in all the rooms? Do you have nameplates on them?' she asked.

'You don't need to label rooms in your own home. Do you?' he asked.

'Well, no, but I only have five rooms,' Anna said.

'There's only thirty-two here,' William said, 'not many really.'

Anna's eyes widened.

'One of my friends has seventy-nine rooms,' he added.

'And he doesn't get lost?'

'Oh, hopelessly. He really should get some name plates.'

Anna looked at him and he glanced quickly at her and then grinned. 'This is one of my favourite rooms,' he said. 'I call it The Gallery.'

'It's fabulous,' Anna said. 'I've never seen anything like it before.'

'And have you seen the garden yet?' he asked.

'Yes. I saw it when I arrived. It's lovely. I love the fruit trees against the wall.'

'What about the pond? And the well?'

It was Anna's turn to look surprised.

'You've only seen the fruit garden,' he said, running a hand through his thick fair hair which resulted in it sticking out even more. 'Come on. I'll show you the rest.'

They headed outside from the patio doors of the dining room and Anna instantly realised that she was in for a surprise. The garden, like the house, was a mass of different spaces on different levels. Stone steps led down into secluded areas with ornate benches. There were pretty ponds and endless borders heaving with shrubs and flowers.

Pale bluebells mingled with dark irises, and honeysuckle scrambled over a nearby wall, scenting the air with its perfumed tendrils of pink and tangerine. But the real show-stopper was the purple wisteria which was growing up the side of a dilapidated shed, its huge grape-like flowers exuding their intoxicating perfume. Anna truly felt as if she'd entered the Garden of Eden.

Gravelled paths wound their way through seemingly endless grounds and Anna soon spotted white doves resting on the slate roof of the dovecote.

'It was a mess of nettles and old farm machinery when I bought the place and it was a while before I got round to breathing new life into it. There was so much to do in the house first,' William said.

'How long have you been here?' Anna asked.

'Eight years. It seems such a short time, though. See the orchard?' he asked, pointing across a low-lying wall. 'It's such a joy to see the trees grow. I plan on planting my own one day – something real and living to leave behind me when I'm gone, full of heritage varieties like Blenheim Orange and Worcester Pearmain that the supermarkets have never heard of.'

Anna's eyes widened and she was desperate to get her notebook and pen out and write down what he'd said but the moment didn't seem right somehow.

She followed him as he led her to a tiny walled area where there was a mini-maze in box hedging.

'The children love this,' he said. 'Not quite Hampton Court but one day…'

She looked at him and his clear grey eyes seemed to be staring right into the future. And here was she thinking that it was only the past that this man was interested in.

'Please feel free to enjoy the gardens at your leisure,' he said.

'Thank you,' Anna replied.

'Now, if you'll excuse me, I have a few calls to make.'

Anna was a little taken aback. 'When will I see you again?' she called after him as he walked away. 'For the book? I need to start making some–' she stopped because she could see that he wasn't listening.

And then something occurred to her: he'd left The Gallery open for her hadn't he? He'd known that no journalist could resist a door left ajar. He'd choreographed the whole morning. He'd shown her around the room that he wanted her to see first and then taken her out into the garden where they'd talked of nothing but nettles and apples.

Anna smiled a knowing smile. Once again, William Kitson had evaded all the questions she'd had planned for him.

CHAPTER 4

It was then that Anna made a decision: she was going to write everything down. If William Kitson was going to play hard to get, she would have to be careful to get every single word of his recorded.

Finding her pad and pen in her handbag, she returned to one of the sunken gardens where she'd spied a blue bench near a square pond. It was a secluded sunny spot and she sat down, pen poised.

Sometimes, as a kind of warm-up exercise, she would write anything that came into her head just to get the words flowing. It was a very freeing experience and she gave it full rein now.

The first thing that strikes you about William Kitson is his affable manner. You can't help liking the man – damn it!

She scribbled out the phrase, *damn it.*

He is, at once, approachable and elusive, revealing and secretive. I wish I'd been given Sam Mornington to interview – he would have been far easier, I'm sure.

She sighed and crossed out the last sentence.

He has the sweetest little smile and his eyes have a naughty sort of twinkle as if he's hiding something which, I believe, he is. Well, I'm going to find out exactly what it is. You can't hide from me, Mr Kitson!

She flipped the page over, warm up done, and began again, writing down everything she'd managed to glean about William in their brief morning together.

She wrote about her bedroom, The Mirror Room. She wrote about The Gallery and William's first sepia photograph. And she wrote about the gardens, endless and exquisite – the garden of a great romantic.

She lost track of all time as she wrote, her pen flying across page after page, her mind lost in a world of words.

'Hello,' a voice suddenly said, causing Anna to leap a foot into the air.

'Oh!' she said, looking up from her industrious scribbling. 'You gave me a shock.'

'Busy?' William asked, cocking his head to one side.

She nodded, hastily closing her pad. 'I was–'

'In a world of your own,' he said. 'I could see that. Is that about me?' he asked.

'No, I'm writing my memoirs.'

'Oh, can I have a look?'

Anna blushed and then cleared her throat. 'It's not that interesting, really.'

'Can I be the judge of that?' he asked, sitting down next to her on the bench and holding his hand out to her.

Anna panicked. She couldn't let him see it. What would he think? She tried not to think about the embarrassing things she'd written about him during her warm-up session and also about his smile and his eyes.

'It's about you,' she confessed.

He gave a little smile. 'But I haven't told you anything yet.'

'I know,' Anna said. 'I'm just making it all up until you *do* tell me something.'

She looked at him challengingly, her brown eyes meeting his grey ones. Would he take the bait and set aside some proper time for her.

'Did you make your calls?' she asked a moment later when it became obvious that he wasn't going to confess to anything that might be interesting.

He nodded. 'Yes.'

'And?'

'What?' he asked.

'All okay?'

'Are you going to ask me about every phone call I make whilst you're here?'

'No, I – I'm sorry. I thought it might be something to do with the collection.'

'It was,' he said. 'As a matter of fact, a friend's just rung about a local auction later today – said there might be an item of interest to me. Are you up for an auction?'

'Will it be good for the book?'

William shrugged. 'I don't see why not. I spend a good deal of time at auctions. It's where most collections like mine begin.'

'Then I'll come with you,' Anna assented, 'provided I can ask you some questions on the way. Some *proper* questions.'

William's eyebrows rose. 'You're making me very nervous.'

'Why?' she asked, tucking a loose strand of her hair behind her ear.

'You've got that hungry journalistic sort of look that I always run away from. I'm beginning to wonder if it was a good idea to agree to this book.'

'Then why did you?'

He shrugged. 'I guess I realised that the collection was more important than me – that I really shouldn't put myself first. I think it's important that people should know about it.'

Anna smiled. At last she had the beginning of something interesting. 'Is there anything particular in the collection you think is important?'

William shook his head. 'I think it's more the collection as a whole. You know that saying about things being worth more than the sum of their total parts?'

Anna nodded. 'Yes.'

'Collections are always something special.'

'And do you think they tell us as much about the collector as anything else?'

William looked at her. 'What are you trying to say?'

'I'm not sure yet but, if I don't say *something*, there's not going to be any book.'

William nodded. 'Point taken. But we do have a whole week,' he said. 'What's the hurry? It's May.'

Anna's eyes narrowed in bewilderment. 'What do you mean?'

'*May*,' he said again as if repeating it would make it clearer to her. 'The most beautiful month of the year with long, warm days full of bluebells and apple blossom. Nothing should be hurried in May.'

Anna felt as if she wanted to laugh. Who was this crazy man, she wondered?

'Okay,' she said and watched as he got up to leave again. 'Mr Kitson!' she said.

He turned round. 'Please, if you're to be my guest, you must call me William.'

Anna nodded. 'And I suppose you should call me Anna.'

He smiled and turned to leave again.

'William!' she called after him. 'Where are you going? Do I get a tour of the house yet?'

He looked puzzled, as if wondering if he'd arranged such a thing. 'Yes, of course,' he said.

'Now?' Anna said. 'I mean, I know it's May and everything but it would be handy to see something of the collection – for the book.'

William nodded. 'I guess we have some time before the auction.'

'Great,' Anna said, jumping to her feet and suddenly feeling like a child on Christmas morning.

It was as they were crossing the lawn back towards the house that two cheeky-faced dogs came running towards them barking.

'Ah! There you are, boys. I wondered where you'd got to.'

'Who are these little fellows, then?' Anna asked, reaching out to pat their small tawny-brown faces.

'Cocoa and Beanie,' William said, patting each head in turn. 'My adorable Border Terriers.'

'What curious names.'

'After my obsession for chocolate.'

Anna nodded knowingly. 'So there's a chocolate room at the house?'

'Used to be but I soon discovered I was no Willy Wonka.'

'What do you mean?'

'I sold it all. I didn't spend much time in there. It seemed it was a passing craze, that's all.'

'Oh,' Anna said.

'You sound surprised.'

'I am. I was just thinking of my sister, Libby. Once something enters her house, it's there for good.'

'She's a collector, is she? What does she collect?'

'That's the problem really – she tends to collect everything.'

'Such as?'

'Well,' Anna said with a large intake of breath, 'ceramics, clothes, jewellery, handbags, hats, ornaments, plates, cups, old telephones, dolls, purses. The latest craze is looking for a blue pig called Montgomery. It drives me crazy!'

'And she has a large house for all this?'

'No, that's the problem,' Anna said, 'I'm afraid she doesn't.'

'Then where does she keep it all?' he asked.

'Everywhere! It's not confined to one room. It's all over the place. In fact, it hits you as soon as you enter the front door. There are piles of stuff in the hallway, the living room, the kitchen cupboards spill over with all the plates and cups and you don't even want to think about the bedrooms. It's a nightmare. Her husband, Charlie, is an absolute saint. I don't know how he puts up with it.'

There was a pause and the two of them bent down to stroke Cocoa and Beanie. Pets were always good for those awkward pauses, Anna thought.

'Perhaps that's why you're single,' she suddenly said.

'Pardon?'

Instantly, Anna realised how rude she'd sounded. 'I mean – perhaps that's why you live alone – because nobody would put up with all your stuff.'

William's eyebrows rose. 'Is that what you think?' he said.

'I'm sorry,' Anna said, biting her lip. 'I didn't mean that to come out as it did.'

'One of your journalist's ways of wheedling information out of me, is it?'

'Oh, no! It just kind of slipped out.'

William gave a little smile but his bright eyes had narrowed at her from behind his glasses and Anna wondered if she'd been truly forgiven.

'Now,' he said, slapping his right leg for his dogs' attention, 'did you want a tour of my bachelor pad or not, Miss McCall?'

'Yes, thank you, Mr Kitson,' Anna said, noting his use of her full name and wondering if he was teasing or if she had really put her foot in it and their relationship had just gone into reverse.

Oh, how she could have kicked herself for that stupid comment. They'd been getting on so well too. Now, she swore there was a certain frostiness about him. The shutters were closed and the drawbridge was up. Well, she thought, architectural comparisons seemed appropriate with this man.

They walked into the house via ten beautiful golden steps which led to a large wooden door.

'The tradesmen's entrance,' Anna said, smiling as she recognised the door from when she'd first arrived.

'As befits a reporter,' William said.

Was he joking? Again, Anna couldn't tell, especially when he had his back to her.

'This passage is actually the old part of the house,' he told her.

'How old?'

'Sixteenth century.'

'No!'

William turned to face her. 'You don't believe me?'

'Oh, *yes*,' she said, 'it's just I've never been in a house older than a hundred years.'

'They're fascinating places,' he said. 'It's one of the reasons I bought the place.'

'Yes,' Anna said, 'I was going to ask you about that. What made you buy it?'

'What made me buy it?' William took a deep breath and exhaled slowly as if luxuriating in the memory and his bright eyes took on a misty quality as though he was travelling back in time to relive that special moment. 'I suppose you could say that it was love at first sight.'

When William Kitson first saw Fox Hill Manor, he knew he was totally smitten. He also knew that it was going to cost a fortune to renovate. Luckily for him, a previous life in the city making an obscene amount of money doing relatively very little meant that his bank account now allowed him to do exactly what he wanted.

He had first seen the crumbling manor house in a country magazine. It was to be auctioned. William was used to auctions – he already had a pretty impressive collection of historical knick-knacks purchased from the great auction houses of London – but he'd never bought a house at auction. That would be a totally new experience: both exciting and nerve-wracking.

At the earliest opportunity, William had arranged to visit Fox Hill Manor, driving through the country lanes of the Cotswold's Elm Valley in his Land Rover. He'd used to own a Ferrari but you just couldn't fit a suit of armour inside one and so he'd sold it. The Land Rover was far more practical and William was often seen loading it up with all manner of crazy things from bone-shaker bicycles to Samurai swords which probably explained why his flat in Fulham was getting a little crowded. He'd long ago stopped asking friends over after work and lady friends were totally out of the question. The women he knew and worked with were far more into Armani than armour.

He'd met the estate agent at the office in the honey-coloured market town of Elmington because they'd been quite sure he wouldn't be able to find the house on his own. So William followed the young man's Volvo through the pretty villages and high hedgerows of the Cotswold countryside. It was a far cry from the crowded streets of London where the only views were those of more houses and more streets, and William knew that his decision to leave the city was the right one.

As soon as he'd bumped down the long winding track which led to Fox Hill Manor, he knew he'd found his home – the place he wanted to live the rest of his life.

'As you can see,' Mr Walton said, 'it needs a little bit of work.'

William tried not to guffaw at the man's understatement as he gazed at the great golden façade. Out of control trees reached high into the heavens and most of the garden was a tangle of brambles and buddleia. Nettles roamed freely and armies of weeds choked the borders.

'Up until a year ago, the property had been in the same family for over two hundred years,' Mr Walton informed William.

'What happened to them?' he asked.

'Oh, they died out. The property passed down to a young woman living in Los Angeles but she had no interest in it. She's just decided to sell it.'

'And you've had a lot of interest?' William probed.

'Oh, yes,' Mr Walton said. 'Several interested parties.'

William could understand why. Viewing the acres of beautiful countryside around him, he could only imagine what a developer would do to the place – sectioning off the house into nasty little flats and building more on the surrounding land whilst bulldozing the garden to make a hideous car park. He couldn't let that happen. He *wouldn't* let that happen.

'You have the keys?' William asked.

'Of course. Follow me.'

William followed Mr Walton up an overgrown path towards the house.

'I should warn you,' Mr Walton said, 'it needs a lot of work doing to it but it has enormous potential.'

'I can see that,' William said, imagining the kind of collection he could have if he owned such a space. At the moment, his precious belongings were hidden away in horrible storage facilities. It broke his heart. He felt like a part-time father who was desperate to spend more time with his children. But here, in this house, he could place everything together for the very first time and he could go on collecting too. He smiled as he thought about a whole future of collecting that lay before him. There would be no limits, he thought, just the limit of his own imagination and that, he knew, was boundless.

Mr Walton had led the way in through a beautiful wooden front door and they had to let their eyes adjust for a moment in the long dark hallway that greeted them. It was completely empty, as most of the house was, apart from a few dusty boxes and a lot of cobwebs.

'The new owner had a big house sale,' Mr Walton explained. 'Sold everything off.'

'I wish I'd known about it,' William said. 'I might have kept a few pieces.'

'If it's any consolation, I heard that there wasn't much of value. A few antique chairs and a rather nice clock but the rest was just junk. At least that leaves room for your own bits and pieces. I believe you're a collector?'

'You could say that,' William said with wry smile.

'And Fox Hill will make the perfect museum,' Mr Walton said.

William winced at the word museum. He'd never liked it. To him it sounded static and permanent – as if a collection never grew or evolved and his did – all the time. He wanted this house to be alive and lived in. He didn't want it to be like one of those places which invites the public in and then tells them not to touch anything or sit anywhere or step over the barriers. That wasn't the point of his collection at all. He wanted it to be enjoyed.

As they moved from room to room, William could imagine it housing his precious things. This room would just suit the Cantonese cabinet and this one would be great for his marble busts. Room after room was examined and silently applauded by William.

Just when he thought it couldn't possibly recommend itself to him any further, another beautiful room would be shown to him. With sloping ceilings and floors to match, they weren't to everybody's taste but, to William, they were heaven: each suffused with its own character whether they had great fat exposed beams, sturdy mullioned windows or beautifully ornate fireplaces.

Then, of course, there were the views, stretching far over the gardens and on into the greens and golds of the Elm Valley. They were the sorts of views that could chase away all the bad moods that the city bred, and William knew right there and then that he wanted to spend the rest of his life looking at them.

Thinking of that first tour of Fox Hill Manor now, he remembered how, for days, he'd carried the picture of the house around with him in his pocket, pulling it out at every available opportunity and staring at the mellow golden building. In his heart, he knew it was his yet he couldn't help feeling incredibly nervous. If it was just for sale, he could go and buy it but, at an auction, there might be competition. What if there was somebody else out there who wanted it as much as he did? William soon realised that he would have to develop a strategy. Yes, a simple foolproof strategy that meant he couldn't fail. And this was it: he would pay any price for that house. No matter how it rose in value, his hand would be holding the winning paddle.

'I heard somewhere that you'd bought it at an auction,' Anna said, bringing him back to the present.

William smiled. 'It was the most exciting auction of my life. It'll never be equalled.'

'And was the house in a terrible state?'

'Well, the garden was nothing more than a mountain of brambles, the house hadn't been lived in properly for years unless you count the mice, pigeons and spiders but you have to see beyond that.' He watched Anna's response. She nodded but did she really understand? She struck him as a neat modern-house sort of a girl who wouldn't know her Art Deco from her elbow. Could she really appreciate a house and a collection such as this?

For a moment, William wondered what on earth he'd done inviting her into his home and agreeing to the book. But that wasn't the only thing that was worrying him. What if she found out that there was more to his collection than met the eye?

CHAPTER 5

Anna was picking up a strange vibe from William as he began the tour of the house. He was polite – as ever – but there was something distinctly distancing about his manner. It really was as if he was giving a guided tour that she – a complete stranger – had paid for.

'You're already familiar with the Mirror Room – your bedroom, of course – and the Sword Passage and The Gallery,' he said.

Anna sighed as William marched forwards. She'd really been looking forward to poking around the old house and finding out more about the collection but his cardboard-stiff manner was making her horribly uncomfortable.

Concentrate, she told herself. *You're a professional. Your interviewees don't have to like you. You're after his story not his friendship, for goodness' sake! Just get on with the job.*

They walked along a dark corridor lined with oak panelling before William turned left into a grand room.

'I call this The Armoury,' he said and Anna didn't need to ask why because the entire room was filled with huge suits of armour from the shiniest of silvers to dark smoky greys. What struck her the most was the fact that the suits of armour were wonderfully complete. Some were even holding weapons in their hands and Anna had the unnerving impression that they were about to come to life at any moment.

'They're amazing,' she said. 'How on earth did you find all these pieces?'

'Patience, perseverance and luck,' William said. 'So often, you'll find them in parts. A helmet here and a breast-plate there. It can take many years to piece together a complete suit of armour and it isn't a cheap hobby.'

'I bet it isn't,' Anna said. 'What's this at the back of the helmet?' she asked, pointing to a piece of metal shaped like a small funnel.

'That's a plume-holder.'

'Oh, wonderful! Have you got one?'

'A plume? No, I haven't.'

'Oh, but you *should*. It would be the making of it – really bring it to life,' she said, suddenly realising that she was far more interested in these old things than she'd ever thought possible.

'Maybe I'll get one,' he said with a little nod.

'The kids would love it,' she told him. 'When you do your school tours. You do those, don't you?' she asked.

'Yes,' he said. 'Although not many.'

'Why not?'

William looked at her and a frown creased his forehead. 'Well,' he said, 'I like to – erm – keep things simple, you know?'

'What do you mean?'

William cleared his throat and looked around at the armour on display in the room, dusting the shoulder of nearby suit with his right hand. 'Just simple,' he said. 'Follow me.' Quickly, he left the room as if it had just caught fire.

Anna followed him and he walked along the corridor and into a room which housed a ginormous canon.

'Wow!' Anna said. 'So this is the famous canon?'

'Famous?'

'The one you used to chase those boys away,' she said, noting that the canon was facing the window as if ready to fire at any trespassers.

'Ah, you've heard about that,' William said. 'Some stories are grossly exaggerated,' he said. 'You should know that being a journalist.'

'What I know – being a journalist – is that there is a grain of truth in every story.' She watched for his response but his expression didn't give anything away.

Anna looked around the rest of the room. There were glass cabinets filled with clothing and she noticed a pair of gloves, pieces of lace, and a woman's bonnet.

'What are all these things?' she asked.

'I call this room Civil War. Everything in it dates from that period. There are documents, clothing, pottery and – as you can see – a few of the weapons of war.'

'Yes, that seems to be a running theme at Fox Hill,' Anna said.

'What, weapons?' William said, as if surprised by her observation.

'Yes. They're everywhere: canons, suits of armour, swords, guns.'

'Then I think it's fair to say that's it's a true representation of the world we live in.'

Anna bit her lip at his statement. He was right, of course, but the thought was a disturbing one.

'Don't you think it strange how time can make these weapons seem beautiful? I mean, look at that canon,' William said. 'It's such a beautiful shape, isn't it?'

Anna walked across the room and dared to touch it. It felt cold and solid under her fingers but was wonderful to touch. 'I wonder how many people this killed,' she said, half to herself.

'But you should see the pleasure it gives people now,' he said.

'How strange,' she said, her eyes taking on a wistful quality. 'It was once a weapon of war and now a weapon of wonder.'

'You should write that down for the book.'

'I think I will,' she said with a little laugh.

After that, William showed her the other rooms on the ground floor and it wasn't long before she felt dizzy with all that was on offer. There were clocks and pots, paintings and pianos, tins and tools, and maps and masks. Huge pieces of furniture vied for space and tiny fragile ornaments jostled for attention. This, Anna thought, was collecting on a serious scale. It suddenly made her sister Libby's seem very innocent indeed. After all, she was only collecting domestic things like cups and handbags. Everybody needed cups and handbags but not everyone needed a room full of masks or half a dozen medieval swords.

'What made you start collecting?' Anna asked. 'I mean, my sister was collecting from childhood. Were you?'

'Oh, yes,' William said.

'So do you think collectors are born rather than bred?'

'That's a very interesting question,' he said. 'I think perhaps it's a bit of both. With me, my mother inspired it. She had a cabinet – the Cantonese one you saw.'

'With all the drawers?'

'The very one. I always adored it. The craftsmanship is exquisite. I could spend hours looking at it and opening those drawers, desperate to find all its secrets.'

Anna smiled. This was exactly the sort of thing she needed for her book. 'Do you think anyone could start a collection like this?' she asked.

William shook his head. 'I think there is a trigger for some collectors but I think a person either has a capacity to collect or they don't.'

'I don't think I have it,' she said. 'I like to pare everything down. I don't like to have things around me that I don't need and I'm the worst when it comes to receiving gifts I don't want. They usually go straight in a charity bag.'

'Now, you see, I'm not like that at all. Everything has to be homed. I can't part with a single item if it has been given with love.'

'That's not at all practical in a house as small as mine,' Anna said.

'And that's the very reason I bought Fox Hill. It allowed me the space to indulge my collecting habits,' he said, running his finger along the edge of a fine balloon back chair.

'How much of a collection did you have before you moved here?'

'Well, obviously not as much. I'd say it was about a tenth of what's here now,' he said, casting his eyes to the ceiling as if mentally calculating.

'And where did you keep it all?' Anna asked, trying to imagine a modern house filled with Samurai warriors and eighteenth-century telescopes.

'It's amazing what you can cram into a London flat when you sell half your furniture.'

'You didn't!' she said with a gasp.

'I most certainly did. I didn't have a choice. But then there was still more. I had to hire some storage which I hated.'

Anna shook her head. At least Libby hadn't started selling her family's furniture yet.

After that, they went upstairs, the great wooden steps creaking under their feet.

'This whole house reminds me of a great ship,' Anna said. 'All this wood and none of it seems quite straight to me. I feel as if I'm on permanent tilt.'

'Yes,' William said. 'The little steps up and down into some of the rooms can easily unbalance you if you've had a glass or two of wine in the evenings. It's the kind of house you don't want to sleepwalk in.'

The views from the first floor were breathtaking. One could see for miles. Anna spotted the nearby farm she'd driven by on her way to Fox Hill Manor, she could see the huddle of Fox Hill village and, way beyond that, the steeple of St George's at the top of Elmington

High Street. The house had been worth buying for these views alone, she thought.

The more she looked around, the more she realized how unique it was and it suddenly occurred to her that she was falling under its spell. Anna had never thought that she'd appreciate an old house. She was strictly modern with all the practicalities that that entailed – like level flooring, she thought with a smile. She liked rooms that were light and airy, she liked white paint and shiny surfaces made out of the latest materials, she didn't like dark beams or wooden panelling – or so she'd thought. Fox Hill Manor must be enchanted because she was beginning to feel at home there. She wasn't even shying away from the enormity of the collection anymore. In fact, it was quite the opposite: she was rushing into each room William showed her, eager to see and to touch whatever treasures it held.

One of the most stunning was the room William called Orchestra because it held a collection of musical instruments from elegant silver flutes to great gold trombones. There were citterns and hurdy-gurdies too and a beautiful mandolin with mother-of-pearl inlay.

'Do you play any of them?' she asked.

'I'm afraid not.'

'Craftsmanship again?' Anna asked, bending down to touch a pale gold lute.

William nodded. 'You'll agree that they're all beautiful?'

'Oh, yes!' Anna enthused.

'And this room always gets people excited. There's something very lively about it – as if the instruments are about to break into song at any moment.'

Anna nodded. It was an odd feeling – rather like the one she'd felt with the suits of armour. What was it about this house, she wondered? It wasn't like a regular museum where everything seemed to be sleeping. There was something inherently alive about this place.

They moved on to a room called Flight which housed all sorts of model aircraft dangling from the beams, then it was on to the very top of the house which was filled with old bicycles. There must have been dozens up there in the roof space, all casting chaotic, interlocking shadows against the beams with their sturdy wheels and finely shaped seats. It was all so mesmeric.

'Please tell me you didn't have these in your London flat?' she said with a laugh, trying to imagine the scene.

'No,' he said, 'these came after. As soon as I saw this space, I knew how I wanted to fill it.'

Anna looked at him as his eyes scanned the room and she couldn't help smiling. She'd never seen anybody so obsessed, so involved with inanimate objects before. Her sister's collection seemed much more about the act of collecting rather than the things themselves and she'd never seen that look on Libby's face which was on William's right now. It was hard to describe but it was like pride, joy and bemusement all rolled into one.

They returned to the first floor via a different staircase which was lined with old oil paintings. Not a single piece of wall had been left unadorned. Space at Fox Hill Manor was there to be filled. That much was certain.

It was as they were about to descend to the ground floor that Anna noticed a corridor they hadn't explored. It seemed darker than the rest of the house and stretched to the very end of the first floor.

'Aren't we going to see these rooms?' she asked, nodding in their direction.

'No,' William said.

'Don't you use them?'

William looked a little vague. 'They're not suitable,' he said.

'Why not?' Anna asked, wondering if they were ravaged by damp or deathwatch beetle or some other old house horror that she hadn't heard of.

But William didn't answer. Instead, he made his way back down to the ground floor and Anna found herself following.

When they reached the Sword Passage once more, Anna couldn't help feeling a little puzzled by the unexplored corridor and William seemed to sense this.

'There's nothing there,' he said, 'and I'd rather you stayed away from those rooms to be honest.'

'Are they dangerous?'

William paused before answering. 'Yes,' he said, 'and you've quite enough to be going on with, I think, with what I've shown you today.'

Anna frowned, not liking to be told such things. Didn't he know that it was a journalist's job to uncover the complete story? It was the very thing that people tried to hide that journalists wanted the most.

'So, are you up for this auction?' he asked, clapping his hands as if trying to divert her attention.

Anna nodded. 'Yes. Let's see you in action,' she said. For the time being, she'd pretend she wasn't interested in that secret corridor but she'd find a way get to the bottom of whatever it was he was hiding there and, if he seriously thought she could be distracted from that by some silly auction, he was more naïve than she'd given him credit for.

CHAPTER 6

Anna had never been to an auction before and the idea of it didn't exactly thrill her. Weren't they just opportunities for people to make as much money as they could from unwanted pieces of junk that really should be given to charity for free?

'This is just a local auction, you understand,' William said as they drove through the Elm Valley towards the outskirts of Berminster where the auction was going to take place in one of those communal buildings that looks part village hall and part farmyard storage facility.

Anna looked in the back of the Land Rover where Cocoa and Beanie were, their eager little faces looking out of the window. They'd refused to be left behind and William had promised them a walk on the way home. She looked at the two furry friends whose little pink tongues were showing and then she turned to the business in hand, opening her handbag and taking out her notepad.

'Oh, you won't have time to use that,' William warned. 'Once you get caught up in an auction, that's it.'

'But I'll just be observing,' Anna assured him.

William gave a half smile as if he knew something that she didn't. 'We'll see,' he said as they turned in to a large field where everyone was parking.

'Come on, boys,' William said as he got out of the car and opened the back door to let the dogs out.

Anna followed them. 'Are they allowed in?'

'Oh, everyone knows Cocoa and Beanie.'

As they entered the building, Anna noticed the small stage where a desk and chair stood. Opposite that were row upon row of wooden benches.

'Not the height of comfort,' William said, 'but it keeps you awake and alert.' He clapped his hands together. 'Just in time to see what's on offer.'

It was then that Anna noticed all the goods lying around the room with numbers on.

'Why are all these things in boxes?' Anna asked, peering into them and seeing great piles of what only could be described as junk, each box carrying a number.

'Sometimes, it's the only way to get rid of stuff,' William said. 'They'll pack lots of rubbish alongside a gem or two and it'll sell and they'll be shot of it all in one fell swoop.'

More and more people entered the room and Anna found herself wondering what on earth they were all looking for. As far as she could see, there was nothing in the room of any value at all. She watched as William went to register, leaving her to look around and she couldn't help sighing. This was going to be a very long afternoon.

Returning with a bidding paddle a moment later, William smiled. 'I was tipped off about some old gardener's tools but I've just seen them.'

'Oh, are they no good?' she asked.

'They're duplicates,' William said, 'and the one I really liked and hoped to get is badly damaged.'

'So we're not staying?'

'Oh, we'll stay,' he said and they took a seat near the back of the room, Cocoa and Beanie lying down beside him, resting their heads on their front paws, obviously knowing that they were in it for the long haul.

'Isn't it better to be at the front?'

'Absolutely not,' William said. 'You can see who you're up against if you sit at the back and you can save the bidding getting sky high if you hold back until the end.'

Anna sat down beside him, her notepad in her hand.

'I told you. Don't even think of writing anything in that notepad of yours. You're going to be bidding for me.'

Before she could protest, a middle-aged woman had climbed onto the stage. The benches were filling up with bidders and the auction was about to begin.

They watched the first few lots and then William gave her a nudge.

'This is our lot,' he told her.

Anna swallowed. She was suddenly very nervous. 'Are you sure you want me to bid for you? What if I get it all wrong?'

'You can't. It's as simple as breathing.'

'What's your budget?' she asked.

'Don't worry, I'll stop you if you go too far.'

'Lot number eight,' the woman on the stage announced. 'A fine collection of crockery and china ornaments.'

'Are you *sure* this is ours?' Anna said.

William nodded.

'Who'll start the bidding at twenty pounds? Fifteen then? Ten to start?'

Suddenly, the bidding was off. Two people at the front of the room were bidding against each other but William motioned for Anna to hang back. Finally, as the price seemed to be sticking, he nudged her into action and she raised her paddle.

'There's still someone bidding against us,' Anna whispered, surprised at how quickly the price was rising.

'Yes, I know. Karl Torman,' William said. 'He's a rival collector. He's probably convinced that there's something in this lot that's really rare and worth having.'

'And there isn't?'

William shook his head. 'Keep bidding.'

Anna raised her paddle as the price rose to thirty pounds. 'If there isn't anything worth having in the lot, why are we bidding on it?'

'Wait and see,' William said.

Anna raised her paddle again, wondering what on earth William was up to. Was this some kind of game he was playing just to wind up this rival, Karl Torman? Was this how antique collectors got their kicks?

'Are you sure you want to go on bidding?' Anna asked as the price rose towards three figures.

'Go up to ninety-five pounds. Torman's about to drop out.'

'How do you know?' she asked but, as soon as the question was out, the auctioneer was saying those magic words: 'Going once. Going twice. Sold! To the lady at the back.'

'Raise your paddle,' William said.

'Number fifteen.'

'We won!' Anna said. 'I'm not quite sure *what* we've won but we won!'

'And here was me thinking that you didn't like auctions.'

'I didn't think I did,' Anna said, her cheeks flushing at the genuine surprise she was feeling. 'I got a real buzz from that.'

'It's even more exciting at the big London auctions. There are bids made by telephone and internet too – from people who live all around the world and can't make the auction. It can be a dangerously addictive way to pass the time.'

'I'm just glad Libby hasn't discovered this way of collecting,' Anna said, thinking of the horror her sister might wreak if she got near an auction room.

They sat through the rest of the lots together and then William got up and smiled.

'Come with me,' he said and Anna followed him. The auction was finishing and now was the time to pay for and collect the goods. Anna stood in the queue with William, curious to see exactly what it was he'd been bidding on. She didn't have to wait long as he soon had the treasured box.

Eagerly, Anna looked inside but all she could see was a couple of old plates and some tatty ornaments. Was she missing something? Who in their right mind would want those?

'I don't see anything,' she said in frustration. 'Is there something valuable here? A piece of Wedgewood or something?'

'Look again,' he said. 'Anything that might complete a collection?'

Anna looked again. As far as she could tell, William didn't collect floral dinner plates nor did he collect chipped china dogs. But then something blue caught her eye.

'The blue pig!' she screamed.

William nodded. 'Montgomery, I take it? One of the *Farmyard Cuties* your sister was after? I saw a blue pig and made a lucky guess,' he said.

'You bought this box for my sister?' Anna's mouth dropped open.

William nodded, a delightful twinkle in his grey eyes.

'Oh, William! I don't know what to say. Except thank you,' Anna said. 'Libby's going to love this. Really, *really* love it!'

'That's the magic of the auction,' William said. 'You never quite know what you're going to find.'

Anna was wrong to think that her sister, Libby, had never been to an auction. She might not have actually set foot in an auction house but there was more than one way to bid in the modern world and Libby had discovered it months ago.

Everyone had a hobby and most people's hobbies involved spending a certain amount of money, Libby reasoned, as she sat down at the computer after having made herself a cup of tea. The family computer became an extension of herself – a friendly face in the corner of the room which promised wonderful gifts literally at the touch of a few buttons. Yes, Libby thought to herself, online shopping was the best of inventions. It could never replace real shopping, of course – what could possibly beat that wonderful feeling one got from walking into a beautiful shop, making a spontaneous purchase and the thrill of leaving with a new carrier bag full of goodies? However, as far as Libby was concerned, online shopping came a close second.

Hours flew by in a blur of mousing and, the happiest thing was, one simply lost track of the money spent. It was as if no money was really changing hands at all. It was all virtual, wasn't it? Like playing a game with pretend money.

It was also the most wonderful of time-fillers. Ever since she'd left her job at the building society to have Toby, Libby had harboured a deep dread of going back to work.

'Don't worry about it,' Charlie had said. 'Have a good break. What's the point of having a baby if you're not going to spend any time with it?'

And so they'd agreed that Libby would be a stay-at-home mum – for the first couple of years at least. Then Libby had postponed things further.

'Just until he's at school,' she'd told Charlie who'd been anxious but understanding. Now Toby was seven and Libby still wasn't showing any signs of finding work. She was well and truly out of the habit and there was no way she wanted to get back into it. The thought of the early morning commute filled her with dread as did the monotonous routine of her old job. Nothing could compare to spending the day at home with unlimited access to the world wide web.

For a moment, she tried to imagine a typical day at work.

'Oh, Libby, did you find that file I asked for?' her boss would ask.

'No, not yet,' Libby would say. 'I've just got to make sure I'm not outbid on this nineteen-thirties photo frame.'

It just wouldn't work, would it? She'd be fired within an hour.

Most of her time was spent visiting her favourite websites. She thought of them as gigantic car boot sales with the added bonus that you didn't have to leave the comfort of your own home and trudge around endless heaps of rubbish to find what you wanted. You could pinpoint exactly what you were looking for or browse items you might never have *thought* you wanted. For example, before Libby had discovered Antonia's Antiques, she'd never known how much she'd wanted to collect porcelain lipsticks. Now, she had a collection of thirty-two. There were still many new shades to discover, of course. She'd only just got into it and had yet to find a *Summer Raspberry* or a *Christmas Kiss* that were in excellent condition. They were just so cute. They were about half the size of a regular lipstick and worked just like a real one: you could take the lid off and wind up the colour. There was even a collectable rack where you could line up the lipsticks and put them on display.

Another of her favourite collections was *Fans From Around the World*, which she had stumbled upon quite by accident at a site called Collector's Delight. Half a dozen were up for auction by someone who had sold Libby a doll's house. An email had arrived about a week after the purchase of the doll's house; Libby had obviously been put on the woman's mailing list which, she thought, was most thoughtful of her. A few weeks later, and Libby had no less than nine beautiful fans.

Nothing beat buying oneself little gifts, Libby thought. First there was the hunting and the choosing of the item, then the excitement of bidding or buying them and then came the day of their arrival and the unwrapping and the admiring of them. Each was like a little Christmas.

Of course, there were some collections that she had to admit were a mistake. The miniature dogs, for example. Libby wasn't quite sure what had made her start collecting those dogs. She wasn't particularly keen on dogs especially small ones which yapped and bit ankles. But now, she had eighteen of them and had decided she didn't like them. At least she'd managed to find a little corner to hide them in.

Overall, her online bidding was a resounding success and she never let it interfere with her role as a mother and a wife. Although there had been that one time that she'd forgotten to pick Toby up from school because there'd been a mad frenzy of bidding at the last moment on a rare perfume bottle which she simply had to have.

Libby sighed. Toby was, perhaps, her biggest problem. Libby had the feeling that he knew exactly what she was up to. He'd look up at her with his big brown eyes and it was as if he could see inside her very mind and read all her thoughts.

'Why do you spend so much time on the computer, Mummy?' he'd ask.

'I don't, darling,' she'd say. 'Not as much as you with those games of yours!'

And he'd look at her, refusing to be brushed off by her attempt at humour and she'd instantly feel guilty. It would pass, of course. His anxious face would be banished from her mind in the rush to get to the computer once she'd dropped him off at school.

What a blessing school was, Libby thought, as she checked her email to see what was arriving and when. Mercifully, most of the packages were delivered when Toby was at school and Charlie at work. There had been that really awkward moment, though, when she'd been expecting a delivery of limited edition plates depicting astrological signs when Charlie had come home ill.

'What's that?' Charlie had called from upstairs after a very loud knock on the door.

'Oh, nothing, darling. It's a package for Mrs Clinton,' Libby had called up the stairs. 'I'll put it in the dining room and take it round to her later.'

Then there was the endless problem of all the boxes. Everything was so beautifully wrapped but it meant a lot of wastage when it was all unpacked. Libby kept a good proportion of the stuff in the very boxes they came in but she had to deal with the rest that she didn't want to keep and that was where the problem lay. She could flatten the boxes and put them in recycling bags to put out on bin day but how would she explain it all? There was only one solution: to stuff the boxes in the garage and then sneak them to the dump in the car when she could.

'I'm just taking the car,' she'd tell Charlie. 'Off round to Tanya's. I won't be long.'

Honestly, sometimes she felt like a naughty teenager and then she'd admonish herself for feeling such guilt. After all, collecting was an innocent enough pastime, wasn't it?

CHAPTER 7

'I can't believe how much fun that was,' Anna said as she and William returned to Fox Hill Manor. It was mid-afternoon and the sunshine was gilding the honey-coloured cottages and stone walls in the valley whilst a light breeze made the cow parsley dance along the hedgerows.

'And to think you didn't want to go,' William said.

Anna nodded. 'You know, I didn't even really want to come here at all.'

William glanced at her. 'To Fox Hill? Why not?'

'I don't like collectors,' she confessed.

'But your sister's one.'

'I know and I've *never* understood it.'

'Because you're not a collector yourself?'

'Perhaps. But I've always rather thought that a collector must be trying to compensate for something – that there's something missing from their lives. Perhaps there's a space to fill.'

'And you think that of my collection?' William asked.

Anna was quiet as they took a bend in the road and splashed through a shallow ford. 'I'm not sure now,' she said at last. 'I mean, I could almost understand it if you had a child. All these incredible things to hand down to the next generation. But what's their use otherwise? They're beautiful and interesting but not all of them have a use, do they?'

'Do things always have to have a use?'

'Yes! Absolutely!' she said, confused that he didn't agree with her.

'In *your* world perhaps but this is my world. You keep conveniently forgetting that,' he said, raking a hand through his fair hair which, like before, just had the effect of making it stick out at a slightly odd angle.

Anna smiled as they turned off the road and drove down the track towards the manor. 'So I do keep forgetting,' she said.

'Anyway, you're a collector too, you know.'

Anna frowned. 'I am not!'

William nodded, a little smile lighting his face. 'Yes you are. Most people collect something.'

'And what is it I'm meant to collect?'

'People. Or, rather, their stories.'

Anna tutted. 'That doesn't count.'

'Why not?'

'Because that's my job,' she said in a self-righteous manner.

William pulled up in the courtyard and got out of the car, Cocoa and Beanie leaping out in anticipation of a slightly longer walk than the one they'd had around the auction car park. 'I think you'll probably be wanting to get on with that job of yours,' William said.

'Oh, right,' Anna said.

'I have something I must attend to,' he said, unlocking and opening the front door for her. 'But first, a walk. Come on, boys,' he said, clapping his hands and Anna watched as he strode into the gardens towards the fields beyond without another word.

She gazed after William, watching the two blurs of fur legging it into the distance and wondering why she hadn't been invited to accompany him. Had he just brushed her off again because she'd been a little too direct honest for his liking? She shook her head.

'It was because you've got work to do – nothing more,' she told herself, walking into the hallway and deciding to make herself a cup of tea before going to her room and having a session on the laptop. It was then that she realised how hungry she was. It had been an age since breakfast and they'd only eaten a sandwich before leaving for the auction.

Entering the kitchen, Anna saw the dishes immediately: a dinner plate, cutlery and a single mug. She knew for a fact that they'd not been there at breakfast because she herself had cleared everything away. She also knew that William hadn't had time to eat a proper meal because he had been with her most of the day. So where had the dishes come from? Had Mrs Boothby come and gone in their absence, done a bit of housework and then helped herself to a meal and not tidied away afterwards? It didn't seem very likely. Or perhaps William had a house guest he hadn't told her about. But why would he hide something like that?

She looked at the dishes again and shook her head. It was probably nothing.

'And I have other things to be worrying about,' she told herself. 'Like book deadlines.'

She made herself a cup of tea, grabbed the end of a baguette and a couple of chocolate chip cookies she found in a jar and went up to her bedroom, smiling at the dozens of reflections that greeted her there.

She was just about to settle down at the laptop when her phone rang.

'Libby!' she cried as she answered it.

'Anna!' her sister cried back. 'I've been waiting to hear from you. How're you getting on? I was having visions of you being locked away in some dark attic somewhere by that mad collector and him refusing to let you out.'

'I'm fine. Everything's fine. I'm in my room at the moment but he certainly hasn't locked me in.'

'So what's he like?'

Anna sighed as she tried to sum up her host. 'Oh, you know – eccentric, mad and bonkers.'

Libby laughed. 'Is he really that bad?'

'No, I'm just joking. He's lovely. He's sweet and interesting and kind.'

'And handsome?'

'Well, I suppose he has certain country charm about him if you don't mind a mass of messy hair and more tweed than you can shake a walking stick at.'

'But you're getting on well with him, aren't you?' Libby said.

'Yes,' Anna said, 'although there was a bit of a blip when I said something silly. He really seemed to clam up for a while.' She paused. 'And I have this feeling he's not telling me everything.'

'Like what?'

'I'm not really sure,' she said, curling her feet up underneath herself on the bed. 'It's just a feeling I'm getting.'

'A journalist's intuition?' Libby said.

'Perhaps.'

'You think there's a story to uncover beyond the collection itself?'

'There might be,' Anna said.

'And here's me chatting away and distracting you from your work.'

'No, it's lovely to hear from you. Is everyone okay? How's that lovely nephew of mine?'

'He's fine. He wants to know if Mr Kitson really does have a canon.'

'He certainly does and mighty impressive it is too.'

'Well, if he finds out you're gossiping with your sister rather than writing that book he might very well fire it at you,' Libby said.

Anna laughed. 'I'll ring you soon.'

'Yes, tell me if you find anything juicy about your mystery man.'

They said their goodbyes and it was just as she hung up that Anna realized she'd forgotten to tell Libby about the blue pig.

It was after seven o'clock by the time Anna stopped typing. She looked up from her laptop and stretched her arms out above her. She hadn't seen or heard William or the dogs since they'd gone for their walk and she wondered where they were. They must be back by now, she reasoned. Perhaps they were in the kitchen. It was certainly time for some tea.

Leaving the silvery Mirror Room, Anna descended to the kitchen but there was nobody there.

'William?' she called out into the hallway. She walked along to the dining room but it was also empty. The sitting room, too, was vacant. Only the sound of the longcase clock could be heard.

It felt funny being in the house on her own. She almost felt as if she was trespassing.

'Trespassing,' she said, sounding the word to herself quietly. As soon as she heard it, a thought struck her. There was only one place in the whole of Fox Hill Manor where it really would be trespassing and that would be the dark corridor William had refused to show her.

She bit her lip and looked around her as if William might spring out from behind the clock or from under the coffee table at any moment.

'I'll just say I'm lost,' she told herself.

Quickly, before she had a chance to change her mind, Anna climbed the stairs up to the first floor and took the turn that led towards the unexplored corridor. She really felt like an explorer who'd been given a blank map to fill. Well, that's what being a journalist was, wasn't it? It was all about filling blank spaces with words. That's all she was doing. It was just an extension of her job and he couldn't blame her for it, could he?

Looking down the corridor now, she wondered if she really was doing the right thing. William had trusted her enough to leave her in his home alone and she was about to betray that trust.

But he won't know, she told herself again, daring to take a couple of steps forward. The wooden floorboards stretched far into the distance and ended in a beautiful mullioned window. There were two doors leading off to the right and three to the left and there was only one way to find out what was behind them and so she walked forward and reached out for the first door handle on the right. Taking a deep breath, she turned it and it opened into a bright room.

'Oh!' she couldn't help exclaiming because the room was completely empty. Not only that but it was in rather a bad state of repair with ancient wallpaper hanging in tatters and a nasty damp smell hanging in the air.

She walked across to the window. The view was still fabulous, despite the awfulness of the room. No wonder William hadn't shown her the day before. He just hadn't got around to making this part of the house liveable for his collection.

Anna wondered what he'd use it for. What else could he possibly find to collect that he didn't already have at Fox Hill? Perhaps a collection of old typewriters. Or shoes through the ages. Now that would be fun, she thought. Or maybe–

'What are you doing?' a voice – William's voice – suddenly startled her, making her spin around to face him.

'Oh, you shocked me!' she gasped, her hand flying to her heart like a bad actress.

'What are you doing up here?' he asked again, the look in his eyes piercing her very soul. She felt the full weight of guilt upon her and felt truly awful.

'I'm so sorry,' she said. 'I was just curious. I wanted to know–'

'But I told you yesterday,' he said, motioning for her to leave the room.

'I know,' she said. 'I thought you were hiding something.'

William frowned. 'Whatever gave you that impression?'

'Just a feeling,' Anna said helplessly.

'What on earth did you think I was hiding?' he asked, his tone angry and confused.

Anna shrugged helplessly. 'I don't know,' she said.

He sighed. 'Look, it's very odd for me to be doing any of this interview stuff at all. I'm finding it hard, if you must know the truth.'

Anna cringed inwardly. She was making him feel uncomfortable in his own home and that was the last thing she'd wanted to happen.

'I'm *really* sorry,' she said again. 'It's inexcusable. It was just that journalistic nosiness again.'

'I guess you fall back on that excuse a lot,' he said.

Anna tried not to flinch at the insult. Instead she took a deep breath. 'I said I was sorry.'

She left the room and started down the stairs.

'Anna,' William said and she wondered what else he was going to throw at her, 'I almost forgot. There's a school party coming tomorrow. Eleven o'clock. There'll be twenty ten-year-olds so you might want to lay low.'

'Can't I join in?' she asked. 'I think it'll be good for the book. And I can help out,' she added, worrying that he might be thinking she'd be just another person to keep an eye on.

'Well, if you really want to.'

'Yes, she said. 'I can keep an eye on any stragglers. Make sure they're not naughty and go wandering off into rooms they've no business being in.'

William looked at her and Anna gave a little smile.

He smiled back and nodded. 'I suppose you'll be able to tell the sort who does that?'

'Yes,' she said. 'Us nosy people know each other instantly.'

'Then my house will be in safe hands,' he said.

CHAPTER 8

There is nothing louder first thing in the morning than twenty excitable schoolchildren crammed into a narrow hallway. Anna was wondering if she should have stayed in the sanctuary of her bedroom but she desperately wanted to see William in action as a tour guide.

Nothing more was mentioned about Anna's private tour of the house and she was intensely grateful for that. Today was a new start and she was going to do her very best not to insult her host nor go behind his back and upset him. She really was.

There were two teachers with the children, a small pinched-looking woman with frizzy brown hair called Mrs Banwell, and a rather round woman with a smiley face called Miss Cole.

'Right,' William said, clapping his great hands together to get everybody's attention. 'I'm William Kitson and I'd like to welcome you all to my home, Fox Hill Manor or FHM as we like to call it.'

Mrs Banwell and Miss Cole gave a polite chuckle each but the children looked nonplussed.

'I'm very privileged to live in such a marvellous old property and I'm hoping you'll all enjoy your time here today. You'll be pleased to hear that there are no worksheets BUT I will be asking some questions at the end of the tour so *pay attention* and there's a special prize for the person who gets most of the questions right.'

Everyone looked really excited at this declaration and William led the way through the downstairs rooms.

It was just as the tour was really getting into its stride when the first drops of rain were heard on the windows. The sky had darkened and so had the rooms, casting everything into gloom. There were whisperings of excitement amongst the children and the two teachers tried to silence them with hushing but they seemed to be fighting a losing battle as, suddenly, everything took on a surreal, underwater hue.

William looked at Anna and smiled. She'd read online that he was a recluse, that he didn't have much to do with anyone and that he was often very rude but, looking at him now, completely surrounded by children, he looked in his element.

She watched in fascination as he captivated the children with his tales from history:

'This cannon was fired at Collingwood Castle in Cuthland during the Civil War and did a lot of damage.'

He told them about his favourite pieces from the collection and he described how he found his beloved antiques:

'Collecting takes you to some strange places. I once discovered an eighteenth-century sword buried under straw in a horse's stable. The owner didn't even know it was there and was so surprised that he let me have it for free, thinking it was just a piece of rubbish.'

And then it was question time:

'If you had to sell something, what would it be?'

'I'd sell my nose or my toes or my ears before I'd sell something from my collection,' William told them and was greeted by a round of giggles.

There were more questions about the children's favourite pieces from the collection, about William and – finally –

'Is this lady your girlfriend?'

William's eyes widened.

Mrs Banwell looked equally surprised. 'Damon! If you haven't got a sensible question then just keep quiet or you can go and sit on the coach.'

'It's all right,' William assured her. 'This is Miss McCall and she's my friend.'

Anna instantly blushed as she caught William's eye. Was she? Was she really his friend? She was just enjoying the warm glow that his comment had produced when Mrs Banwell suddenly broke the spell.

'Where's Nicholas?' she asked.

William and Anna looked around. Who was Nicholas and what did he look like? And how long had been missing for?

'Who's his partner?' Miss Cole asked.

'I am,' a boy with bright red hair said.

'Ah, Billy! I might've known,' Mrs Banwell said. 'And when did you last see him?'

Billy shrugged and Anna felt sorry for him. Why should he be made responsible for somebody else? Anna knew that not one of the children would be monitoring their partners when there were swords and masks to look at.

'Mr Kitson, I'm afraid it appears that we've lost Nicholas,' Mrs Banwell said.

'Okay,' William said, 'then we'd better look for him. Why don't you guys sit in the Sword Passage and pick something to draw?'

'Good idea,' Miss Cole said. 'Come along, everyone and – for goodness' sake – *keep together!*'

Anna looked at William. 'Where could he be?' she whispered to him.

'Well, he can't be far away, can he?'

'I suppose not,' Anna said, noticing that William sounded far more concerned now that they were on their own. 'Perhaps he needed the toilet.'

William nodded. 'Yes,' he said, 'I pointed that out to them on the way in, didn't I?'

'Hey!' Anna said, grabbing his arm as he went to leave the room. 'It'll be all right.'

'I know,' he said, but his pale face looked as if he didn't quite believe it.

They both left the room and went off to check the downstairs toilet but it was empty.

'Where would he go?' William asked.

'Well, if I was a boy, I'd probably want to see something exciting. Maybe he went back to see the armour?'

'Yes, yes!' William said, nodding wildly.

But Nicholas wasn't there either.

'Might he have gone upstairs?' Anna asked.

'Why would he have gone upstairs?' William said.

'Because he's a boy,' Anna said, 'and they like to go where they shouldn't.'

For the first time, William looked more than anxious. He looked annoyed.

'This must have happened before,' Anna said.

'No, never. If you'd been keeping an eye on everyone–'

'Me? It wasn't *my* fault!' Anna said, angry that William should suggest that it was.

But William didn't appear to be listening. He had his back to her and was already heading up the stairs. Anna followed behind him. It was getting increasingly dark and an angry patter of rain rattled the window on the landing as if a handful of tiny stones had just been thrown.

'Maybe he's scared of storms?' Anna suggested. 'He might've run away to hide.'

'But the storm's just started and we don't know how long he's been missing for.'

They continued up the stairs and William began searching the rooms.

'Nicholas!' he shouted, his voice strained and fretful.

'Nicholas?' Anna called, trying not to scare the boy even more.

The whole house had darkened into deep shadows and it was becoming hard to see. William started switching lights on but still the boy could not be found.

'Where the hell is he?'

Anna flinched at the angry tone of William's voice.

It was then that voices were heard from downstairs.

'Is that him?' William asked, bounding down the stairs. Anna followed, her feet clattering loudly behind him.

When they rejoined the school party, everybody seemed to be talking at once, all crowded around a small dark-haired boy.

'QUIET!' Mrs Banwell shouted, desperately trying to restore order.

'Where've you been?' Anna said. 'Everyone's been so worried about you!'

'I got lost,' the boy said but he didn't sound very convincing. Anna noticed how white his face was.

'Nicholas!' Mrs Banwell cried. 'I told you all not to go wandering off! Where *were* you?'

'In a room,' the poor boy said, pointing vaguely in the direction of upstairs. 'There was this old woman,' he said, 'with really white hair and scary eyes.'

There were sudden mutterings amongst the children.

'Nicholas has seen a ghost!'

'It's haunted!'

'Fox Hill Manor's haunted!'

'Shush!' Mrs Banwell said. 'I'm sure it's no such thing, is it, Mr Kitson?'

'But I *saw* her!' Nicholas protested.

Anna looked at William who was standing at the back of the

room. His face was white too.

'Is there a ghost, sir?' one of the boys at the front asked.

William laughed. 'This is an old house with many secrets. Who knows if there is a ghost?'

Mrs Banwell didn't look at all pleased with this answer. 'I'm sure Nicholas just caught his reflection in a window or a mirror or something,' she said.

'Yeah!' another boy said. 'Nicholas looks like an old lady.'

Anna looked at the poor boy. Now he looked white, frightened and angry all at the same time.

Miss Cole decided to take charge. 'I think it's probably about time for lunch,' she said. 'Mr Kitson?'

'Ah, yes,' William said, looking relieved that he could be excused duty for a while. 'If you'll follow me,' he said.

Provision had been made in the kitchen where the children all jostled along the two great benches at the trestle table. It was as if it had been made for such an event and Anna smiled as they all emptied out the rucksacks that had been placed there earlier and William made cups of tea for Mrs Banwell and Miss Cole.

'Anna?' he asked.

'Thank you,' she said. 'Milk, one sugar.'

With two teas for themselves, they left the pupils and teachers, promising to be back later on, and then walked through to the small sitting room. William still looked pale and had lost some of the sparkle with which he'd greeted the children earlier.

'What do you make of Nicholas?' Anna asked, sipping her hot tea and watching William closely for his response.

'He's a boy with a vivid imagination is what I think.'

'You don't think he saw an old lady?'

'He probably just saw a portrait in the half-light or got spooked by his own reflection. These things happen in big old houses – especially during storms.'

Anna looked out of the window. There hadn't been any thunder or lightning yet but the rain was far from over. The Elm Valley looked dejected and depressed under the bruised sky and angry clouds, and the flowers in the garden seemed to be groaning and drowning.

'Anna?' William suddenly said.

'Yes?'

'I'm sorry about before.'

'Oh,' she said. 'Don't worry.'

'It wasn't your fault and I shouldn't have blamed you like that.'

'Are you only apologizing so I don't write about it?'

William stared at her.

'I'm joking!' she said. 'Relax!'

He gave a little smile. 'You asked me why I didn't do more tours. That's why!'

'Do many people get lost, then?'

'No,' he said, 'not many. And that's the way I intend to keep it.'

'But everyone was having such a good time. You really should do more of them.'

William shook his head. 'I don't think so.'

Anna was disappointed. 'You're very protective of this house, aren't you?'

He looked at her and, for a moment, he didn't speak. 'Of course,' he said. She then watched as he got up. 'I'm just going to let the dogs out for a stretch before question time begins.'

'But it's still raining,' she said as he left the room. She frowned. Sometimes, she really felt that she didn't understand this man at all.

Putting down her cup of tea, she decided to go up to her bedroom and see if he really was going out into the garden. She had a good view from her window and, once back in her room, positioned herself in such a way that she could see out but so that she wouldn't be spotted.

It was still pouring with rain and everything looked grey. Surely Cocoa and Beanie wouldn't want to go out in such weather. Anna watched, her eyes scanning the courtyard and the garden for signs of dog walking. She'd almost given up when she suddenly saw William. Dressed in a big waterproof coat with a flat cap on his head, he strode out into one of the walled gardens, Cocoa and Beanie following behind. The dogs were each wearing a little jacket and didn't seem to mind the rain at all as they trotted after their owner.

She was just about to sit down on her bed and open her laptop when William stopped walking and looked back at the house, his neck craning slightly. Watching, Anna gasped as he waved a hand in the air. Had he seen her? No, he couldn't have. Anyway, he was waving up to another part of the house. Then, he continued down the path with the two terriers in tow.

'What was all that about?' Anna asked herself. Had he spotted one of the teachers? No. They were both downstairs and he had definitely waved upstairs.

She sat on the edge of her bed mulling over his strange behaviour and then she remembered what Nicholas had said. Something about a lady. A white-haired lady. Was that whom William had been waving to? Was there a white-haired lady living at Fox Hill Manor? And, if there was, who was she and why was William keeping her a secret?

CHAPTER 9

Anna hadn't seen William since the school party had left. He'd followed everyone outside to wave them off and then made some vague excuse about seeing somebody in town and left. Feeling somewhat disgruntled, Anna had returned to her bedroom and got to work on her article. Cocoa and Beanie had followed her upstairs and were lying by her feet as her fingers danced over the keys on her laptop.

'I know,' she said to them as she deleted an angry paragraph she'd written about William as a warm-up, 'he's left me without so much as a by-your-leave too. Very rude, your owner.'

One of the dogs – she wasn't sure which – cocked its head to one side and looked sympathetic. Anna smiled at him and sighed. Then, flexing her fingers, she determined to get on with her work, the minutes rolling into hours as she lost herself in her writing.

She wrote about the history of the house and how William had first discovered it and the work he'd done on it, breathing new life into the old stones and bringing it to life with his collection. She wrote about the rooms and picked a few of the key items which stood out like the Cantonese cabinet, the Samurai swords and the boneshaker bicycles, and she wrote about the school tour and how the children had responded to the collection.

It wasn't until there was a loud knock at the door and the dogs started barking that she lifted her head from the bright screen of her laptop. Cocoa and Beanie were up, jumping and barking as the knocking continued. Anna looked at her watch. It was after nine – much later than she'd thought. She hadn't meant to work so late and then felt horribly guilty that she hadn't even thought about the poor dogs.

'Come on, boys,' she said, getting up to see who it was. They ran out of the room ahead of her and down the stairs towards the door.

It couldn't be William, Anna thought. The dogs would recognise him and wouldn't be barking like that, surely?

Anna suddenly realized how dark it was in the hallway and switched on a lamp, flooding the narrow passage with soft light. At least that was better but she was still aware of how vulnerable she was in the big old house all on her own. It was some way even to the main road and anyone could just drive down and knock on the door.

'Don't be silly,' she told herself. 'You've been watching too many horror movies.' And, with that, she opened the door.

The dogs were outside before she could stop them.

'Cocoa! Beanie!' she shouted after them, and then she saw the tall man trying desperately to shelter in the doorway.

'Hello, boys!' he called cheerily as the dogs tore past him and Anna thought she recognised his voice. 'Oh,' he said, turning to face her, 'hello. I've come to see William.'

'He's out, I'm afraid,' Anna said, and then wondered if it was wise to say that.

'Any idea when he'll be back?' the man asked.

'No,' Anna said. 'I'm sorry – who are you?'

'George,' he said, presenting her with his hand. 'George Kitson.'

'William's brother?'

'Big brother,' he said.

'He didn't tell me.'

'And you are?'

'Oh, Anna. Anna McCall. I'm a writer.'

'And girlfriend?'

'Gracious, no! I'm a journalist.'

George frowned. 'A bit late for interviewing, isn't it?'

'I'm here for a book,' she said.

'Which you can tell me all about once you've invited me inside for a drink. I'm absolutely soaked!'

'Well,' Anna said, 'if you're sure you're William's brother, I suppose I should invite you in.'

'Before I drown right here on the doorstep. Come on, boys,' he shouted at the dogs and they trotted inside, shaking their little wet bodies in the hallway before anyone could think off rubbing them with a towel. 'Off on one of his blasted hunting trips, is he?' George asked.

'William? I've no idea. We had a school party this morning and then he left straight after. Didn't say where he was going.'

'Sounds about right,' George said, shaking off his wax jacket and hanging it up on a hook where it dripped melodiously.

'Would you like a coffee?' Anna asked.

George raised an eyebrow. 'So William hasn't told you all the secrets of his house yet?'

'What do you mean?' Anna asked, immediately thinking about ghosts and hidden wives up in the attics.

'Like where he keeps his fine wines.'

'Oh!' Anna gasped.

'Fancy having a journalist to stay and not telling her where the alcohol is,' George said, leading the way into the sitting room and making straight for a beautiful wooden cabinet at the far side.

'Glass of red?' he said as he opened the double doors to reveal the hidden treasures.

'Well, I'm not sure–'

'Relax,' George said, 'he won't begrudge his brother a glass or two of wine.'

Anna smiled uneasily. She still wasn't at all sure about this strange man whom she'd found on the doorstep although he did look a lot like William, she thought. He shared William's height and had the same tousled fair hair and bright, inquisitive eyes but his manner was so different. He seemed at ease with her straightaway and there wasn't that awkwardness about him that William often displayed.

Anna sat down and Cocoa and Beanie settled by her feet and the fug of warm, wet dog soon filled the room. She watched as George helped himself to two crystal glasses, filling each with deep red wine.

'Ah!' he said, sniffing his glass appreciatively. 'You have to give it to William. He knows his stuff.' He walked across the room and handed Anna a glass and then plonked himself down in a chair as if he was in his own living room.

'You're not at all like him,' Anna said and then blushed. 'I mean, you are to look at.'

George nodded. 'Perhaps because we're not really brothers.'

Anna suddenly felt a wave of panic and she felt the colour drain away from her face. Had the brother tale just been a line to get inside the house?

'We're half-brothers really,' George explained.

Anna felt herself relaxing once again. '*Oh!*' she said with a sigh of relief.

'Share the same father,' George said. 'But, when William's father died, he came to live with us – me and my mother, Paula.'

'But what about his own mother?'

'Oh, she'd left to live with someone else years before,' George said, taking a sip of his wine. 'Wasn't interested in her son at all apparently.'

'God, that's awful. Poor William,' Anna said, trying to imagine the young, displaced boy.

'Oh, don't feel too sorry for him. Born survivor is William. My mother made sure of that.'

'How do you mean?'

'Well, he didn't always get on with Paula. You see, she made the mistake of selling something of his.'

'What?' Anna asked.

'Some cabinet or other. I don't remember. Anyway, he made a real fuss about it and they've never spoken since.'

'Not the Cantonese cabinet?' she asked with a frown.

George frowned. 'Rings a bell.'

'But that's here – in Fox Hill Manor.'

'Yes,' George said, 'I heard he'd managed to track it down. Like a bloodhound with antiques is young Will.' He laughed.

Anna's eyes widened. She'd had no idea that William had had such a strange childhood.

'Look, I'm not sure if I'm meant to have said all that,' George suddenly said, sitting forward on the sofa. 'I mean, you're a reporter, aren't you?'

'Not really,' she said. 'I'm a freelance writer. Mostly biographies, features in national magazines and that kind of thing.'

'Same thing, isn't it? Someone tells you something and you write about it,' George said matter-of-factly.

'Well, if you're worried, I promise I won't mention anything you've just told me,' she said.

'Oh, I'm not worried. You can write what you want just don't tell young Will where you got it from. He has a memory like an elephant and I'd never be made welcome here again. In fact, I'm not sure I'm that welcome here now.'

'What do you mean?'

George looked towards the door as if expecting an angry brother to walk through it and throw him out into the rain. 'Let's just say we don't see eye to eye on a few things,' he said with a sigh, running his hand through his hair in a manner that reminded her of William.

'Like what?'

George paused before answering. 'Just how much do you know about the collection here?' he asked. But Anna didn't get a chance to answer because it was then that Cocoa and Beanie sprang up as they heard the front door open.

Anna and George sat perfectly still, staring at each other anxiously as they waited for William to enter the living room.

'Anna? You there?' he called above the deafening bark of the dogs as he closed the door behind him. 'Quiet boys!'

'Yes, I'm here,' Anna said, springing up from her chair. She looked at George and he held a finger up to his mouth.

'I want to surprise him,' he whispered.

Anna walked out into the hallway and saw William taking off his coat. 'What a night!' he said. 'The roads are like rivers out there. Dogs okay? They been out?'

'Yes, they're fine. We went for a walk before and they've had their tea. Where've you been?' she asked.

'Cirencester,' he said. 'There's a guy who has the most amazing antiques shop out that way. Keeps an eye open for me. I like to keep in touch with him – tell him what I'm looking out for.'

Anna nodded but she wasn't really listening. 'William – there's someone–' but she didn't get a chance to warn him because George had left the living room and was standing in the hallway, his glass of red wine in his hand. 'Hello, Will,' he said. 'Haven't you got a welcome for your big brother?'

The rain became progressively heavier as the night continued and soon the heavens were rumbling and flashing. Libby was catching up on some neglected mountains of ironing, wondering where it had all come from and debating whether it had actually been multiplying on its own in the laundry basket when a small head peeped around the kitchen door.

'Toby?' she cried. 'You should be in bed!'

'I can't sleep. The thunder's got into my head,' he said, shuffling into the room in his bright green dragon-embroidered slippers.

'There's nothing to worry about,' Libby said, switching off the iron and ruffling his tousled hair.

'But it sounds so close,' Toby said.

'It isn't really. It just likes to make a big old fuss. Come on, let's get you back upstairs,' she said, taking his hand and leading him out of the kitchen. She was glad of an excuse to get away from the laundry.

'I don't want to go to bed,' Toby complained.

Libby bit her lip. 'Your dad's in bed,' she said, thinking of the snoring form of Charlie who had to get up extra early the next morning and wouldn't want to be disturbed. 'He's not worried about some silly little storm.' As soon as the words were out of her mouth, she regretted saying them because Toby looked genuinely terrified. 'I tell you what,' she said, 'why don't we search for dragons?'

Toby's eyes widened. 'What do you mean?'

'Ah! Wait and see,' Libby said, taking him into the spare room that doubled as a study. They had to climb over a couple of bin bags to get in there and Libby made a mental note to sort them out as soon as possible before Charlie started asking awkward questions about their contents. Truth be told, she'd forgotten what was in them. They could either be the nineteen-sixties dresses she'd bought online, the job lot of cushions from the car boot sale or the twelve teddy bears she'd liberated from a local charity shop where they'd looked so forlorn on the shelves above the ladies' shoe rack.

'Right,' she said, 'let's get comfy.'

Switching a computer on in a thunderstorm probably wasn't the wisest of moves but Libby couldn't think of anything else to do to take Toby's mind off things. Anyway, she reasoned, they had one of those protector things in case a bolt of lightning did find its way down to earth via their house.

'I find that a quick surf around on the internet auction sites always takes my mind off any problems,' Libby said, kissing the top of Toby's head as he sat on her knee to get comfortable. 'Now, what models are you looking for at the moment to complete your collections?'

'Some Fire-breathing Beasts,' Toby said, getting into the swing of things immediately.

'Of course,' Libby said as she quickly logged on. 'How could I forget?'

'I'm still after the Dragon of Death Vale,' Toby said, 'and the Dragon of Ruby Mountain, and Dark Water Dale.'

Libby nodded. That was plenty to be getting on with.

Toby watched as his mum's fingers flew across the keyboard,

searching, clicking, and comparing sites. He could tell she was a pro and their faces glowed in the light from the screen and they both soon forgot the raging storm outside.

Twenty minutes later, they had found a near-perfect Dragon of Ruby Mountain at a bargain price.

'There we are,' Libby said with a big smile, 'it only takes a bit of time.'

'Thanks, Mum!' Toby enthused.

'Oh, look at that dinosaur!' Libby said, returning her gaze to the screen. 'Is that part of your collection?'

'No. That's different.'

'It's very cute, though, isn't it?' she said. 'It would look perfect on your bedside table, don't you think?'

Toby gave a little shrug.

'Would you like it?' she asked him, her eyes wide with excitement and her finger hovering over the 'Buy it Now' button.

For a split second, Toby looked a little unsure as if he was being tested, perhaps, but then he nodded and a big grin found its way across his face as his mum clicked through to the PayPal site.

Things weren't quite so happy back at Fox Hill Manor. William was staring at his brother George without the faintest trace of pleasure at seeing him.

'Don't worry about pleasantries,' George said, 'We've introduced ourselves,' he said, nodding towards Anna.

'What are you doing here?' William asked bluntly.

'That's no welcome for your old bro,' George said with a grin.

'I see you've helped yourself.'

'Only in anticipation of you offering me a glass,' George said. 'You should pour yourself one and take the edge of that mood of yours.'

There was a moment's pause when nobody spoke.

'Perhaps I should go to my room?' Anna suggested.

'Now, why would you want to go and do that?' George asked. 'You've been a perfect companion whilst waiting for my dear brother to come home.'

Anna waited for William to say something. 'Shall we all sit down? I could get you a drink?' she said.

At last, William nodded and the three of them went into the living room.

'So, you've been shopping, have you?' George said with a little smile.

'It's not exactly shopping,' William said angrily.

'Hmmm, let me see,' George said. 'You drive halfway across the county in a thunderstorm to talk to some guy about spending an obscene amount of money. That sounds like the very worst shopping-addict I've ever heard of.'

Anna suddenly realised that she was holding her breath and exhaled quickly before she turned red in the face. She'd never felt so uncomfortable in her life.

'What do you want?' William asked. 'Because it seems to me that we've nothing to say to each other.'

A stony silence filled the room and then George sighed. 'Mum's dead,' he said. 'Died the night before last.'

'Paula?' Anna said.

'How do you know about Paula?' William asked.

'We were just having a nice friendly chat before you came home,' George said. 'Believe it or not, some people are capable of that.'

'Gosh, I'm sorry to hear about your mother,' Anna said to George.

'Thank you, my dear,' George said with a little nod.

'When's the funeral?' William asked.

'Next Tuesday. Three o'clock.'

William nodded.

'You'll be there?' George asked. 'I believe she's left you some money. She said something about making amends.'

'I don't need to be bribed by money to attend a funeral,' William said.

'Right,' George said, draining his glass of wine and standing up. 'I'd better be off.'

William stood up too. 'Why did you come all this way? Why didn't you just ring?'

George shrugged. 'I had some business in Cheltenham. I thought I'd stop by on the way back.'

'You're not driving far tonight, are you?' Anna asked as they walked through the hallway. 'The weather's appalling.'

'No, I've got a hotel booked nearby.'

'Oh, couldn't you stay–' Anna began.

'I'm best suited to a hotel,' George interrupted her. 'Very nice to meet you, though.' He leant forward and kissed her cheek. Anna was a little taken aback and saw the dark frown on William's face.

'She's a great girl, Will. You should tell her about your collection before she finds out for herself.'

Anna looked at William. What exactly hadn't he told her?

'Goodbye, George,' William said curtly as he opened the door.

'See you on Tuesday,' George said, crunching across the gravel in the pouring rain to where he'd parked his car.

'Shouldn't you have invited him to stay?' Anna said following William back into the house.

'He's got a hotel.'

'That's not the point, though, is it?' Anna said.

'He wouldn't be at home here,' William told her.

'No, I can see that,' Anna said. 'You didn't exactly make him feel welcome, did you? And what did he mean about the collection?'

'He meant nothing. He just likes to make trouble. Now, it's been a very long day,' he said. 'If you'll excuse me.'

Anna sighed. In her opinion, William needed a lot of excusing.

CHAPTER 10

As soon as William reached his bedroom, he closed the door behind him and exhaled a long, slow breath. He hated being rude. It wasn't in his nature at all and yet the last few days had forced him into being so, culminating in the arrival of George that evening.

He ran a hand through his hair and then took his glasses off and rubbed his eyes. Whatever must Anna think of him now? First he'd shouted at her over that affair with Nicholas the schoolboy and now she thought him heartless for throwing his brother out in the middle of a storm just after he'd told him he'd lost his mother. Things weren't going well. But then, what had he expected?

When he'd invited a journalist into his home, he'd had no intentions of befriending her – that hadn't been part of his agenda at all. He'd wanted nothing more than a slightly prolonged business-like meeting, allowing him to make his collection understood. Instead he'd found – he'd found – what? He sighed. He'd found a bright and very sweet woman whom he liked spending time with and, what was more, she seemed to understand his collection. Okay, so there'd been a lot of resistance at first but he'd seen those rigid ideas of hers slowly dissolving. He'd watched her face as he'd shown her the rooms, explaining the items and sharing their magic. He'd seen the light in her eyes and the joy behind her smile. But he'd also seen the accusation at what she'd thought was the cruel treatment of George.

He closed his eyes. He couldn't have had George stay at FHM. His brother knew his secrets and he was just the sort of person to reveal them too. In fact, William was worrying that something might have been said already. What exactly had passed between George and Anna before he'd got home? He dreaded to think what might have happened if he hadn't arrived home when he had done.

And now, on top of everything else, there was Paula's funeral to contend with. He knew he'd have to go. It would seem churlish of him if he didn't, even though it had always been perfectly obvious to everyone around them that they hadn't gone on. She may well have taken him into her home after his own mother had died but she'd never let him forget the fact. He was the son of the second Mrs Kitson – the woman who had broken her family apart.

He walked over to the bedroom window and looked out into the darkness. Anna had asked him when he'd started collecting and, although the interest had always been there – with the gift of his mother's Cantonese cabinet – he'd really started at that dreadful time after his mother had died. The early eighteenth-century piece of furniture had been her pride and joy and, together, they would open the black double doors to reveal the exquisitely gilded interior and the tiny drawers opened by even tinier keys.

When he'd inherited it, he'd filled it with tiny objects and curios like fossils, coins and shells which he either found or bought with his pocket money. They hadn't been collector's pieces but, at the time, they were his entire world. His little treasures, he called them.

He also had a Georgian dolls' house he'd bought at a car boot sale. It had been in an appalling state and he'd spent months restoring it before collecting the furniture. Thinking about it now, it was like Fox Hill Manor in miniature – each room was filled with beautiful objects: clocks, tables, chairs, a piano – each of the items lovingly chosen and, most importantly, the craftsmanship had always been exquisite.

'That's girls' stuff,' George had said cruelly when he'd forced his way into William's room and picked up one of the chairs.

'Careful!' William had cried. 'It's fragile.' And he'd watched helplessly as George had casually crushed it between his fingers.

'So it is,' he'd said.

And that was George. Oh, he may have seemed charming and affable – Anna had certainly been taken in by him – but, underneath, he was no more than a thug, bent on destroying whatever was most precious and that was why William didn't want him anywhere near Fox Hill Manor and certainly nowhere near Anna.

It was no use. Anna couldn't sleep. She'd always been nervous of storms once night fell and couldn't understand how anybody could possibly sleep during them. It was like trying to sleep through an angry Beethoven symphony, she thought, as she swung her legs out of bed and found the soft comfort of her slippers.

A sudden silvery lightning strike lit up the bedroom, flashing off the mirrors and filling the room with wild light. Anna braced herself for the rumble of thunder which would surely follow, a great grumbling, belly-turning sound that was mighty and monstrous. She shivered. She didn't want to stay in this room. The walls of mirrors made the whole experience nightmarish and she kept half-believing that there were ghoulish faces staring back at her from out of the silvery depths. She had to get out of there.

Opening the door of the Mirror Room, Anna looked up and down the corridor, hoping for signs of life but William was obviously sleeping or already downstairs with a comforting hot drink.

Fox Hill Manor was the strangest of houses. Cosy and comforting during the day, its personality seemed to undergo a change once night arrived, as if it had taken a drink of Doctor Jekyll's potion and had metamorphosed into the architectural equivalent of Mr Hyde. The wooden panelling became darker than any forest and the corridors seemed to hold all sorts of menaces in their shadows. Anna tried to avoid the spookiest of the rooms. She had no intention of crossing paths with the Samurai warriors on such a night nor did she want to see William's collection of axes, rifles and guns.

There was only one place of comfort and that was the kitchen. If one was going to be kept up all night, one might as well do it with a sandwich and a cup of tea, she reasoned.

She crept along the corridors slowly as her eyes adjusted to the dim light. William was not one to leave on more than one light on each storey and Anna began to curse him now for his conservation-addled brain.

'A light would be very welcome right now,' Anna whispered to herself as she tried to avoid glancing into the shadows.

A sudden bolt of lightning lit up the passageway from the landing window she was passing.

'Not *that* kind of light!' she cried, her heart pounding in shock.

Finally, she made it to the ground floor and was filled with a sense of disproportionate relief that a light was already on in the kitchen. William hadn't struck her as being the type to be bothered by storms but she was glad he was there. It would be good to have someone to talk to until the heavens had calmed themselves.

However, as Anna entered the kitchen, she soon realised that it wasn't William sitting at the table at all. It was an old lady.

Anna stood by the door, surprised into stillness. The woman didn't appear to have heard her and Anna was able to observe her for a moment. She was taking delicate sips from a mug of tea which was clutched in great gnarled hands. Her hair was shoulder-length, straight and as white as a summer cloud and her skin was astonishingly pale and looked as fine as tissue paper.

Nicholas's white-haired lady, she thought. So the boy hadn't been lying at all; *William* had.

Anna was reluctant to disturb the old woman – she looked so peaceful – but the need for a companion overrode this as did her curiosity and she took a step forward.

'Hello,' she said, hesitatingly.

The old woman leapt up in her chair.

'Are you okay?' Anna said, walking forward quickly.

'Oh!' the old lady exclaimed. 'You did give me a shock.'

'I'm sorry,' Anna said quickly. 'I didn't mean to. Did you spill your drink?'

The old lady looked up but Anna wasn't sure if she could see her properly. Her eyes – which were a pale, pearly blue – looked cloudy.

'My drink? No. It's finished.'

'Then let me get you another. I was going to make one for myself.'

'I'd better not, dear, or I'll be tripping to the toilet for the rest of the night.'

Anna smiled and moved towards the kettle to boil it. As she reached for a mug, she turned to look at the old lady again, wondering who she was. Was this the woman whose cups and plates she'd been finding? And why on earth hadn't William told her about her?

She was glad that William was sleeping through the storm because it gave her the opportunity to find out as much as she could. But she'd do it tactfully. She didn't want to scare the woman.

'I couldn't sleep,' Anna said, pushing her hair away from her face. 'I hate storms.'

The old lady nodded. 'Me too. Always have and I've seen many. I still remember the great storm of seventy-two. What a horror that was.'

Anna smiled. 'I don't remember that one.'

'Of course you wouldn't,' the lady said. 'You're far too young. A real wild night, it was. Brought the church steeple down and countless trees. Fair shook my bones, it did, and they were old back then.'

'I've always been an absolute baby with storms. Don't mind the rain but I'll never understand the need for thunder and lightning,' Anna said as she made her cup of tea with an extra large spoonful of sugar. 'I mean, it's a lot of fuss and noise with no end product as far as I can see. Except damage. Do you think this old house will be okay?' Anna suddenly looked around the room as if it might cave in at any moment.

'This one's built to last,' the old lady said. 'Like me.'

Anna took her mug of tea to the table and sat down.

'You must be Anna,' the old lady said. 'William's told me all about you.'

'Has he?' Anna said, genuinely surprised.

'Oh, yes. He's very impressed with you,' she said with a little chuckle that sounded like a meadow stream. 'He says you work too hard.'

'Oh, did he now?'

'Yes. That's very ageing, you know. And I should know!'

'What sort of jobs did you do?' Anna asked, trying to make it sound as casual a question as possible.

'Me? Oh, let me see if I can remember. I was a farmhand for a time, a ladies' maid, a shop assistant, a nanny–' she stopped as if trying to remember if she'd left anything out.

Anna nodded. 'A bit of everything, then?'

'Oh, yes. But nothing – you know – that required reading. I never got the hang of reading although I've tried many a time.'

Anna frowned. She didn't know of anyone who couldn't read. Even her young nephew, Toby, raced through book after book. Anna couldn't imagine her world without the printed word. It would be bleak and barren. Half a world, really.

'Have you tried listening to audio books?' Anna asked. 'I always have a few in the house.'

The old lady nodded. 'William bought me some a while back but they all sent me to sleep and so I never found out what happened in the end.'

Anna laughed. 'Do you like films?'

The old lady shook her head. 'My eyes won't let me, I'm afraid. I can only make out a bit of a blur.'

Anna watched her, fascinated by who she was. 'What's your name?' she asked.

'My name?' the old woman chuckled. 'You want to know who I am, do you?'

Suddenly, Anna was aware of a figure standing in the kitchen doorway. It was William.

'Oh, William, my dear. Did the storm wake you?' the old lady asked, obviously having sensed William's presence too.

'No,' William said. 'I heard Anna get up.'

'I couldn't sleep,' Anna said unnecessarily, her eyes still on the old lady.

'Hadn't you better get back to bed?' he asked, moving towards the woman and offering an arm to help her up. 'It's not very warm down here.'

'Oh, what a fuss. Always fussing after me, he is,' the old lady said, smiling at Anna as she was hoisted out of the chair.

'You'll be comfier upstairs,' William said. 'You should've called me if you needed something.'

'What nonsense. I'm not going to disturb you every time I need something.'

'But you should.' William led her out of the kitchen. Once he was in the hallway, he turned to face Anna. 'You should go to bed,' he said.

Anna's mouth dropped open. He had no intention of introducing her to this woman at all, did he?

Anna watched as they disappeared down the corridor together and then drained her mug of tea, frowning at William's intensely bad manners.

Predictably, the morning after the storm was calm and bright, making Anna wonder if she'd imagined the whole thing; it certainly had a dream-like quality about it now. The Mirror Room had returned to its silvery self, beautiful and without a shred of stormy eeriness about it, and the wooden floorboards no longer looked like the entrance to some deep dark abyss.

Peeping out of her curtains and gazing out over the garden, Anna saw that it was bathed in early morning sunshine. The dovecote was covered in white doves and the warm golden stone of the walled garden seemed to glow. There was also a pair of Border Terriers flopped on the neatly cut lawn which told Anna that William was out and about – a perfect time to question him because there was one memory of the night before which she didn't want to shake from her head and that was the strange old lady she'd met in the kitchen.

Getting washed and dressed, Anna raced down to the kitchen for something quick to eat. Finding the fruit bowl full of peaches, she grabbed one and ate on the move, not wanting to miss William in the garden when he was likely to be in a good mood.

Stepping out into the sunshine, Anna inhaled deeply. The rich dark earth smelt wonderful after the rain and all the plants looked especially green and lush. The air was apple-fresh and a pair of swifts flew over the garden, their cries piercingly beautiful.

Almost at once, Cocoa and Beanie saw her and trotted down the path towards her.

'Hello, boys,' Anna said, bending down to ruffle their hairy heads. 'Where's your lord and master, then?' She looked down the path and saw William half-hidden in one of the borders as he tackled a plant.

'Good morning,' she called.

He looked up from out of his cultivated jungle. 'Good morning,' he said, stepping back out onto the path. 'Did you manage to get to sleep?' he asked as Anna and the dogs approached.

'Yes. Finally.'

'Good,' he said.

'Nothing damaged, is there?' Anna asked, looking around the garden.

'Not really. I was just straightening a few things. Have you had breakfast?'

Anna held up her peach and William frowned.

'It's fine,' she said.

'It absolutely isn't. I insist on a fully cooked breakfast,' he said. 'Come with me.'

Anna sighed but then thought that if they returned to the kitchen, it would be easier to bring up the subject of the old lady who'd been sitting there last night.

'Okay,' she said, following William back to the house.

On entering the hallway, Anna had to give herself a second for her eyes to adjust as the garden had been so bright but the dogs charged ahead, believing that food would be on offer at any moment.

'What would you like?' William asked as they entered the kitchen. 'Scrambled egg on toast okay to start?'

'Fine,' she said, sitting down at the table and watching as William busied himself.

It was strange having a man cook breakfast for her. Anna had never experienced that before. She thought back over her sorry list of boyfriends: Andy whose idea of spoiling her had been taking her to a football match, David who had attempted to cook spaghetti Bolognese one evening and had burnt a pan and set fire to a wooden spoon, and the lovely but rather useless Lucas who never went near a kitchen and only ate takeaways on the move.

'You look surprised,' William said.

'Oh?' Anna said, suddenly aware that William was looking at her. 'I guess that's because I am – pleasantly so, I might add.'

William laughed. 'Well, I'm not saying I'm a five-star chef or anything but it's fun to have a go.' With that, he popped up the toast, placed the slices on a plate and spread them with the buttery scrambled egg.

As he sat down at the table, Anna wondered if now would be a good time to question him. He obviously wasn't going to bring up the subject himself, was he?

'William,' she began.

'Yes?'

'That old lady last night – who was–'

'Just look at that,' William interrupted. 'That gorgeous yellowness. Free-range organic, these eggs. From Hawthorn Cottage just outside the village. Betty Turner's chickens. I keep meaning to get a few of my own but really don't need to with these on my doorstep.'

'*William!*'

'What?' He looked genuinely surprised.

'That woman last night. Who was she?'

'She's a friend,' he answered simply.

'A friend? I assumed she was your grandmother. The white-haired woman that poor Nicholas stumbled upon – that everyone thought was a ghost.'

'No,' William said. 'I wish it were as simple as having a ghost.'

'So how come she lives here?'

'Because this is the best home for her.'

'Is she from the village? Someone who couldn't afford care?'

William shook his head. 'It's nothing like that.'

'Or did you bid for her at some old people's auction?' Anna said and couldn't help smiling at her joke.

'I told you, she's just a friend.'

Anna frowned. He was being deliberately vague and it was winding her up. 'You didn't tell me there was somebody living here.'

'Should I have?'

'I think it's only polite. I mean, it was only a matter of time before I bumped into her,' Anna pointed out. 'It might be a big house by most people's standards but we were bound to meet at some point.'

'Meg doesn't usually leave her room,' William said.

'Meg?' Anna said, pouncing on the name instantly.

William flinched, obviously not having meant to reveal so much. 'Yes, her name is Meg,' he said with a sigh.

Anna nodded, delighted with this long-awaited piece of information. 'And she normally lives upstairs somewhere? One of those rooms I didn't explore that day but in that wing you didn't want me poking around, am I right?' Anna thought back to the plates, cups and cutlery she'd seen left out and the food that Mrs Boothby had prepared.

'There's no reason for her to leave her room. She's very frail and she's comfortable there.'

'Doesn't she go into the garden at all?'

'I wouldn't be happy for her to leave the house.'

'William!' Anna said astounded. 'You can't keep her prisoner here.'

His eyes widened in surprise. 'She isn't a prisoner!'

'She's not allowed out of her room. She's not allowed in the garden. It sounds like she's a prisoner to me!'

'It's not like that at all. You're exaggerating things.' He took his glasses off and pinched the bridge of his nose.

Anna sighed. This wasn't going the way she wanted it to. The last thing she wanted to do was attack William. She took a deep breath and started again.

'How long have you known her for?' she asked.

'A few years.'

Anna did her best not to throw her plate at him. He might cook the best breakfast in the world but he was terrible at answering questions. But maybe she was being too direct. Perhaps he'd respond better to a more oblique approach.

'There's something very odd about her – otherworldly,' Anna said. 'Do you know what I mean?'

William looked unimpressed. 'I thought you were writing an

article about *me.*'

'Don't be like that,' Anna said. 'I'm a writer – I'm interested in people.'

William put his glasses back on and got up from the table, taking the plates to the sink. 'I've got to go out this morning,' he said.

'Okay,' Anna said. 'Is it somewhere I should go too?'

'No,' he said.

Anna flinched. She'd pushed him too far with this Meg woman and now he'd clammed up completely.

'No,' he said again, more gently. 'It's nowhere really – just a warehouse in the back of beyond.'

Anna nodded. 'When will you be back?'

'Mid-afternoon. I've left some old photographs out for you in the study. They show the state of the house when I bought it. I thought they might be of interest for your book.'

'Thanks,' she said, secretly thinking that, with William out of the house, she might be able to go in search of Meg.

'Please don't think about bothering Meg,' William said, as if reading her mind.

'I wouldn't dream of such a thing.'

'No,' he said. 'Of course you wouldn't.'

They looked at each other. Anna didn't know if he was about to laugh or, perhaps, threaten her with eviction but he did neither. He simply nodded to her and left the room, Cocoa and Beanie trotting after him.

CHAPTER 11

Anna took a cup of tea into William's study and began looking through the photographs until she was quite sure he'd left Fox Hill Manor. For half an hour or so, she was completely absorbed in the pictures. The house had been a complete wreck when he'd taken it on. She remembered him telling her about his first sight of it with its overgrown garden spilling brambles and nettles and all the borders choked with weeds. Many of the windowpanes had been broken and the golden stonework had been crumbling away. How could anyone let such a beautiful place fall apart like that? It was like burying a diamond.

She sat back in the wooden chair, gazing at the photographs. There were endless windows hanging with spider web hammocks, masonry on the floors of rooms, beams riddled with woodworm and towering piles of rubbish and rubble everywhere. William had had to camp out in the garden whilst he made the house safe and habitable. Which reminded Anna of Meg. When had she come to Fox Hill Manor?

Anna suddenly got excited. Had Meg come with the place? Had William discovered her under a pile of rubble one day? No, that was being ridiculous. Still, with William out of the way for a few hours, Anna had ample opportunity to find out, didn't she? If she could find Meg, that was.

Putting the photographs away, Anna returned her mug to the kitchen and found a tin of biscuits in the cupboard. Food was always the best way into a conversation, she found. She'd lost count of the number of people she'd interviewed over the years who only really began to open up once the tea and biscuits had been served.

Making her way up the creaking stairs, she looked down the forbidden corridor. The wooden floor sloped dramatically in this part of the house and Anna could imagine that it would be somewhat hazardous for an elderly lady to be roaming around in the depths of a stormy night. No wonder William had been worried about her.

There were five doors leading off the passageway and Anna had only opened one of them before.

'Where to start?' she said to herself, walking up and down in the hope of hearing some signs of life. And that's precisely what happened.

'And, our next episode of *Oh, to be in England*, will be at the same time, eleven o'clock, tomorrow. Bye-bye for now.'

A radio! Meg was listening to the radio.

Anna cleared her throat and knocked on the door. There was no answer. She knocked again.

'William?' a voice came.

Anna opened the door an inch and stepped inside. 'It's Anna. May I come in?'

Meg was sitting in a pretty red armchair near the window, the radio on the sill.

'Oh, yes,' she said enthusiastically. 'I don't get many visitors.'

Anna walked into the room and looked around. There was a large brass bed and heaps of white frilly bedding and pillows. There was an enormous dressing table and mirror, its dark wood gleaming, and there was a bookshelf on the far wall which was lined with dozens of audio books.

'What a wonderful collection of audio books,' she said.

'William keeps buying them for me,' Meg said with a little nod. 'He's so kind.'

Anna nodded, remembering their conversation of the night before. 'You'll have to tell him that they send you to sleep.'

'I was just trying to listen to a story on the radio by that nice H E Bates but I was nodding off, I'm afraid.'

Anna smiled.

'Why don't you come and sit down?' Meg asked.

Anna moved forwards to a matching chair that stood opposite Meg's own.

'What a gorgeous view,' she said, looking out of the window across the garden and out to the valley beyond.

'William says it's the best view of the garden. I just wish I could make it out properly.'

'Do you find your sight a great problem?'

'Oh, I shouldn't complain. I can still see vague shapes and colours. I guess I'm lucky.'

'How old–'

'And I'm not in any pain. I have to count my blessings. We all do, don't we?'

'Yes,' Anna said. 'Do you mind me asking how old you–'

'You can't take anything for granted, you see. If there's one lesson I've learned, it's that. You can't expect anything – not from anyone.'

Anna nodded patiently. 'William told me your name's Meg,' she said.

Meg nodded. 'Meg. Meggie. Margaret. Mags. I've had many names down the years.'

'Meg suits you.'

'That's what one of my husbands said. The last one, I think. Or maybe it was the one before. I can't remember,' Meg said with a chuckle.

'It sounds like you've led a very interesting life,' Anna said, offering her a biscuit.

She shook her head politely. 'Oh, you wouldn't believe it if I told you.'

'Try me,' Anna said, noticing how white and fine Meg's long hair was against the red of the chair.

'Well, I've always been up for a challenge,' Meg said.

'Great!' Anna said, not believing how well this was all going. 'How's about I go and get my notepad and pen and then you tell me everything?'

'You mean you're going to write it down?' Meg said in surprise.

'Of course,' Anna said.

'But why?'

'Because it might make a good article. Would you mind me writing about you?'

'What would William say?' Meg asked, her gnarly hands knotting themselves together in her lap.

'He'll probably just be a bit jealous that I'm interested in you as well as him but I'm not his private journalist. I can write about whom I want.'

Meg smiled and nodded. 'But I won't know where to begin.'

Anna thought 'How about with these husbands of yours? That might be a good angle and I should very much like to hear about them.'

'But I might not be able to remember everything,' Meg said, worry clouding her face.

'That's okay. We can skim over anything that's a bit vague,' Anna assured her. 'Shall I go and get my things then?' Anna waited and then Meg nodded. 'And do have some biscuits. I stole them from the kitchen and they're absolutely delicious,' she said, rushing out of the room before Meg had a chance to change her mind.

Grabbing her notepad and pens from her room a moment later, Anna stopped, catching her reflection in one of the many mirrors. She looked at herself, noticing that she had that gleam about her – the one that meant she was onto a winner. She could feel that wonderful buzzing sensation that she always felt when ideas for new stories landed.

'I'm sorry, William,' she told her reflection, 'but I have to do this. It's just too good to miss.'

It was when Meg was telling Anna about her fourth husband that she became suspicious. Meg's personal history seemed to be no more than a collection of extraordinary stories made up by Meg herself. Not that they weren't entertaining – they were: there was Richard, a soldier who had lost a leg; Marcus, a baker, who was allergic to dough; Jeremiah, a butler who, it turned out, was already married when he married Meg; and Marcus, a gardener, who was more in love with his brassicas than with Meg.

Anna's notes became more and more haphazard as she realised she was being woven a lot of nonsense. Here was a woman who had nothing to do all day but make up stories. She couldn't read stories – stories on tape or radio sent her to sleep – and so she made them up. Everybody, Anna believed, needed stories in their life and she really couldn't blame Meg for creating a few of her own.

'There are others, of course,' Meg added after a slight pause, 'but I'm afraid I can't remember all their names. I did warn you I wouldn't be a very good subject.'

'No, no,' Anna assured her, noticing the small square diamond ring Meg was wearing and wondering which husband had given her that. 'You've been wonderful.'

'You can't really be serious about using all that, can you?' Meg said, munching on another biscuit.

'You never know. I'm sure there's a story in here somewhere.'

'Everyone has a story inside them, isn't that what they say?' Meg said.

'Yes, it is,' Anna said.

'Mine might just be a little longer than most.'

A tiny silver clock on Meg's bedside table chimed softly.

'It's two o'clock,' Anna said in shock. 'We've missed lunch.'

'And eaten all these biscuits,' Meg said with a chuckle.

'Can I get you anything?'

'I usually have a small bowl of soup for lunch,' Meg told her.

'Is that all?'

'That's all,' Meg said.

'I'll bring it up for you, then.'

'Oh, no, I'll come downstairs.'

'Are you sure?' Anna asked. 'It's no trouble for me to–'

'My dear, it's the only exercise I get. If I didn't get up occasionally, I'd find myself welded to this chair, wouldn't I?'

Anna smiled as she took Meg's elbow and helped her up out of the chair. Meg felt incredibly fragile, like a piece of antique lace.

'Don't worry,' Meg said as if reading her mind, 'I won't break. Well, some bits of me might, I suppose,' she added. 'I just have to take things slowly.'

And they did. It was a long, slow progress down to the kitchen but they made it in one piece.

'It must be frustrating for you,' Anna said as Meg took a seat at the table.

'What's that?'

'Not being able to get out and about.'

Meg waved a hand. 'I've been there and done that,' she said. 'Isn't that the right phrase?'

Anna laughed. 'And so you're ready for retirement?'

'Oh, yes,' she said. 'If only you knew.'

Anna opened the cupboards and found a large tin of soup, some bowls and a pan.

'How about some bread?'

'One slice,' Meg said.

'You sure? It doesn't seem much.'

'I don't need much these days.'

Anna got on with preparing things and the two of them were soon sharing a simple lunch.

'Meg?' Anna began, knowing that she just couldn't sit and eat opposite somebody like Meg without a few dozen questions vying for freedom.

'Yes?'

'Your husbands,' Anna said, 'you don't think there were too many of them?'

Meg swallowed a spoonful of soup and Anna watched her closely. 'I only had one at a time, my dear,' she said. 'Not too excessive really.'

Anna couldn't make it out. Meg seemed to completely believe that what she was saying was the truth and yet it couldn't be possible. Only Hollywood actresses had more than three husbands, didn't they?

'You're not married, I take it?' Meg said.

'No,' Anna said.

'Let me guess. You haven't met the right man yet?'

'Something like that,' she said and she suddenly felt rather shy admitting such a thing to this world-wise woman.

'And what do you think of our young William?'

Anna almost choked on her soup. 'Well, I– I'm not really–'

'So, you like him?' Meg said with a chuckle.

Anna grinned. 'Yes. I like him but I've not proposed to him yet if that's what you mean.'

'He's very handsome, is he not?'

'He can be rather cute, I suppose,' she said.

'When he's not ordering you about, that is?'

'You've heard him?' Anna said.

'William does like to be in control of things. It's his one fault. He must learn to relax and let things tick along on their own.' Meg looked thoughtful. 'I think he's one of these people who's always been self-reliant. He knows what he wants and he feels very strongly that only he can get it.'

'He doesn't give much away,' Anna said.

'You mean of himself?' Meg asked. 'No. I've been trying to get to know him for ages and it seems very unfair because he knows all about me.'

'But *I* don't,' Anna said, feeling that this was another good opportunity to question Meg. 'In fact, there are some things I'd love to ask you.'

But she didn't get to ask her questions because it was then that she heard the front door open and the scamper of terrier feet on the stone passageway.

'I expect we're about to get another telling off,' Meg whispered.

'Yes,' Anna agreed with a sigh, and they were right because it didn't take William long to reach the kitchen.

'Meg!' he said in surprise. 'What are you doing down here?'

'What does it look like?' she answered with gusto. 'Having some lunch with my new friend, Anna.'

William glared at Anna but soon returned his gaze to Meg. 'I thought I told you that the stairs are too much for you. Heaven knows, they're too much for *me* most days.'

'Then you should take more exercise, William,' Meg said.

Anna laughed. She couldn't help it. Meg was priceless.

William cleared his throat. 'Well,' he said, 'it looks like you've finished your lunch. It's time for your nap.'

'Oh, you are an old fuss pot,' Meg said, unhappily allowing herself to be helped up from the bench. As they left the kitchen, William turned to Anna and she knew she was in big trouble.

Anna wasn't the only one in trouble. Libby was too only she was denying it. It had begun as she was getting Toby ready for school and the post had arrived.

'I'll get it,' Charlie had called.

'No,' Libby said, rushing into the hallway to snatch up the envelopes. It was annoying, really, because Charlie should have left ages ago. He was normally well clear of the house before the post arrived.

Libby examined the envelopes. It was just as she'd thought: they were all for her and they were all bad news. There was only one thing to do with them: put them in her bad news wardrobe later. In the meantime, she stuffed them in the shoe cupboard under the stairs. Charlie never looked in there because it was filled with nothing but Libby's shoes.

'Anything for me?' Charlie asked, popping his head around the door.

'Oh, no,' Libby said vaguely.

'Okay, then, I'll be off,' he said. 'Oh, and if you find my striped shirt, let me know. I haven't seen it for weeks.'

Libby swallowed hard. She'd burned a terrible hole in the middle of the left sleeve of Charlie's favourite shirt when she'd been distracted by the end of an auction on eBay.

'I can't think where it is,' she told him innocently.

'And, darling?' he added.

'Yes?'

'You couldn't have a tidy around, could you? Only, it's impossible to find anything. The house is such a–'

'Yes, yes! Of course!' she said.

'Only if you have time,' he said with a tight smile.

'Are you going to drop me off, Daddy?' Toby asked hopefully. It was always more fun to be taken to school in his dad's beaten up van than being walked there by his mum.

'Are you ready?'

Toby nodded.

'Don't forget your packed lunch,' Libby said, running after him as he legged it down the hallway.

'Bye, Mum.'

'See you later,' she said.

Charlie and Toby leant forward to kiss her and she watched them both getting into the van, breathing a sigh of relief as the two men in her life left for the day.

As she opened the shoe cupboard, she realised she was shaking. Picking up the bills, she walked as calmly as she could upstairs. She would open one. Just one. Sitting on the edge of the bed, she picked an envelope at random and opened it, sliding out the credit card statement before looking at the amount due.

Eight hundred and forty-six pounds.

Libby blinked and then swallowed. That couldn't be right, could it? She hadn't bought that much on this card this month, had she? Her heart started racing. She hated that feeling and so stuffed the statement back into the envelope and took the small bundle over to the wardrobe where she hid them in the pocket of an old winter coat she no longer wore since replacing it with three others that had begged to be bought.

Last month, Libby had discovered a new way to shop. She'd been idly flicking channels when she'd stumbled across a programme called *Price Plummet*. At first, she'd thought it ridiculous but she'd soon been sucked in by the format and, before long, her hand had reached for the telephone.

She'd never thought to collect jewellery before because it was so expensive but then the TV presenter had said that every woman deserved to have a treat, didn't they? And Libby had agreed with her. Why shouldn't Libby have some lovely pieces to wear like the Art Deco-inspired diamond earrings? And there were only fifteen pairs left. She must ring now if she wanted a pair. Just look at the way those diamonds caught the light! They were practically blinding the TV presenter – she'd said so. And she'd confessed that she'd never seen anything like this on the high street – not at such a good price. Your friends will be so jealous, she'd said. It was too good an offer to miss. You won't get it for that price again. Ring now to avoid disappointment!

So Libby had rung. It had been so easy and the payments were to be spread over four months which really brought the price down. The only thing was, Libby hadn't stopped at the earrings. There had been that fascinating and unique white gold bracelet – so highly polished, and the amethyst ring. They were all so beautiful and Libby could imagine wearing each piece a thousand times. Charlie was sure to love them too if she introduced them to him gradually and told him what a bargain they had been.

But the jewellery was just the tip of the iceberg this month. Libby didn't even dare think about the other things that she'd bought. No, she told herself, she wouldn't think about it. It was too grim and it was such a lovely day. The storm of the night before had passed and a golden sun was smiling down on Elmington. Libby looked at the clock. It was nine already. Just time to make a cup of tea and then do a bit of window shopping on TV.

Just window shopping today, she told herself.

CHAPTER 12

Anna didn't want to hang around the kitchen any longer so decided to return to the study but it didn't take long for William to find her.

'You weren't just having lunch, were you?' he said as soon as he entered the room, not wasting any time with small talk.

'What do you mean?' Anna asked, being deliberately vague in a manner she'd learnt well from William.

'You went upstairs, didn't you? After I'd asked you not to.'

'I must say, I don't like your accusatory tone,' Anna said.

'Then tell me I'm wrong,' he said, his eyes wide and fixed on her.

Anna put down the photograph she'd been holding and gave him her full attention. 'I was lonely,' she said. 'I wanted to talk to someone.'

'You're a journalist. You don't talk to people – you interrogate them.'

'That's not fair!' she cried.

'But it's true,' William said, 'isn't it?'

Anna sighed and pursed her lips. 'Okay. What do you want me to say? I'm a journalist – as you're *so* keen to point out to me every five minutes. I want to know things. And if you have an old lady living in your house who isn't your grandmother and who you won't introduce me to like any civilized person then I'm going to do my best to find out who she is myself.'

William ran a hand through his hair. 'But I asked you not to.'

'And I'm sorry I didn't do as you asked.'

They were silent. Anna's eyes returned to the photographs and then William pulled up a chair and sat down. Anna waited for him to speak.

'What did you ask her?' he said at last.

'Oh, the usual. What's your name? How old are you? Where do you come from? Were you married?'

William flinched and his face drained of colour. 'And what did she say?'

Anna frowned. 'What do you mean? She told me she was Meg.'

'Nothing else?' William asked, obviously puzzled.

'Only that she'd had about half a dozen husbands which, of course, I didn't believe. She's a very sweet lady but I think she has a tendency to make things up, don't you?' Anna said, catching William's eye.

'She can get a little muddled at times,' he said slowly.

'A little?' Anna laughed. 'She told me she had six husbands that she could remember and that there were probably more!'

'Yes,' William said.

'She's told you the same, then?'

William nodded. 'When I first met her, she told me of eleven she could remember. Her memory's obviously fading.'

'But you didn't believe her, surely? Gosh, she must be in the *Guinness Book of Records.*'

'No,' William said. 'She leads a very quiet life – that sort of fame wouldn't interest her at all.'

Anna was becoming more and more frustrated. 'William!' she half-shouted. 'Just tell me who she is!'

William shifted uncomfortably in his chair. 'She's Meg.' He shrugged.

'That's not good enough! Why's she here? Why are you living with a barmy old lady?'

'She's not barmy,' William said quickly. 'She's just old.'

'Yes,' Anna said. 'She wouldn't tell me how old she was.'

'No,' William said. 'She knows better than to do that now.'

'What do you mean?'

William didn't answer at first but then he sighed and Anna had the feeling that he was going to open up – that her constant battering of him with questions had worked and that, at last, he was going to answer her.

'I expect she told you about the great storm last night?' he said.

'Yes. She did,' Anna said. 'The storm of seventy-two. A bit before my time.'

'And mine too. She meant *seventeen* seventy-two.'

'What?' Anna frowned at him. 'What do you mean?'

William didn't speak for a moment.

'Oh!' Anna said. 'You mean she's some sort of historian. Is that why she's staying here?'

William shook his head and looked closely at her. 'No, Anna,' he said, 'Meg's not a historian. She's three hundred and fifty-five years old. Give or take a decade.'

At first, Anna didn't respond at all. Perhaps she wasn't sure how William wanted her to respond. A laugh? Yes, perhaps a laugh. She tried one out but he frowned at her.

'You're kidding, right?' Anna said. 'I mean, she looks pretty old. In fact, she's the oldest-looking person I've ever seen.'

'That's because she is.'

Anna laughed again. 'Right.'

'No, Anna, she really is. You asked me who she is and I'm telling you. I want to be honest with you. It's finally time to tell someone.'

They stared at each other for what seemed like an eternity.

'Let me get this absolutely clear,' Anna said, holding her hands in the air as if that might help to keep herself sane, 'because I'm a little bit muddled. You're saying you've got a three hundred and fifty-five year old woman in your house.'

'Yes, that's absolutely what I'm saying.'

'Okay,' Anna said. 'I'm beginning to think that coming here to interview you wasn't the smartest move I've ever made. You don't need a journalist, William. You need a novelist because this is the best story I've heard in a very long time.'

'Anna, I can assure you, this is not fiction,' he said. 'I'm telling you the truth – Meg's truth.'

Anna pushed her chair back abruptly. 'I think I'd better go home for a bit,' she said, getting up to leave.

'Wait, listen–' William said, grabbing her arm.

'I really don't know who that sweet old lady is but I think you should probably find out.'

'You don't believe me?' he said.

'Of *course* I don't believe you!' Anna said with a laugh. 'What do you take me for? It's just another of your stories – another part of this incredible house. Is that what you tell the schoolchildren who come here? You wheel out your old lady from the village every so often and say, *Hey, kids, meet the oldest woman in England*. She's your party piece, right? Well, I'm not one of your children so don't treat me like one.' Anna shook his arm from her and she realised that her heart was hammering.

'Anna! Listen to me. I've never told a living soul about Meg before

– precisely because this is the reaction I knew I'd get. But Meg is real and her story is real. You've got to believe me,' William said sounding wild.

'Why should I? You've kept her hidden away from me all this time and then tell me to have nothing to do with her. What's going on, William?'

William's face was drained of all colour and his eyes were filled with anxiety. 'Come with me,' he said. 'I think I'll need a drink to do this properly.'

Anna followed him into the living room and watched him open his secret cabinet of drinks which George had helped himself to the night before.

'Are you okay?' she asked, shaking her head as he offered her a drink.

'No,' he said. 'I'm not okay with any of this but you've come this far now and found out what you have and, being who you are, it's inevitable that you'd find the rest out at some point too.'

Anna frowned. That sounded like an insult to her but she didn't say anything because she was far too intrigued by William's behaviour. She watched as he poured himself a tumbler of whisky and sat down opposite her and then he began.

'Meg came to Fox Hill Manor four years ago. She'd heard that I was a collector. Somebody had read out an article about me to her from a local newspaper. It was November and bitterly cold. I'd been gardening all morning and was just scraping the mud off my boots when I saw this tiny figure walking up my driveway. At first, I thought she was lost. We don't get many visitors at Fox Hill Manor and I was just about to turn her away – as politely as possible, of course, when she said my name. "I've come to see Mr Kitson," she said. "I think he might be interested in me." It was as simple as that,' William said, swilling the golden whisky in his glass before taking a sip and continuing.

'I invited her in, gave her a cup of tea and listened to her story. I'll never forget how cold her hands were when she first shook mine but how bright her eyes were even though she said she couldn't see me properly. You know, the only thing she brought with her was a small tapestry holdall and there really wasn't very much inside it. "I always believe in travelling light," she told me. "It really is the best lesson life can teach you."'

'And she told you how old she was then?' Anna asked.

William nodded. 'Not straightaway. She told me she'd been travelling, looking for a home and that it was harder than you might imagine when you've no family and no money.'

'How on earth has she coped in the past?'

'By the kindness of strangers,' William said. 'She told me she's never had a problem finding a home. Everyone is so kind. I find it hard to believe that but I do think she has the sort of personality that appeals, you know? Once, she said, she was hanging around a shopping centre when a young mother asked her if she was all right. She lived with that family for six years.'

'But what on earth did she tell people?' Anna asked.

'As little as possible. She just keeps things vague and says she has no family and refuses to go into a home. Apart from being frail, she's very well which is rather remarkable so she isn't a burden to anyone. In fact, she often helped out. The young mother, for example, was able to take a part-time job whilst Meg looked after the children.'

'Was she really able to do that?' Anna asked.

'Oh, they were at school and very sensible. She just went to collect them and made them tea.'

Anna shook her head. 'And she's got no family?'

'Do you think you would after three hundred and fifty-five years?'

'Well, I've never thought about it before,' she said.

'Do you know all *your* ancestors? I didn't even know all my grandparents,' William said. 'Anyway, all her family died out centuries ago.'

'But she hasn't always lived around here, has she?'

'No, not at all. When she was younger and married, she moved all over the place. Norfolk, Suffolk, Oxfordshire, Worcestershire, London and now the Cotswolds.'

'And there's nobody in those places who could take care of her?'

'She told me there wasn't but I think she's a very proud woman. I don't think it's in her nature to ask for help,' he said.

'But she asked you,' Anna pointed out.

'That's different. She thought I'd be genuinely interested in her,' William said and then he smiled.

'What?' Anna asked.

'When she first arrived, she said, "You collect old things, don't you? Do you want to add me to your collection?"'

Anna laughed. 'But this age thing – what did you make of that?'

William's eyes widened. 'I didn't know what to make of it. At first, I was as dumbfounded as you looked when I told you. I mean, I could see she was old but why tell me she was over three hundred? We talked for hours. Well, *she* talked; I listened. I had questions for her, of course, but I was just swept up in her story. And I really did think it was all a story at first. A well-constructed story. But there was such attention to detail, such colour and emotion that I really began to wonder.'

'You can't say that you believe her, William?' Anna said.

William frowned. 'Why not?'

'What do you mean, *why not*? Three hundred and fifty-five years old? It's not humanly possible!' Anna shrieked.

'Just because you've never heard of it before?'

'No!' Anna cried. 'Because a human's lifespan isn't that long! Even those really, really ancient people in India and China and goodness knows where else – even they don't live much beyond one hundred!'

'But Meg's our proof,' William said.

'How? Does she have a birth certificate? Is there documentary evidence? Has she got a personally addressed letter from George III or someone?'

'Of course not.'

'Then we can't prove a thing,' Anna said.

'But the stories – the human stories.'

'Are very likely made up,' Anna insisted. 'People invent stories. We're surrounded by them constantly. TV, films, books. Stories are as natural as breathing. Meg's just probably overdosed on a few historical documentaries or – more than likely – costume dramas and has cast herself in the role of heroine in her very own version.'

'But she doesn't watch films. Her eyesight isn't great.'

'But it once was,' Anna pointed out.

'You don't give her story any credibility at all, do you?'

Anna sighed, seeing that her views upset William. 'I'm a journalist. I have to try and find the truth in every story.'

'Then you're not like any journalist I've ever met before.'

Anna tutted. 'Yeah, well, some of us prefer the truth to fiction.'

They were quiet for a moment. Anna was the one to speak first.

'Look,' she said, 'Meg's an amazing person. I really think she's wonderful and I'm sure she has many incredible stories to tell about her *own* life. But you can't seriously tell me that you believe her when she tells you she's centuries old, can you?' She looked at William. His face was calm and she found it hard to read his thoughts. 'William,' she said, 'I think you've been spending far too much time surrounded by all these old things. It's starting to affect your judgement.'

He shook his head. 'No,' he said, ruffling his hair, 'You don't understand.'

'But I *do* understand. Meg's a very persuasive lady and I can absolutely see why you want to believe her. Who wouldn't? Just think of it – a three hundred and fifty-five year old woman! It would be amazing. Think of all the questions you could ask her. Think of all the things you could learn. She'd be a one-woman show. People would come from miles around to hear her speak – from all over the world!'

'Anna,' William said cautiously, 'you mustn't think like that. It would be like turning her into some sort of King Kong.'

Anna laughed. 'I'm not saying that will happen, silly! I'm saying, that might happen if she really *were* that old.'

William sighed and it sounded as if all the air in his body was leaving him in frustration. 'I guess we're going to have to disagree, aren't we?'

Anna looked at him. He was completely earnest about this , wasn't he?

'I guess we are,' she said, studying him. 'Does Mrs Boothby know about Meg?' she asked after a moment.

'She knows she lives here. She cooks for her sometimes and does bits of shopping for her but she thinks she's my great aunt.'

Anna nodded. 'Does anyone else know about her? Does George?'

'No,' William said. 'He has his suspicions. He knows I'm living with someone but he thinks it's an old girlfriend.'

'A *very* old girlfriend!' Anna teased.

William raised a smile but it disappeared in an instant. 'Look, Anna,' he said, 'I've never told anyone Meg's story and you must swear to me that all this remains secret. It must never leave FHM, do you understand?'

Anna frowned. 'Yes, of course,' she said.

William shook his head. 'This piece you're writing – it mustn't contain anything about Meg. There must be no mention of her whatsoever. I'm her guardian, you see. It's up to me to protect her.'

Anna was beginning to get annoyed by William now. She thought he was taking himself far too seriously. 'She's just an old lady, William.'

'No,' he said, 'she isn't and you mustn't think of her as such.'

For a moment, they sat staring at each other.

'You don't believe me, do you?' William said at last. 'You don't believe a single word I've said.'

Anna looked at him, taking her time in answering because her head was buzzing with conflicting ideas but, at last, she spoke.

'I know you're not the kind of person who'd lie,' she told him. 'But you're right. I don't believe you.'

CHAPTER 13

After spending half the night lying awake, Anna decided that it really would be best if she were to return home. Time out. For her and for William. Things had become a little surreal of late and she needed to concentrate on what really mattered: her deadline.

Still, she knew it was going to be awkward leaving and, when William saw her standing in the hallway with her suitcase and laptop the next morning, he looked puzzled and a little upset.

'You're really going?' he said.

Anna nodded. 'I think I've plenty of notes to be getting on with,' she said, doing her best to avoid eye contact with him. 'You've been so kind and helpful.'

William just frowned. 'It's about Meg, isn't it? You're leaving because of what I told you?'

Anna swallowed. She really didn't know what to say. 'I'm not here because of Meg. I'm here to write about your collection and I should really get on with that.'

'But you can do that here. Surely it would be better to write *here* – with the whole collection around you?'

Anna was puzzled by his reaction. She'd thought William was uncomfortable with her in the house – that she made him anxious – but now he seemed to be trying to keep her there.

'I thought you didn't like me sneaking about,' she said.

'I didn't. I don't. But I've kind of got used to it now,' he said and then he took a step towards her. 'I've got used to you,' he said in a low voice.

Anna wasn't quite sure she'd heard him correctly. She looked at him. He was right beside her now and she could see her own face reflected in his grey eyes.

'Willia–'

She didn't finish his name – she couldn't – because he'd taken her face in his hands and kissed her. Anna was so delightedly surprised by finding herself desired first thing in the morning that she did absolutely nothing to stop him but, instead, found herself kissing him back, dropping both suitcase and laptop in an instant.

She couldn't remember the last time she'd been kissed and she certainly couldn't remember the last time she'd been kissed so well. Her heart was racing faster than it had in a long time and Anna could almost feel the rest of the world dissolving away. Nothing mattered: her deadline, the bills waiting for her at home, the confusion about Meg… it all slipped away as they kissed in the hallway to the ticking of three longcase clocks.

'Anna!' he whispered when they'd stopped kissing.

'WILLIAM?'

They stopped. It wasn't Anna who'd spoken.

Anna and William stared at one another.

'WILLIAM?' the voice called again. Meg's voice.

Leaving Anna in an instant, William rushed to the foot of the stairs. 'Meg? Are you okay?'

'YES!' she called from the first floor landing. 'But I'm afraid I've spilled my tea.'

'It's all right. I'll be up in a moment.'

He walked back over to Anna. 'She's okay,' he said, giving a little smile.

Anna smiled back. She felt wonderfully light-headed.

'What on earth happened?' she whispered.

'She probably just knocked her cup over,' he said.

'No!' she said with a laugh. 'Between us! Just now?' It was a silly question, she knew but it was buzzing around her head and she couldn't think of anything else to say.

'I – well – erm –' William stumbled and then laughed.

Anna laughed too. 'I wasn't expecting that,' she said. 'I didn't think you liked me very much.'

'Whatever gave you that idea?'

'Oh, I don't know. The way you talked to me. The way you behaved.'

William shook his head. 'I'm so sorry, Anna. I don't know what you must think of me.'

'And neither do I now!' she said.

'I guess I can be a little over-protective of this place.'

'Just a little bit,' she said.

'I worry,' he said. 'That's all it is. I don't mean to be rude and I certainly didn't mean for you to go.'

Anna bit her lip. 'But my job is done here.'

They looked at each other and Anna felt that perhaps she would like to stay forever.

'I have a home of my own and I have to write this article.'

'But why not do that here?' William said. 'You have your trusty laptop. And I can let you have a bigger table if you need. Or anything else,' he said, and there was a magical light in his silver-grey eyes. 'Anything,' he said and then he was kissing her again.

His mouth was warm and firm and Anna closed her eyes and thought of nothing else but the moment. William Kitson was kissing her. The famous recluse. The man who terrified trespassing children. The person who threw his brother out in the middle of a storm. And the man who believed in miraculously old women.

Anna hadn't intended this to happen. Yes, he was cute – she'd admitted as much to Meg – but she hadn't imagined this. He wasn't her type, was he? She liked modern and he liked antiques. She liked empty spaces and he liked clutter. They weren't compatible at all, that's what her mind was saying but, as they kissed, her body was telling her something completely different.

'William,' she said at last, pulling away from his embrace and managing to get his whole name out without his mouth taking hers prisoner again. 'I really should go.'

He sighed. 'You seem quite determined although I don't know why.'

'My home – there are things to do.'

She looked up at him and suddenly wished that she'd left Fox Hill Manor in the middle of the night and not had this marvellous muddle to contend with now.

'Right,' she said, picking up her suitcase and laptop.

'Here, let me help you,' William said.

'No, no, I'm okay.'

For a split second, she saw a look of panic cross William's face. 'I'll see you again?'

'Yes,' Anna said. 'Of course you will.'

'Do I have your number?' He started searching in his pockets for a pen.

'Here,' Anna said, putting her suitcase down again and finding a business card for him.

William took it and frowned and Anna realised what he was thinking because she was thinking it too: it seemed so cold and business-like after what they'd just shared.

'I – erm – don't know what to say,' William said.

'No,' Anna said. 'This is all so – unexpected.'

'But not unpleasantly so?' he asked, his eyes anxiously searching hers.

Anna gave a little smile. 'No,' she said, 'not unpleasantly so. Quite the reverse, in fact.' She opened the door, picked up her things again and walked the short distance to her car. William followed, his hands deep in his jacket pockets. Cocoa and Beanie had shot out after him and were waiting with him as Anna got in the car.

'Oh, dear,' Anna said to herself as she got in and started the engine. 'This wasn't meant to happen at all.'

Putting the car into reverse, she looked in her rear-view mirror and saw William raise a hand to wave her off. A breeze tousled his fair hair and the morning light bounced off his glasses and Anna realised how easy it would be to stay a little while longer. But she didn't. Instead, she raised a hand in response to his and began the drive down the track, leaving Fox Hill Manor for home.

William watched Anna's car until it had disappeared around the first bend in the driveway, went to clean up Meg's spilt tea, and then whistled for the dogs and went for a long walk. He needed to think and a good long walk through the gardens and out into the fields and the wood always cleared his head.

He hadn't felt like this in a long time. His mind was racing in sync with his overworked heart. He was flying. He was soaring. He was in love!

'Oh, my God!' he said, causing his dogs to pause in their sniffing and look back at their master. Cocoa had had his nose deep in a clump of cowslips and Beanie had been on the scent of something small and furry. 'I'm in love,' he told them.

He leapt over the ditch that separated the end of his garden and the adjacent field, and strode across the golden-green countryside, breathing in great lungfuls of air as if he'd been asleep for a very long time and was only just waking up.

Beautiful sweet Anna with the inquisitive eyes and the yielding mouth. He'd never met another woman like her. When she'd first arrived, he'd been so terrified of what the next few days would involve that he hadn't really thought about her as a woman at all. She'd been a journalist – enemy number one. And – boy – had he put up the defences good and proper.

He must have known she'd find out about Meg, though. He wouldn't have thought very highly of her abilities as a journalist if she hadn't. And now, looking back, he realised that he didn't mind. It had been a relief to tell somebody about her because, up until now, he hadn't told a soul. Meg's story had been for his ears only. Not Mrs Boothby, not George – not anyone – knew of his unusual house guest.

As he entered the beech wood beyond the old stone wall, he sighed. He might have shared Meg's secret with Anna but it was quite plain she didn't believe him and he felt strange about that. There was a feeling of frustration that she should shut out the possibility that this was true but he felt relief as well. After all, she was a journalist and there was no telling what she might do with such a story handed to her.

He inhaled the sweet air of the wood, gazing at the brilliant green of the beech leaves and admiring the smooth silvery trunks which always reminded him of church organs. He'd tried to buy one of those once for FHM but the seller had mistakenly thought William's budget was bottomless and he'd had to walk away. William wondered what Anna would think of that. She'd really begun to love the collection, he could see that.

He smiled. His collection had always come between him and women in the past. For one thing, it meant he didn't get out much and socialise. His hunting trips usually involved tobacco-smoking dealers or farmers in ancient overalls who had 'something of interest' in one of their barns that they wanted shifting. He didn't often get to meet beautiful young women.

There'd been Fiona, of course. He'd met her after an auction where he'd outbid her on a beautiful old table she'd wanted for her father. Things had started promisingly with her. Okay, so she'd got a bit tipsy on that bottle of red but she was smart and sophisticated and attractive – albeit in that haughty horsey sort of way. But then there'd been that misunderstanding and he'd invited her home to show her his collection. He'd never forget the look of horror on her face.

'I thought you said you liked antiques,' he'd said.

'No,' she'd said, her face scrunching up in bemusement. 'I thought you said *bou*tiques.'

Tara hadn't been much fun either. She'd had a real live panic attack in the middle of The Armoury and he'd had to find a paper bag for her to breathe in to in order to calm her down.

And then there'd been Beth who'd just laughed at the whole thing. He hadn't managed to get a sensible word out of her. Anna was the first woman in a long time who seemed to understand and that made him smile.

As he walked through the woods, he felt that everything was well with the world. But then he remembered something. Paula's funeral. No, he wasn't going to think about that today. Today was for happy thoughts only. He took a deep breath, luxuriating in that wondrous scent of a wood after rainfall and, thinking only of Anna, continued on his walk with Cocoa and Beanie.

When she arrived home, there was a pile of post to meet her. Bills, bills and more bills. Anna rolled her eyes to the ceiling. She hadn't realised quite how comfy and cosseted she'd been at Fox Hill Manor. It had been like living in a beautiful bubble with nothing to worry about and, now she was home, she began to realise how much she'd loved it there.

Walking through to the kitchen, she filled the kettle and made a cup of tea.

'Tackle nothing before tea,' she said, remembering the words of her late grandmother.

A few minutes later, she walked through her tiny house with her cup of tea warming her hands. It felt so strange to have a house you could walk around in less than a minute. There were no long passageways or secret rooms to discover, no creaking, sloping floorboards or ancient wooden doors. She was back home. It was light and bright and modern and, for the first time in her life, she wasn't totally in love with it.

'How strange,' she said to herself as she realised that she was missing the mullioned windows and the craggy oak beams of Fox Hill Manor. And William? Her heart raced as she thought about him. Once again, she was in the hallway, half lit by the pale morning light that streamed through the square glass panes of the door. How warm she had felt, how warm and safe and – she paused and then giggled - seriously, deliriously sexy, and that was something she definitely hadn't bargained for when taking the assignment, not even when she'd first met the mysterious Mr Kitson. He'd been attractive, yes, but she'd never really gone for that country tweedy look and rather preferred her men to be well acquainted with their local barber. But now, she found her fingers itching to touch those unruly locks and to feel that scratchy jacket against her.

Her eyes widened as she thought about him. What was happening to her? She was behaving like a schoolgirl. And it feels wonderful, she thought, thinking that she must tell somebody right away.

'*Libby!*'

Anna nodded to herself. Yes, Libby would understand. She'd call Libby.

'You *idiot!*' her sister shouted down the phone a few minutes later. 'What on earth are you doing back home after that?'

Anna rolled her eyes. She should *never* have told Libby. She should've known she wouldn't understand.

'I have work to do.'

'Work? You're talking about work at a time like this? When you've just discovered true love and–'

'Hey! Slow down a minute,' Anna cried.

'*You* were the one who said the earth moved!' her sister told her.

'Well, that might just have been the rickety floorboards,' Anna said with a giggle. 'This is all so unexpected, though.'

'You're telling me!' Libby said. 'You don't even like antiques. You didn't even really want to go to Fox Hill Manor.'

'I *know*,' Anna said.

'What's happened to you, Anna? Are you in love?'

Anna took a deep breath and then let it out slowly. 'You know,' she said, 'I think I just might be.'

CHAPTER 14

But it didn't take Anna long to come back down to earth. Two days later and the memory of William's kisses was beginning to fade as she got on with her work. She was a very practical girl at heart and, no matter how good a kiss was, it wasn't going to pay the bills. So she got on with the article book, writing up her notes about William and his collection, breathing life into it with an account of the school trip, how he'd acquired certain objects though his 'hunting trips' and the exciting atmosphere of an auction room when you were bidding against your rival.

Finally, she had a first draft and was, she had to admit, quite happy with it. It was far more fun a piece of writing than she'd imagined it would ever be when she'd taken on the assignment. And yet … it wasn't exceptional.

For a while, she sat tapping her head with a pencil. She knew what was wrong, of course. Her journalist's mind had already disconnected with William and the Fox Hill Manor collection and had started working on something else. Meg's story.

As with every writer, the burning question 'what if' wouldn't leave her. What if Meg's story was true? What if she really was over three hundred years old? And what if Anna was the first person to find out more?

The first thing to do was some research so Anna did a bit of surfing on the internet. From what she could make out, the oldest people in the world had only ever lived to between one hundred and ten and one hundred and twenty-two. Anna smiled to herself. 'Only,' she said, as if she thought that age was laughably young and unimpressive compared to Meg's three hundred and fifty-five.

There also didn't seem to be any rhyme or reason as to why these people lived longer. For one thing, they lived all over the world from China to the USA. Some lived healthy lives, others smoked. Some had huge families and others didn't. There was no correlation – no secret ingredient to living to a ripe old age.

The other thing that got Anna thinking was the whole issue of ageing. Meg looked old but she didn't look much older than your average eighty-year old. Perhaps that was the thing with old age. Once you were old, that was it. You just stopped. A body could only age so much, perhaps. Wrinkles couldn't grow more wrinkles, could they?

Anna already knew that, because of improvements in health care, diet and lifestyle, people were living longer but she hadn't known that a new phrase had been coined for such people: supercentenarians. Females, in particular, were increasingly living longer.

Anna sat back in her chair at her desk. The only problem was verifying such claims. Records had improved down the decades but there were still many disputes about people's claims as to how old they were.

Anna wondered and pondered for a while. Even if Meg wasn't as old as she claimed, she was still pretty old and it would make a great story if she were perhaps the oldest woman in the UK, wouldn't it?

All at once, she became excited as she thought about all the things Meg may have lived through: the invention of TV, computers and the internet, electricity, cars, the rocket and the telephone, Elvis Presley, Marilyn Monroe…

And, if she really was as old as she claimed: Two world wars, Darwin, Dickens, Napoleon and Nelson, Queen Victoria, the Industrial Revolution…

'But surely not?' Anna said. Still, she couldn't help thinking, couldn't help dreaming. 'Just imagine. If she'd *really* been born in – when was it? Sixteen-fifty something.'

Anna searched the internet again. The seventeenth-century was a complete mystery to her. It was just after the English Civil War, she discovered. Oliver Cromwell had become Lord Protector. Well, even Anna had heard of him. There was the restoration of the monarchy, the Great Plague and the Great Fire of London.

And then there was the eighteenth-century with the great composers Mozart and Beethoven, and the poets Wordsworth and Coleridge and, of course, the French Revolution.

This was immense. Could someone possibly have lived through all of that? Anna mind raced at the thought of it and she knew what she had to do. She had to see Meg again.

'Tuesday,' she whispered. William would be away at Paula's

funeral. It would be the perfect time to go back to Fox Hill Manor.

Suddenly, Anna was buzzing again. This was it – the next story she wanted to write. Even if it wasn't true. Even if Meg's story was the biggest hoax of all time, Anna was going to write about it. And William wasn't going to be there to stop her.

'Mrs Boothby!'

Anna bit her lip as she remembered her but then shook her head in dismissal. She might not even be there. She was only part-time, after all.

Smiling once again, Anna knew that this was absolutely the right thing to do.

For William, Tuesday came round all too quickly. He'd driven up to London the night before, leaving Mrs Boothby in charge of Meg, Cocoa and Beanie at FHM.

Nobody liked funerals but perhaps it was especially miserable to be attending one of a person whom you didn't even care for in life. At least, that's how William felt as he hopped in a taxi to take him to the crematorium on the outskirts of London. It had been a wet start to the day but the sun had come out as if to mock the pain of the mourners who gathered to await the service. William's taxi pulled up and he paid the driver, wishing he could just ask him to take him back to his hotel instead but it would all be over quickly enough, he reasoned, forcing himself to go through it.

As he got out, he noticed that there weren't many people there and William felt a little comfort in the fact that perhaps he hadn't been the only one to receive the sharp edge of Paula's tongue. A funeral was a testament of a life, wasn't it?

William did his best not to dwell on negative thoughts. He was going to get through the day as quickly and as painlessly as possible. Paula was part of his past; today was just one way of making sure she stayed there.

'Will!' a voice suddenly called and William turned to see George walking towards him. 'You made it. I wasn't sure you would.'

'I said I was coming. I always keep my word,' William said.

'So you do,' George said. 'And I have something for you.' Before William could say anything, George's hand disappeared into his pocket and he produced a dark cream envelope. 'This is for you.'

William scowled. He really didn't want it, whatever it was.

'Come on, Will,' George said. 'Just take it.' He thrust the envelope at William and then turned to walk inside the crematorium where the service was about to begin.

It was about this time in the Elm Valley that Anna's car turned into the long sweep of the driveway at Fox Hill Manor. It seemed funny to be back, especially knowing that William wasn't going to be there. Not for the first time, Anna almost felt as if she were trespassing which was silly really because she had every right to be there, didn't she? William had wanted her there and had begged for her to stay. That's what she'd been telling herself she'd say if she came across Mrs Boothby. But, as she pulled up next to the outbuildings, she was relieved to see that there were no cars around. Meg, it seemed, was on her own.

Nipping into one of the old stables, Anna reached up to unhook an old firebucket which was hanging from a rusty nail. Sure enough, there was the key to the side entrance door. William had told her about it in case she found herself locked out of the house and it was most welcome now.

As Anna climbed the steps up to the door, she couldn't help smiling. She had so many ideas about Meg that her head was spinning with excitement at the titles of pieces she could write about her. She could be restrained and prosaic:

Meet Meg – the world's oldest woman.

She could go all sensational:

Meg – a – Star! The woman's who's set to wow the world.

Or she could go for the tabloid angle:

Cromwell's kid!

She grinned. It was the gift of a lifetime for a freelance journalist and she couldn't wait to get started on Project Meg.

Opening the door and stepping inside the hallway, Anna allowed her eyes to adjust to the dim light. She heard the friendly tick of the longcase clocks that William loved so much and could smell the comforting scent of beeswax. Almost at once, Anna felt at ease. This was a place she had slowly come to feel a part of and leaving it – just for a few days – had made her realise how much she loved it.

But there was no time to be poetical. There was work to be done and the sooner she was upstairs with Meg, the better.

Unfortunately, that wasn't going to prove so easy because, as soon as Anna reached the foot of the stairs, she heard a voice.

'Is that you, Miss McCall?'

Anna gasped in surprise and turned to come face to face with Mrs Boothby.

'Oh! I didn't think you'd be here,' Anna said.

Mrs Boothby smiled. 'I wondered who it could be.'

'I didn't see your car in the driveway,' Anna said.

'No. It's at the garage. My son dropped me off.'

Immediately, Anna wanted to ask when he was picking her up again but thought that might sound rude.

'I didn't mean to disturb you. It's just I had to come and check a few things for my article. William said that would be okay.'

'And he told you where the key was, I see,' Mrs Boothby said with a friendly nod.

'Yes, thank you.'

'Because I'll be leaving as soon as I'm ready.'

Anna breathed a secretive sigh of relief. 'That's okay. I can lock up.'

'Good,' Mrs Boothby said. 'I've fed the dogs. Might be an idea to let them have a sniff in the garden before you go. If you have time, that is.'

'Yes, of course.' Anna looked at her, wondering if she was going to mention Meg. As far as Mrs Boothby was concerned, Anna had no idea that there was an elderly lady living upstairs.

'I'll be off then,' Mrs Boothby said. 'There's the end of a Dundee cake in the tin by the kettle if you get peckish.'

'Thank you.'

'Will I see you again?' she asked as she reached the door.

'Oh, I expect so,' Anna said.

'Perhaps there'll be a glamorous book launch to look forward to?'

'Perhaps,' Anna said. Just then, a car horn tooted outside.

'That must be Carl,' Mrs Boothby said. 'I'll be off, then,' she said with a little wave, her neat little handbag resting in the crook of her arm like the queen.

'See you later,' Anna said and, as soon as she heard the car pull away, she skipped up the stairs to Meg's room.

'Meg?' she called, tapping lightly on her bedroom door and hoping she wasn't disturbing her.

'Anna? Is that you?' her light voice replied.

'Hello, Meg,' she said, opening the door and entering the room. 'How are you?'

'As well as can be expected,' Meg said with a little smile that lit her face up. 'But we weren't expecting you, were we?'

'Not exactly.'

'William's away.'

'Yes, I know.'

Meg nodded. 'I see.'

Anna frowned. 'What do you see?'

'You've had an argument.'

'No. Nothing like that,' Anna said and Meg's eyes instantly sparkled.

'Then it must be love.'

'What makes you say that?' Anna asked.

'Because you wait until the minute he goes away to come and see me. You're avoiding him, aren't you? You've been wanting to ask me more questions, haven't you? And you know he doesn't like that.'

'If that's the reason I'm avoiding him, why did you think I was in love with him?'

Meg chuckled. 'Because you're two young people. What else is there to do? Either you're going to fight or fall in love.'

It was Anna's turn to laugh. 'You are funny!'

'But he's a lovely boy, our William, isn't he?' Meg persisted.

'Yes,' Anna said, humouring her.

'Sweet William,' Meg said and gave a girlish giggle. 'I've often thought, if I was a bit younger–'

Anna smiled. 'What, say three hundred years or so?'

Meg nodded. 'Thereabouts.'

Anna watched her expression and, once again, Meg looked completely earnest. Sitting down in the chair opposite, she looked out of the window. 'It's such a lovely afternoon.'

'Tell me,' Meg said.

'Everything looks newly washed after the rain and there's that wonderful smell. It's all woody and earthy, you know?'

'I know exactly. I used to live near a wood – a long time ago – and I would pray for rain just so I could smell the earth afterwards. Tell me more.'

'Well, the sky is so blue today. I had to put sunglasses on to drive here because it was so bright, and the hedgerows have sprung up to such a height. The cow parsley is all frothy and foamy and the campion looks so pretty too.'

'That's the pink flower?'

'Yes. The bluebells are past their prime now, though.'

'Such an elegant flower, I've always thought. So graceful.'

'William said that the poppies around here are spectacular too although it's a bit early for them.'

'What else?' Meg asked.

Anna looked up into the sky. 'The swifts and swallows are about – all dive-bombing in the fields. You should see them,' she said and then she paused.

'What is it?' Meg asked as if anticipating Anna's thought.

'You *should* see them!'

'What do you mean?' Meg said.

'I mean, why don't I take you out? Instead of just sitting here telling you all about it – why don't we go out and get you amongst it all? Out in the garden and the fields and the woods!'

'I can't walk very far, I'm afraid.'

'You won't need to. I have my car. I could take you for a drive through the valley and the villages. It would be wonderful. We'd have so much fun!'

Meg smiled. 'I like cars,' she said. 'But I haven't been in one for ages.'

'Doesn't William take you out for a spin?'

'He told me his car isn't very suitable. What did he call it now? Ah, yes – a boneshaker!'

Anna grinned. 'Well, mine's a little more comfortable. Oh, *do* say you'll come, Meg. We could have so much fun!'

Meg looked very serious. 'Now, let me see. I can either sit here on my own getting rigid and stiff in this chair or I can go out and have fun in a car with you.' A small smile spread across her face. 'Let's get going, then,' she said and Anna clapped her hands in glee.

CHAPTER 15

It was a lot faster getting Meg ready for a day out than Anna had supposed. She just got up from her chair, grabbed her handbag and put her coat on. 'I'm ready,' she said.

Anna laughed. 'Then let's go.'

Another thing that surprised Anna was how sprightly Meg was. She managed the first part of the stairs with gentle grace, one hand placed on the banister and the other on Anna's arm. Anna smiled. Three hundred and fifty-five, indeed. She probably wasn't a day over eighty.

'Oh, there is just one thing I should bring,' Meg said as they reached the landing before the final sweep of stairs to the hallway.

'What's that?'

'My mobile,' Meg said. 'Some strange phone which William makes me carry around.'

'Oh,' Anna said. 'Do you really think we'll need it?' The last thing Anna wanted was William able to contact them wherever they went.

'He does like me to have it,' Meg said. 'But we're not going to be long, are we?'

'I'll have you back in time for tea,' Anna said, taking Meg's arm to help her down the last few stairs.

Suddenly, a scraping noise was heard as the outside door was opened.

'What's that?' Anna asked but she knew what it was. It was Mrs Boothby.

'I thought she'd left for the day,' Meg said.

'Yes,' Anna said, 'so did I. You'll have to hide, Meg!' Anna said, knowing there wasn't enough time to get Meg back to her bedroom.

'Why?'

'Because she'll know I'm up to no good with you.'

'But where am I going to hide?' Meg asked anxiously.

Anna looked around. They were halfway down the stairs and had reached the landing where a large suit of armour stood by a huge window. It would have to do.

'Get behind this and keep still. If you move, it'll clank. With any luck, she'll stay downstairs and not see you.'

Meg was so skinny that she was practically invisible behind the suit of armour but Anna was still worried she'd be seen. She'd have to make sure she distracted Mrs Boothby so she quickly ran down the stairs.

'Mrs Boothby! You're back,' she said, meeting her in the hallway and willing her not to venture upstairs.

'I left my umbrella,' Mrs Boothby said. 'Took it out to dry after the downpour this morning and left it behind. Silly really but you can't get far without one, can you? Not in our country.'

'No,' Anna said with a smile as she followed her to the kitchen where the forgotten item stood drying next to the range.

'And there it is,' Mrs Boothby said, bending down to pick it up. 'Carl is so cross with me. *Mother*, he said, *you'd forget your head if it wasn't screwed on.*' She gave a light laugh. 'Not very original, my son. And now I've made him cross because he's going to miss the start of some game show he's hooked on. Oh, dear.'

Anna followed her out into the hallway again and was mightily relieved to see her close the door behind her.

'Are we safe?' Meg called from behind the suit of armour on the landing.

'I think so,' Anna said, rushing up to help Meg. Once Anna had reached the landing, Meg walked out to greet her but bumped into the armour, sending it swaying. Instinctively, Anna reached out to grab it but the impact loosened the helmet which came crashing to the ground, rolling down the stairs and landing at the bottom with a loud clank.

'Oooops!' Anna yelped, tearing after it. 'I hope I've not damaged it.'

'I'm sure it's fine,' Meg said. 'William won't notice if there's another dent in it.'

Anna lifted up the dislodged helmet and examined it. 'It doesn't seem to be any the worse for wear but it's hard to tell.'

'It's so old, what's a few more knocks when it's survived goodness knows how many battle fields?'

'It's a good job that didn't happen when Mrs Boothby was here,' Anna said, her face paling at the thought.

'Oh, just imagine!' Meg said and started to laugh. Anna joined in and went to return the helmet.

'Come on, let's get out of here before we bring the whole place tumbling to the ground.'

They left Fox Hill by the side door and Anna returned the key to the secret bucket in the old stables. She then helped Meg into her car and did her seatbelt up before starting the engine and heading down the driveway.

'Now, this *is* an adventure,' Meg said.

'Where would you like to go?' Anna asked.

'We're in the Cotswolds, aren't we?' Meg asked.

'That's right,' Anna said.

'Excuse me for asking but I sometimes forget and have to check with people. I've lived in so many places, you see, and it's easy to forget.'

Anna smiled. She was a girl born and bred in the Cotswolds, never more than a stone's throw from the Elm Valley, and it was hard to imagine living anywhere else.

'Tell me more about where you've lived, Meg,' she said.

Meg looked across at Anna. 'You know, don't you?'

'Know what?'

'That I'm very old.'

'Yes, of course,' Anna said.

Meg shook her head. 'William's spoken to you, hasn't he?'

Anna bit her lip, not wanting to betray the bond between William and Meg. 'Yes,' she said, 'he's spoken to me.'

'Because I didn't think you believed me when I told you which is okay,' Meg said, 'because I'm used to people not believing me.'

'It's not that I don't believe you, Meg,' Anna said. 'I want to, I really do. It's just difficult. You see, you seem to be one of a kind.'

'Yes,' Meg said, 'it would certainly appear that way.'

Anna stopped at the gateway to let a tractor drive by and then turned onto the road into Fox Hill. 'Perhaps you can tell me more about yourself, though.'

'Is that why we're going on this little trip?' Meg asked.

Anna's eyes widened. 'Certainly not!' she lied. 'I just thought you might like–'

Meg laughed. 'I'm just teasing.'

A wave of relief hit Anna although she couldn't stop feeling guilty too. 'Not too breezy for you?' she asked, changing the subject as the car picked up speed and she opened the windows.

'Not at all. It's wonderful. Like flying.'

'Have you ever flown, Meg?'

'What do you mean?'

'In an aeroplane.'

'Oh, those things,' Meg said with a groan. 'I've heard about them but I must say that I don't like the sound of them.'

'So you've never left Britain?'

'Never left England,' she said.

'Really?'

Meg nodded. 'No need to.'

'But there's so much to see,' Anna said. 'Didn't you ever want to see the pyramids of Egypt or Niagara Falls?'

'No.'

'Or the Grand Canyon or the Great Barrier Reef?'

'No.'

'What about Chamber's Cross?' Anna tried.

'That's here, isn't it?'

'It's gorgeous and has one of my favourite views of the Elm Valley,' Anna said. 'I know this perfect little seat. Shall we head there?'

Meg nodded and, once they'd driven through the village of Fox Hill, Anna headed for the long twisting lane that led straight up to the very top of the Elm Valley.

They drove through honey-coloured villages where cottage windows had been flung open to make the most of the sunshine. Lines of washing blew in gardens and there were children paddling in a stream, glad to be free of school for the day.

The road narrowed and Anna slowed down as she overtook two chestnut horses.

'Just listen to that,' Meg said as the clip-clop of their hooves reached her. 'Isn't that the nicest sound? I've always thought so.'

Anna smiled. 'And they smell so great too, don't they? We used to live in a house that backed onto a field with three horses and I would bury my head in their necks just to smell them.'

'They can be great companions,' Meg said, 'and far more reliable than a lot of cars.'

Anna sneaked a look at Meg. Was this another reference to her past, she wondered?

As the road steepened, they left the beech woods behind them and the fields opened up so that you could see the gentle dip and swell of the land for miles.

'Not far now,' Anna said, turning round a bend and spotting the lay-by up ahead. Parking quickly, she put the windows up and got out of the car, walking to the other side to open Meg's door and undoing her seatbelt. She reached behind and grabbed a woollen rug which lived on the backseat and then she held out her arm for support.

'I've got you,' she said, leading Meg along a narrow footpath lined with long grasses to where a little lichen-covered bench stood. She spread the rug across it and Meg slowly lowered herself onto the bench. 'I wish I'd thought to bring a picnic,' she said, making sure Meg was comfortable.

'Perhaps another time.'

'Yes,' Anna said, realising what a nice thought it was to be planning another outing with Meg. 'So, what do you think of my bench?'

'I heartily approve. The air is so sweet up here. There's the most wonderful smell,' Meg said. 'Is it bluebells?'

'I don't think so,' Anna said. 'Most of them have withered away now.' She searched around and then spotted a bright blue clump of flowers under a group of trees. 'There!' she said. 'You're right. There's a pretty little patch of bluebells under the trees.'

'So they've escaped frying in the sun, have they?'

'Yes. They're fresh and gorgeous.'

Meg took a deep breath and then sighed it out slowly. 'I always feel sad when they leave us even though I've had so many years of them. What's that wonderful poem that talks about blossom and the passing of time?'

'A E Housman?' Anna said. 'We had an English teacher at school who was crazy about him. Used to recite him at any opportunity. *Loveliest of trees, the cherry now*, is that the one?'

'Yes,' Meg said.

'*And since to look at things in bloom, Fifty springs are little room.*'

'That's it. That's the one,' Meg said with a sigh. 'And so true.'

Anna was on instant alert. This, she thought, was the perfect opportunity to talk her about her age.

'But surely you can't complain. You've had so many springs,

haven't you?'

Meg chuckled. 'Perhaps but not all with perfect sight.'

Anna instantly felt appalled by what she had said. 'I'm sorry.'

'It's all right. It's all part of growing old,' Meg assured her.

'Can you see much of the view?' Anna asked, now completely distracted from asking the probing questions she'd planned.

'A few blurry colours. Perhaps you can fill the detail in for me?'

'I'd love to,' Anna said. 'Where to begin? There's so much. We're right at the top of a hill here which rolls away into fields. There's every shade of green imaginable but, if you look to the very distant fields, they're far bluer.' Anna paused, looking around for other things to describe. 'There are sheep too. Great white fluffy balls with their noses down. Some of them are sitting and they look as if they're admiring the view too.'

Meg laughed.

'There are a few small farm buildings and I can see a red tractor.'

'Can you see Fox Hill Manor?'

'No. Not from here. It's tucked away behind those trees,' Anna said, pointing without really knowing if Meg could see or not. 'But you can see the spire of St George's in Elmington.'

'And that's where you live?'

'Yes. And my sister too.'

'Is she married?'

'Yes. They have a little boy. Toby. He's perfect.'

'You have children?' Meg asked.

'No,' Anna said. 'I'm not even married.'

'But you don't need to be married to have children. Not these days at least.'

'I know,' Anna said. 'But it still seems the right way round. Perhaps I should have said I don't even have a boyfriend.'

'Yet,' Meg added with a little smile.

Anna smiled. 'You're the cheekiest three hundred and fifty-five year-old I've ever met.'

Meg laughed and didn't contradict Anna at the mention of her age.

They sat for a little longer, listening to the sweet song of a robin in a nearby branch of hawthorn and the distant bleat of sheep. The sun, which had been so bright a few moments ago, had disappeared behind a big bank of cloud and Anna shivered.

'Shall we get going?' she asked.

Meg got up slowly and inhaled deeply, as if locking away the scent of the bluebells.

Walking back to the car with the travel rug over one arm and Meg on the other, Anna asked, 'Where to next?'

Meg sat back in her seat and let her head loll onto the headrest. 'I really don't mind, Anna. You choose. I'm having so much fun.'

'Okay,' Anna said, checking the road before pulling out. 'We'll just take things nice and easy. Drive around and see what we see.'

And that's what they did. The Cotswold roads were a perfect enticement for a leisurely drive with each new turn promising another stunning view. They drove through a market town that was jostling with after-school activity, and then on down a tree-darkened lane before turning into a lush valley filled with grazing cows.

They reached the main road leading to Burford and Anna looked at Meg.

'When was the last time you got out, Meg?'

'Oh,' Meg said, surprised by the question and floundering to think what the answer might be, 'I don't think I've been out since I arrived at the manor.'

'Not at all?' Anna asked in dismay.

'Not beyond the garden.'

'And you don't miss it? You don't get bored?'

'William is very good to me. Everything is taken care of for me,' Meg said, nodding.

'Oh, I know. I didn't mean to suggest that he wasn't looking after you,' Anna said hastily.

'Everything seems to come to me these days. There's very little reason to venture out of doors,' she said.

'Why William, though? Why did you choose him to stay with?'

Meg sat quietly as if pondering on this herself. 'The last family I was staying with had all died,' she said.

Anna glanced at her. It was the oddest statement she'd ever heard.

'It was quite embarrassing, really,' she continued. 'I'd lived with them for years. I think – quite rightly – they expected me to pop my clogs – isn't that the phrase? – a lot sooner than them. But I didn't. On and on I went. I outlived the father, the mother, both daughters and then their son. I was passed from one to the other.'

'And they weren't at all suspicious about your age? I mean, didn't they think it odd that you were so old and kept going on?' Anna said.

'Nobody said anything. I guess they just got used to having me around. I can be very useful, you know. When these busy youngsters were out working all hours, I would tidy around for them and do some cooking. I liked to make myself useful.'

'But then they all died?'

'Yes,' Meg said with a sad sigh. 'It seems to be the story of my life. I have seen so many come and go and I'm obliged to go on without them.'

Anna swallowed. It was one of the saddest things she had ever heard.

'Around the time Marcus died, I heard about William. Marcus had a sweet neighbour, Emily, who would come and read to me and there was an article in a newspaper about this collector who'd just bought some item for thousands of pounds in an auction in London. I forget what it was now. Anyway, it caused all sorts of interest and there was lots written about him and his house. I remember thinking, he sounds like just the sort of mad person I've been looking for. And then Marcus died shortly after that and I remembered this William and got on a train to the Cotswolds.'

'What about the family's things? Marcus, I mean – did he leave you anything in his will?'

'Oh, yes. He left me his house and a sum of money too. I'm not sure what's happened to it now. I've been left all number of houses in the past but what good's a house with nobody in it?'

'But you could hire help. Have a live-in nurse,' Anna said.

Meg shook her head. 'It would be like a prison. There'd be me sitting in this one house with an endless stream of nurses coming and going. Wouldn't that be awful?'

'But isn't William just like a nurse?'

'Oh, no. He's very much his own man. His life doesn't revolve around me and that's the way I like it. I want to be a part of life still – in my own way. I don't want to interfere but I like to be a part of things. And William sounded so – *right* for me. Does that make sense?'

'Oh, yes,' Anna said, quietly wondering if he might also be right for her as well. She hadn't thought about him for a while and wondered where he was. It was early evening now and the funeral would be over.

'He's staying in London tonight, isn't he?' Anna asked.

'Yes. He said there were some people he'd like to see in town whilst he was there.

Anna nodded. That was good. She wouldn't have to rush back with Meg and answer a lot of awkward questions about where they'd been. In fact, they could stay out as long as they liked, she thought.

It wasn't long after this idea had occurred to Anna that Meg noticed the traffic. 'This is a busy road,' she said.

'Yes. It's the main road. We seem to have left the country lanes, don't we?'

'And all these signs too. What do they all say?'

'That last one actually said how far it was to London.'

'London?'

'Yes,' Anna said, and then she smiled. It was naughty, it was wicked and it was completely reprehensible. 'Meg,' she said. 'How do you fancy a trip to the capital?'

CHAPTER 16

The funeral was over mercifully quickly and William was just wondering if he could ring for his taxi and sneaking away when a heavy hand landed on his arm.

'You can share my car to the wake,' George said. His face was sombre and, despite their differences, William didn't have the heart to say no. Getting in the funeral car, George cleared his throat. 'Did you read the letter?'

William frowned. 'What, in the middle of the funeral?'

'I'm sorry. There's not been any time. Read it now.'

'Right now?' William asked, not liking to be bullied into doing it.

George nodded.

'You know what it says?' William asked.

'No. That's why I want you to read it now. See if the old girl's mentioned me at all.'

William sighed. This really was the strangest funeral he'd ever attended. He reached into his pocket and brought out the envelope, opening it in one neat tear and pulling out a letter. Unfolding it, another piece of paper fluttered out.

'It's a cheque,' George said unnecessarily, picking it up and whistling. 'Don't spend it all at once,' he said, handing it to William.

William looked at it. Two hundred pounds. It wouldn't even cover his costs to get to the funeral.

'What's it say, then?' George persisted.

William read the letter quickly. There wasn't much to read.

Dear William. I feel I owe you – not an apology – but at least some recompense for the item of furniture which I sold. I don't need to explain why I sold it but taking charge of a second child when I already had one of my own was expensive and I needed the money. I hope the enclosed allows you to replace your chest of drawers.

William chuckled. Chest of drawers, indeed.

It wasn't easy for me living with the child of the woman my husband left me for and I know it must have been hard for you too. I trust you and George are now friends and can console each other over my demise.

William frowned. 'She knew she was dying?'

'Of course,' George said. 'She'd been ill for months.

William looked at the sign off.

Sincerely, P Kitson.

He shook his head. Cold and callous to the end, he couldn't help thinking. George ripped the letter from his hand.

'She didn't mention me!' he cried.

'Didn't she leave you a letter of your own?'

'No, she didn't, the nasty cow.'

William frowned. And to think that he'd felt sorry for his half-brother.

'Don't look so shocked,' George said. 'I hated her as much as you did. She was the one who drove Dad away. He couldn't stand her either. Practically goaded him into leaving her.'

'Why?' William asked in surprise.

'Because that's the way she was. Oh, she wanted the house he'd bought her. She just didn't want him living in it.'

The car turned into the grounds of a hotel.

'But I thought you two were close,' William said.

'When a mother's all you've got, who else do you turn to?'

'There was me,' William said, surprising himself.

'But you were "the other woman's son",' George told him.

'Is that what Paula used to say?'

George nodded. 'And worse. She used to make me side against you. Told me to say things. *Do* things.'

'What things?'

George looked down at the blackness of his shoes. 'Damage things. Like that dolls' house of yours. She hated it.'

In a flash, William saw the scene before him again with George crushing the delicate miniature chair in his hand. 'I thought it was *you* who hated it.'

George looked puzzled. 'I never hated it. I rather liked it!'

'You're kidding?'

'No. Mother told me to smash the whole thing to pieces but I wouldn't. I couldn't. When you were out, I used to sneak into your room and look at it. It was fascinating. All those tiny wardrobes and tables. And that dinner service – extraordinary! For god's sake, don't tell anyone this but I used to make up stories about the sort of people who might live there.'

William laughed. He couldn't help himself. 'I don't believe it.'

'I didn't think you would,' George said. 'But the things that Lord Albert and Lady Agatha got up to in that house would make your eyes water.'

'Lord Albert? Lady Agatha?'

'I told you – they were my characters – the people who lived there. Kitson Manor, I called it. On George Street. I gave it a postcode and everything.'

William looked at George. 'You're absolutely serious, aren't you?'

'I've never been more serious in my life!' His eyes were wide and full of delight.

A small smile spread across William's face. 'We could have been friends.'

George's face broke into a smile too and William was surprised to see how very similar it was to his own. 'We can *still* be friends. I think we have a little time.'

Meg was staring at Anna as if she were quite mad. 'London?' she said. 'We can't go to London.'

'Why not?' Anna asked. 'It's only a couple of hours away. I'm sure my car's up to the challenge if you are'

'But what would William say?'

'William's away,' Anna pointed out again.

For a while, Meg didn't say anything and Anna continued driving but she could feel that the atmosphere inside the car had changed. It was as though she and Meg had tuned into the same wavelength and, all of a sudden, knew each other's minds. She took a quick look at her. She was smiling.

'We should go, shouldn't we?' Meg said.

Anna smiled, feeling a great bubble of excitement rising in her stomach. 'I'm afraid I don't have any provisions.'

'We can get some. What do we need?' Meg asked.

'Everything. Clothes, cosmetics–'

'We can buy some.'

'Yes. We can. This can be a kind of holiday. I haven't had a holiday for ages.'

Meg's hand disappeared into a pocket of her jacket. 'Will this help?'

Anna gasped as she saw a roll of twenty pound notes. 'Where did you get that?'

'When you've lived as long as I have, you learn to save and I've been saving this for a special occasion. Even William doesn't know about it.'

Anna laughed. 'Well, we'll be able to find a nice hotel for that.'

'And make sure you take some for petrol too. It's not cheap, is it?'

'Meg, you're amazing!' Anna said. 'However did I manage before you came along?'

'People are always saying that to me. I often wonder too.'

'You must've had a lot of adventures.'

'One or two,' she said.

'And you'll have to tell me all about them,' Anna said.

'Is this what this trip's really about?'

'What do you mean?'

'You getting me away from William so you can ask me lots of questions?'

'I didn't plan a trip to London,' Anna said. 'I may have planned a trip out this afternoon. I wanted to see you again. You're interesting, Meg. You surely must realise that.'

'And I'd be happy to answer any of your questions.'

'You would?'

'Of course. I've got nothing else to do, have I?'

'Oh!' Anna suddenly cried. 'What about Cocoa and Beanie?'

Meg shook her head. 'Don't worry. Mrs Boothby is going to pop back tonight to let them out.'

Anna looked anxious. 'But won't she check up on you and raise the alarm?'

'No, no. I left my bedroom light on and she tends not to disturb me.'

'Really?'

'She knows I like my independence,' Meg said.

Anna sighed in relief and grinned from ear to ear. 'Great,' she said. 'Oh, Meg! We're going to have *such* a great time. Just wait and see.'

The last thing William had expected from his trip to London was a reconciliation with George. How strange life could be sometimes, he thought, as he returned to his hotel room and lay down on the bed. He'd spent the whole evening with George, ringing up the antiques dealer he was meant to be seeing and cancelling their appointment. Who would have thought that he'd rather spend time with his half-brother than poking around a basement full of goodies? It was certainly a first for William. And who would have thought that George could be so *nice*. William had spent years of misery living in relative isolation with George and Paula, believing both of them had hated him, resented him being there. But George had assured him that that just wasn't true.

'I'll never forget the evening Mum sat me down to tell me you were arriving. I'd never seen her looking like that before,' George had told him earlier that day.

'What did she look like?'

'Purple,' George said. 'I swear. Her skin was purple. I thought she was going to explode or implode at the very least.'

William watched as George continued. 'Your father had made provisions for you in his will,' George said, 'but he'd also made provisions for Paula too. The only thing was she couldn't get her hands on the money left for her without taking care of you. It was a condition of the will, you see.'

'Ah,' William said. 'And I don't expect she was happy with that.'

'She was *livid*. I've never seen anybody do livid quite like Paula. She had expressions that would chill the blood inside your veins, and I was her only sounding board. It was horrible.'

'I know. I was there.'

'Unfortunately, the will didn't have anything that said she had to be nice to you and, I'm afraid, she made life rather unpleasant, didn't she?'

William nodded. 'Let's just say that it was enough to put me off the idea of family life for a while.'

'Really?'

William nodded.

'God, that's terrible,' George said, running his hand through his fair hair. 'But you're with someone now, right?'

'What do you mean?'

'The lovely Anna?' George said, his eyes sparkling and suggestive.

William couldn't help but smile at the mention of her name. 'Well, she's very special but it's early days,' he said.

'Ah, but the early days are the best,' George said. 'So, you're serious about her?'

'I think so,' William said.

'It's strange but I never imagined you with someone like Anna.'

'What do you mean?' William asked.

George shrugged. 'She just seems to be very much her own woman, doesn't she? And I always imagined you with someone a little more – homely.'

William grinned. 'Like Mrs Boothby?'

'You know, I did use to wonder. I could've sworn you had someone stashed away in that old house of yours. I even warned Anna about it.'

William laughed at the accuracy of George's perception.

'Seriously,' George said, 'you've got a good girl in Anna.'

'I know,' William said, thinking of her lovely face and her bright, inquisitive eyes.

'You know,' George said, 'one way or another, I always end up envying you.'

'What?' William said, startled.

'Yeah. Well, for a start, you didn't have Paula as a mother. You could walk away as soon as you were sixteen and never look back.'

'But you could've done that too,' William said.

George shook his head. 'It's not so easy when you're related, is it?'

They were quiet for a moment. 'What about now?' William asked.

'A good time for new beginnings,' George said. 'I broke up with someone a couple of months ago but I'm ready to start looking again,' he added with a grin. 'Now that I don't have the worry of introducing them to Paula and risk scaring them off.'

'Did she scare anyone off?'

'One or two, I think. She can be – *could* be,' he corrected, 'very domineering. There was the time when I was cooking dinner after work for Elizabeth. She was gorgeous. Funny, smart and sweet. Well, we'd just sat down when we heard the front door open and Paula was standing there. She looked in a right state. Hair tattered, make-up running and tights laddered.'

'What had happened?'

'She said she'd been mugged.'

William's eyes narrowed. 'But she hadn't?'

'Had she heck! She told me he'd taken her purse but when I took her home and she went to have a bath, I found it in her handbag. There was sixty pounds in it. She'd not been mugged. But she'd played *me* for a mug! Completely wrecked my date.'

'Did she know you were seeing someone that evening?'

'Yes, of course' George said and then sighed. 'I'd made the fatal mistake of telling her. Can you believe that?' He shook his head. 'She was what you'd call a possessive mother. I don't think she ever thought I'd move away from home, let alone get married.'

'At least you're free of those worries now, though,' William said.

'Yes,' George said. 'It's rather a liberating feeling. I know one shouldn't really be happy on the day of a funeral but I can feel the tiniest of smiles growing inside me. Is that awful of me?'

William shook his head. 'In the circumstances, I'd say that was perfectly understandable.'

Back in his hotel room, William thought of the strange conversation he'd had with George and the fact that he'd told George about Anna. He hadn't meant to do that but he had to admit that it felt right.

He hadn't been able to get her out of his head. Everywhere he looked, he saw Anna. And he'd come to a decision – he was going to tell her just how he felt about her. Today had taught him that time shouldn't be wasted. Life could take some unexpected turns, many of which couldn't always be controlled by you, but he was going to make sure that he was in charge of this one thing.

Suddenly, William was packing, flinging his clothes into his small suitcase. He had to leave London as soon as possible and get back to Fox Hill Manor.

CHAPTER 17

But William's girls weren't at Fox Hill Manor. They were at a hotel near Marble Arch. With rare on-street parking and an ensuite twin room overlooking a small but perfect London square, Anna was very pleased with their find.

They checked themselves in and then decided to go late-night shopping, taking a taxi to nearby Oxford Street where they dived into a department store for the necessary clothes and toiletries for an impromptu trip to the Big Smoke. Meg insisted on paying, buying herself a pretty cream blouse and raspberry wool skirt. Anna chose a red and white checked shirt and a pair of jeans.

'I once tried jeans,' Meg said, 'but they didn't agree with me.'

Anna grinned, trying to imagine Meg in denim.

'But I must say that I did breathe a sigh of relief when women were allowed to wear trousers. Dresses and skirts are so draughty, aren't they?'

Anna laughed. 'And thank goodness for bras without wires, I say.'

'Wires? You wouldn't get wires anywhere near me,' Meg said. 'A simple vest for me. Luckily, I've never had much to worry about in that department and, at my ripe old age, there's barely anything left to worry about at all.'

The young shop assistant, who had casually sidled over to them in the hope of some sales, looked rather shocked by Meg's confession.

'Just look at that,' Meg said, sticking out her non-existent chest. 'Like a couple of peanuts, they are. I could almost be a man. In fact, I must tell you about the time when I was mistaken for a man. Caused all sorts of complications.'

Anna tried to hide her amusement in front of the sales assistant but it was a losing battle.

They chose some underwear and night garments and then took everything to the till. The assistant followed them and took the clothes, scanning the price labels and folding them neatly to put into bags.

'Meg, are you sure you can afford all this?' Anna said.

'Of course I'm sure. I've got this plastic thing here. William gave it to me. I hand it over and everything gets paid for. It's marvellous.'

'A credit card,' Anna said, assuming William paid the bills and hoping he wouldn't baulk at an armful of designer labels.

'Yes, a credit card. It was William's idea. He said it made life a lot simpler only I don't get many opportunities to use it being cooped up at the manor all the time.'

'No, I don't suppose you do,' Anna said. 'But we'll make sure we give it a bit of exercise whilst we're here in London, won't we?'

When the sales assistant told them the total, Meg handed her card over to Anna. 'I'm not sure what you do with it,' she said.

Anna put it into the machine. 'You have to type in your four digits,' she told Meg.

'Four digits? What four digits?'

'It's a code – to allow you to pay for your goods. You have to type it in or we can't pay.'

'Oh, dear!' Meg said.

The sales assistant didn't look very impressed. 'Are you buying these items or aren't you?'

'Yes,' Anna said, 'just give us a moment.' She turned to Meg. 'Are you sure William didn't give you a number for the card? It might've been a date or something. It's usually a date that you can remember – something significant.'

'Oh!' Meg suddenly exclaimed. 'That's right. He told me it was one six-'

'Shush!' Anna hushed. 'You're not meant to say it out loud. Just type it into the machine here.'

Meg peered at the strange contraption Anna was pointing at. 'I can't see any numbers. Why don't I just tell you the number and you can do it for me?'

'Well, you're not meant to tell anyone else,' Anna said.

'Why not? You're not going to steal from me, are you?'

'No, of course not,' Anna said. 'But you really shouldn't be so trusting of people.'

Meg bent forward and whispered the number to Anna. 'One. Six. Five. Nine. 'It's my supposed date of birth,' she said. 'William thought it would be a good idea to use that so we sat down one day and worked out exactly when I thought it was.'

'You haven't told anyone else, have you?' Anna asked, keying the number in quickly.

'I've never been shopping with anyone else before. This is the first time I've used the card outside the manor.'

'Good,' Anna said, completing the transaction and taking charge of their carrier bags.

'Thank you,' Meg said, aiming a smile at the sales assistant. 'I'm sorry if I embarrassed you before and the confusion with my card but I can't read the numbers. I'm not as old as I used to be.'

'Don't you mean not as *young* as you used to be?' the sales assistant said.

'No,' Meg said. 'I meant what I said. I'm three hundred and fifty-five.'

The sales assistant frowned deeply and then turned her attention to some cardigans that needed folding.

'Meg!' Anna whispered.

'What is it? Have I done something else wrong?'

'You can't just tell people how old you are like that.'

'Why not? They don't believe me anyway,' she said.

'But you didn't need to say anything at all about your age.'

They took the escalator down to the ground floor, Anna guiding Meg so that she didn't stumble.

'I've embarrassed you, haven't I?' Meg said with a little sigh.

Anna shook her head. 'No, you didn't embarrass me.'

'I'm *always* embarrassing people. I shouldn't be allowed out. I should just stay in my room.'

'Don't say that, Meg. Of *course* you shouldn't. And we *all* misbehave every now and again. It's one of the great joys of life. Wouldn't it be dull if we were all perfectly behaved all the time?' she said, navigating Meg through a forest of extended arms proffering innumerable perfume bottles.

'But I seem to get myself into trouble more often than most people,' Meg said, narrowly avoiding being squirted by an over-zealous assistant.

'Nonsense,' Anna said. 'You just have to be careful whom you talk to. Not everyone is understanding, you know?'

They walked by the in-store cafe and the warm aroma of coffee hit them instantly, the espresso machine hissing loudly in the corner.

'Now, that is something I adore about living now. All the different teas and coffees that are available,' Meg said, a delightful smile gracing her face as she inhaled deeply. 'It wasn't that long ago that they were luxuries, you know – kept under lock and key in caddies by the lady of the house. You couldn't just go and make yourself a cuppa anytime you wanted. Oh, how lucky you young girls are today.'

Anna smiled as they left the store and were swallowed up into the crowds on the pavement.

'Meg?' Anna said after a moment as she noticed that Meg's steps were getting shorter and slower. 'Are you okay?'

'Yes, yes,' Meg said quickly. 'I think I just need a little something to eat and a lie-down. I usually nap during the afternoons but we've been so busy, haven't we?'

'Of course,' Anna said, instantly feeling awful at having worked her so hard. 'It is late and it's been such a long day.'

They got a taxi back to their hotel and Anna helped Meg unpack the necessary items for washing and bed. 'I love this nightdress you chose,' she said, holding up the pretty blue dress-like item. 'And my pyjamas are so cute!'

'Perhaps we should go shopping again tomorrow,' Meg said with a smile. 'It was so much fun.'

'I don't think William would approve of our little shopping spree,' Anna said. 'Oh! Should we ring him, do you think? Let him know where we are?'

Meg shook her head. 'He was going to stay in London tonight,' she said.

Anna breathed a sigh of relief. She still felt like a schoolgirl who was skipping off lessons but at least she didn't have to worry about William until tomorrow.

It was long dark by the time William arrived at Fox Hill Manor. It had been an easy journey and he felt his usual joy at having returned to the Cotswolds. The welcoming silhouettes of the hills and trees always made him smile and, turning off the main road and onto the track that led to the manor house, he couldn't help but be happy at this particular homecoming.

He'd thought long and hard about his future on the way back, realising that it was the first time that he'd done such a thing. Usually, William spent most of his time thinking about the past rather than the future. For years, he'd been so focussed on his collection that there'd been very little time left to think about anything else. His mind had been as cluttered as his house with thoughts of armour and armoires, and clocks and coffers. There'd been very little time left for thinking about the female of the species.

As he opened the front door, Cocoa and Beanie came charging out of the sitting room, greeting him in a blinding mass of fur and paws. William bent down to fuss them.

'Hello, boys! Did you miss me?'

They nuzzled his leg in response, Cocoa giving a little jump and pawing at his trousers and Beanie rolling over onto the floor and presenting him with a furry belly to rub.

'Meg upstairs, boys?' he asked. 'She'll get a surprise, won't she?' he said, giving them both one last tickle before standing up and making for the stairs.

It was good to be home. As he passed all the familiar objects around him, he felt a sense of contentment and peace. He also felt excited. His mind was beginning to run away with him as he thought about the future. He was going to tell Anna that he loved her and he felt pretty sure that she felt the same way about him. And that meant endless possibilities were in store for them.

She loves Fox Hill, I know she does, he thought to himself. But would she want to move in with him? That was a big step. It would be a big step if he had a normal home but the manor was far from normal.

You're running away with yourself, he told himself. Wait until you've spoken to her. Don't start planning your whole future together.

But, there was a part of him that just couldn't help it. The thought of Anna seemed to go hand in hand with happy-ever-after.

'Meg?' he hollered up the stairs, forcing himself to return to the present. 'I'm back.' His feet creaked on the wooden landing as he reached the top. 'You're never going to guess what happened in London,' he said, reaching her room and opening the door.

The light was on but Meg's room was empty.

'Meg?' he called, checking her bathroom but she wasn't there. He returned downstairs to the kitchen, thinking that she might be having a spot of supper. 'Meg?'

The kitchen was empty.

William was beginning to get worried now, moving from room to room looking for Meg but she was nowhere to be found. There wasn't even an indication as to where she might have gone like a scribbled note.

'She never leaves the house,' he said to himself. 'Where could she have gone?' William had no idea. There was only one thing of which he was certain: Meg wasn't at Fox Hill Manor.

Anna watched the sleeping figure of Meg. Her skin looked so pale, it was almost translucent. She was still worried that they'd overdone things that day. She had to remember that Meg spent most of her time in her room at FHM and wasn't used to afternoons out followed by long drives to London and hours of shopping.

She thought about their time together and couldn't help grinning as she remembered the blushing sales assistant Meg had embarrassed. But why had Meg felt the need to tell a stranger a lie like that, Anna wondered? It was such a strange thing to do. Usually, women were found guilty of reducing their age not increasing it by hundreds of years. What made a person do that?

Unless, of course, it was true.

That's what today had been all about – getting closer to Meg and finding out why she said such things. She didn't seem at all like the kind of person who would tell great fibs and, indeed, William believed that she was telling the truth. So maybe it was time that Anna started to believe her too.

CHAPTER 18

After having an uneasy night, William woke the next morning. He'd tried Meg's mobile five times but it was obviously switched off and he'd had to leave messages.

It seemed strange to have Fox Hill Manor to himself. Meg had been living there for four years and, although she didn't interrupt his day-to-day routine, he found that – now she wasn't there – he missed her. He supposed it was just the knowledge of having another person in the house that was a comfort. If you were feeling a bit lonely or bored, you could go and have a chat or share a cup of tea together.

He tried her mobile again but there was no reply. Had she left him? Had she finished her time with William and decided to move on to her next home? The thought had never occurred to him that she might just decide to leave one day. But then an idea entered his mind.

'Anna!' he said. Why hadn't he thought of it before? Meg might be with Anna.

Breakfast in Marble Arch was a sumptuous affair with croissants, hot buttered toast and creamy hot chocolate. Anna felt she was in heaven without having the inconvenience of dying first. Meg looked as if she was enjoying herself too, although her portions weren't quite as large as Anna's and she didn't leave a clean plate.

'I've eaten enough to fill an army,' she said, dabbing her mouth politely and taking a sip of tea.

Anna smiled. 'This is such a treat. Normally, it's a bowl of dusty muesli for me.'

'And what do we have planned for today?' Meg asked. 'I feel so much better after that night's sleep. I'm sorry if I wasn't much company last night.'

'Don't apologise. I had a brilliant day,' Anna said. 'I feel like I'm on holiday.'

'Me too,' Meg confided and her pale blue eyes sparkled.

'So, anything you want to see?' Anna asked.

Meg looked thoughtful. 'Actually, there is somewhere I'd like to go.'

'Okay,' Anna said, wondering what Meg had in store for her.

'I haven't been to London for years,' Meg said. 'It seems a lot noisier now than it used to be.'

'When were you last here?'

Meg sighed and scrunched up her eyes as she thought. 'Well, it was a long time ago. Maybe the 1860s.'

Anna almost swallowed the end of her hot chocolate the wrong way. 'Meg, you do say the strangest things.'

Meg smiled. 'You still don't believe me, do you? I can see you've been having a bit of a battle. You *want* to believe me, am I right?'

'I want to know more,' Anna said. 'That's part of the reason I came to see you yesterday. You intrigue me, Meg. I've never met anyone like you.'

'Neither have I. I wish I had sometimes. It gets rather lonely being me,' Meg said. 'Nobody really understands what it's like, you see, and nobody shares the same memories as I have. Well, not beyond the last ninety years, that is.'

Anna smiled and stared at Meg. Everything she said seemed perfectly sincere. There was no difference whether she was talking about something as mundane as breakfast or something as extraordinary as life in a previous century. She really didn't seem to be acting or lying. It was most perplexing and intriguing and Anna could have sat there watching her and listening to her all day but they didn't have the luxury of time so she got up from the breakfast table.

After a quick wash and brush up, they left the hotel.

'So, what's this place you want to see?' Anna asked, feeling as if she was on the brink of a great adventure.

'It was somewhere I used to live,' Meg said. 'Now what was the name? I'm terrible with names but, then again, I've had so many to remember.'

'Can you remember roughly where it was?' Anna asked, wondering, perhaps, if this wasn't just another of Meg's yarns. 'London's a big place.'

'Let me see,' Meg said, casting her eyes up to the sky. 'If only I could remember the name. Ah,' she said after a moment, 'I seem to remember that it was named after that big family who owned great chunks of London.'

Anna frowned. 'The Dukes of Bedford?'

'No. Not Bedford. But it was a duke. Let me think.'

They walked the short distance towards Oxford Street.

'*Cuthland!*' Meg suddenly shouted. 'That's it. Cuthland Square. Or just off it, I think. A crescent, it was – something beginning with B.'

'It might help if we had an A–Z,' Anna said, spying a newsagent's. They went inside, found an A–Z and paid for it.

'Cuthland Square?' Anna said and Meg nodded. Flicking through the pages, Anna found what they were looking for. 'Here we are,' she said.

'Anything beginning with *B*?' Meg asked.

'Just a mo.' Anna scanned the surrounding streets. 'Amberley Street. Pennington Road. *Here!* Bretton Place just off Cuthland Square.'

'That's it!' Meg said in triumph. '*That's* the one.'

'It's not far from here,' Anna said, suddenly excited. 'If we get on one of those tour buses and hop off at the next stop, we could walk. Are you up for a bit of a walk?'

'A bit,' Meg said.

'We can link arms.'

'Like old friends.'

'Yes,' Anna said, taking Meg's arm through hers and patting her hand. 'Like old friends.'

Anna had a little bit of cash on her and she paid for two day tickets for the tour bus. They opted for downstairs seats so that it would be easy for Meg to get off the bus when their stop arrived.

'So, when did you live in Bretton Place?' Anna asked. 'In the nineteenth-century?'

Meg turned to look at Anna. 'You said that with a smile in your voice.'

'No I didn't.'

'Yes you did. Don't deny it, Anna dear. You think I'm potty and that's that.'

'I wish you wouldn't think that, Meg. I don't think you're potty at all.'

'No? You're sure? Because I wouldn't blame you if you did. I often wonder what would happen if I met me coming down the street. Have you ever wondered that?' Meg asked.

Anna shook her head. 'No, I haven't.'

'Well, *I* have,' Meg said. 'Would I like myself, I wonder? Would I believe what I said?'

'And would you?'

'Well, I don't really know. Probably not. So I don't blame *you* for not believing me because I probably wouldn't either.'

Anna pursed her lips, not knowing what she should say. She wanted to believe Meg – she really did – and she got so excited when she thought what it could mean if Meg was telling the truth. As a journalist, she knew that Meg's story was as wacky and wonderful as they came but there was something holding her back from believing it: proof. Okay, so most journalists today didn't let truth and hard facts get in the way of a good story but Anna wasn't one of those journalists. She needed to believe that her written word was true.

'Meg,' she said at last, 'I'm trying to believe you. I really hope I can – and soon – just give me a bit more time.'

'Time,' Meg said, 'is something I've always had plenty of.'

William took Anna's card out of his wallet and looked at it, remembering when she'd handed it to him and closing his eyes briefly as he recalled the moment. But he couldn't think about Anna now; he had to put Meg first and, looking at the card, he saw Anna's address. It wouldn't take long to get there and he thought it was probably best not to ring first. He had a slight suspicion that Anna had taken advantage of him being away and was probably interviewing Meg right now for a book of her very own. So, after checking on Cocoa and Beanie, he let himself out of the house and drove the short distance to Elmington.

The more he thought about it, the more he was convinced that Meg was with Anna and he wasn't sure how he felt about that. He'd asked Anna to leave Meg alone but it was looking like she might have ignored his wishes. Still, he mustn't jump the gun. It was possible that Meg might have just upped and left Fox Hill Manor. Maybe she was bored of life in the Elm Valley and wanted a new family. The thought had never crossed William's mind until yesterday. He thought of Meg as being a permanent fixture, a family member, and he didn't like to think of Fox Hill Manor without her. But maybe life with him was just too dull. He was a single gentleman, after all, and Meg had been used to living with young families. What did he have to offer in comparison?

'Oh, God!' he exclaimed, taking a bend in the road a little too fast. *What do I have to offer anyone*, he wondered? How could he ever expect Anna to want to live with him if Meg couldn't even stand to stay there?

He shook his head. He was running away with himself again. He had to calm down until he was in possession of all the facts.

As he entered Elmington, he glanced down again at Anna's address. He knew the road and soon found it. She'd been right when she'd told him it was small. He wouldn't fit one roomful of his collection in this place, he thought, but it looked neat and tidy and very *Anna.* There was a silver pot by the front door step with a sensible evergreen plant inside and an immaculate coconut mat greeted his old shoes as he knocked on the front door.

Please let them be in, he chanted to himself, and, as he heard the front door open, he thought he was in luck.

'Hello,' a pretty young woman with chestnut hair said.

'Hello,' he said back.

'You're William Kitson, aren't you?' she said, her dark brown eyes scanning him.

William nodded.

'I'm Libby – Anna's sister.

'Oh,' William said, holding out his hand to shake hers. 'How do you do?'

Libby smiled and shook it. 'Would you like to come in?'

'Thank you,' he said, following her into a long neat hallway in which was hung one small square mirror.

'It's pretty sparse, isn't it?' Libby said. 'Far too sparse for me. Anna's problem is she's never understood ornaments. It's such a shame. She misses out on so much.'

'You're the collector, aren't you?' William said.

'Yes,' Libby beamed back at him. 'She's told you about me?'

William nodded. 'Sounds like you have quite an impressive collection.'

'Oh, yes. It's marvellous. The only problem is I don't have enough space for it all. That's why I'm here today – dropping some things off for safe-keeping until I've found some room for them at home. Only don't tell Anna.'

'She's not here?' William said, his smile dropping.

'No, of course not. I thought Anna was with you at Fox Hill Manor?'

'No. I've not seen her. She seems to have disappeared.'

'Oh, dear,' Libby said.

William sighed.

'I'm sure she'll turn up,' Libby said. 'She usually does sooner or later. Probably following the scent of some story. You know what she's like.'

'Yes. I think I do,' he said, dreading to think what must have happened to Anna and having every suspicion that Meg was also involved.

'I was just about to make a cup of tea. Would you like one?' Libby asked.

William nodded and followed her through to the kitchen. Again, the room was neat, tidy and completely devoid of unnecessary ornamentation.

'Isn't it dull?' Libby said. 'No pretty mugs on display, no fridge magnets, no notice board – *nothing!* I can't stand it.'

William grinned, thinking of his own collection of blue and white china, and gleaming copper pots as well as the general mess that comes with being a single man in a kitchen. And then he noticed something.

'What's that in your hair?' he asked.

'What?' Libby said in panic.

William took a step closer. 'It looks like cobweb.'

Libby brushed her hair quickly with frantic hands. 'Is it off? Oh, how horrible! No spiders, I hope?'

'I can't see anything,' William assured her. 'How did you get cobweb in your hair?'

Libby blushed a little. 'It must have been from the attic. I'd just coming down the ladder when you knocked on the door. You know,' she said, 'those boxes I told you about. I was putting them away. Our attic's full now.'

'Right,' William said.

'I'm sure Anna wouldn't mind,' Libby said. 'But best not to tell her all the same.'

'You mean, she doesn't know?'

Libby shook her head. 'She's never understood my collecting. Blimey! I completely forgot!' Libby suddenly exclaimed.

'What?'

'The *Farmyard Cutie* you found for me. That was *so* kind. Anna told me about it. I can't thank you enough.'

'It was my pleasure,' William said. 'Anything to help a fellow collector. We have to stick together, don't we?'

'Nobody else gets us, do they?' she said, a sad, faraway sort of look on her face.

William looked thoughtful. 'You know, I think your sister might be beginning to understand.'

'Really?' Libby sounded surprised.

'Yes. She's quite taken with Fox Hill Manor.'

'How *extraordinary!*' Libby said. 'I mean, no offence, but she was dreading going there.'

'I know. She made that perfectly clear to me,' William said with a little smile.

'I hope she wasn't rude,' Libby said. 'She can be very rude about *my* collecting sometimes.'

'No, she wasn't rude. Just – set in her ways.'

'But you think she's coming round?'

'Yes,' William said, thinking again of their long warm kisses. 'I think she might be.'

'Here we are - the nearest stop to find Bretton Place,' Anna said, checking her A–Z once again. 'Are you ready?'

Meg nodded.

As soon as the tour bus had come to a standstill, Anna took Meg's arm and they got off, looking up and down the road as the bus pulled out and went on its way.

'Well,' Anna said, 'I can safely say that I've never been here before. Does it look familiar to you?'

Meg looked up and down the street. 'It's hard to say.'

'What did the house you lived in look like? Do you remember?'

'It was one of those houses that look like a wedding cake.'

'Georgian?' Anna suggested.

'Tall with those lovely long windows.'

Anna nodded. 'I know what you mean. Shall we try to find it?'

They were the only ones to have got off the bus at Cuthland Square, Anna noticed. There were no museums here, and no planetariums or zoos. This was a little bit of London left to the Londoners and Cuthland Square was at the centre of it.

The square was one of those little oases which always attracted those who were in need of peace. Plane trees with their stripy bark soared into a peerless blue sky and clouds of pearly-grey pigeons flew overhead.

The warm sunshine meant that nearly every bench was full and occupants sat eating packaged sandwiches and watching the world go by. A group of children was chasing each other around a fountain in the centre of the square and Anna wondered if they should sit and enjoy the scene for a while but Meg seemed determined to crack on.

According to the A–Z, Bretton Place was a road off the far side of the square and, as they reached it, the world seemed to be placed on a mute setting – the noise of London being left behind them.

'I think we're here,' Anna said, looking up at the road sign as they crossed from the main square.

'Are you sure?' Meg asked.

'Pretty sure,' Anna said, nodding towards the road sign. 'Look.'

'Oh,' Meg said.

'What's wrong?' Anna asked.

'It feels so different,' Meg said, her face clouding with disappointment.

'Places don't stay the same forever,' Anna said, 'especially in London.'

Meg sighed. 'I suppose not.'

They walked along the length of the road. Most of the houses seemed to be modern.

'It's all so new,' Meg said.

'What did you think was here? Those Georgian buildings you described? The ones like wedding cakes?'

Meg nodded.

'I can't see any. And these ones are very new,' Anna said as they passed a block of apartments.

Meg looked confused. 'It should have been here. It was here, I'm sure of it.'

'You've got the right street?' Anna asked, wondering if she'd perhaps got confused.

'Yes. *Yes!* Meg said in frustration. 'There was a row of them white buildings. All tall like temples.'

Anna suddenly stopped in her tracks. Just ahead of them, with the sun bouncing off its clean white front, stood a short row of Georgian houses.

'Is that it?' Anna asked.

Meg squinted and the two of them walked towards the houses.

'My goodness,' Meg said. 'I do believe you've found them.'

'There's only – one, two, three, four. Only four.'

Meg shook her head. 'But this whole street was lined with them.'

Anna looked up and down, noting the new apartments again. 'Perhaps they were pulled down to make room for the flats,' Anna suggested.

Meg drew a sharp intake of breath. 'They wouldn't do that, would they? How dreadful!'

'Do you remember what number the house was?' Anna said.

'Of course not,' Meg said, getting tetchy now.

Anna sighed. This wasn't working out quite as she'd expected and she, too, was becoming frustrated.

'Shall we go and sit down?' she said.

Meg nodded. She seemed totally defeated.

Returning to the square, they found a bench and sat down. 'I'm sorry you haven't found what you wanted,' Anna said.

'It's no longer here, is it?'

'No, I don't think so,' Anna said, wondering if it had ever been there in the first place.

It was then that she spotted a small tour group on the other side of the square.

'Are you all right sitting here for a moment?'

Leaving Meg to dose in the sun, Anna approached the tour group. There were about twelve people in the group and the guide was a middle-aged woman wearing a stifling navy suit. Anna waited for an opportunity to interrupt and one soon came when the tour guide pointed to a statue in the corner of the square and everybody rushed towards it with their cameras at the ready.

'Excuse me,' Anna began, 'can I ask you something about this area?'

'Yes, of course. How can I help?' the woman said.

'I was wondering if you knew much about Bretton Place over there,' Anna said, pointing. 'About the architecture, I mean.'

'Well, it used to be one of the most beautiful parts of London. The whole area was Georgian but there was a lot of damage during the Blitz, particularly in Bretton Place and, as you can see, the buildings have been replaced by these modern flats. But don't get me started on that!' the guide said, her eyes rolling to high heaven.

Anna stood dumbfounded as the guide moved on, walking towards her group who was still photographing the statue of some duke or other.

Bretton Place had been Georgian. The whole street had been lined with – as Meg called them – wedding cake buildings. How had Meg known that? Had it just been a lucky guess or was there more to it than that?

Anna returned to Meg and sat down on the bench. 'Meg?' she said.

'Yes?'

'Tell me more about your time here.'

CHAPTER 19

If she was perfectly honest, it wasn't Anna's whereabouts that concerned Libby so much as if her sister would notice that somebody had been in the loft. As soon as William had left, Libby returned upstairs, climbing the ladder into the loft once more and shifting her stuff to make it look as inconspicuous as possible which wasn't at all easy as she'd practically taken over the entire space.

It had been an awful rush too because Charlie had decided to spend the morning doing paperwork in the front room and Libby had spent an anxious few hours looking out of the window for delivery vans, hoping against hope that her new dolls' house wouldn't turn up. But, of course, it had.

'Delivery for Mrs Elizabeth Robertson,' the man bellowed when Libby opened the door as quietly as she could.

Libby winced as the man took a huge box out of the back of his van and entered the hallway with it.

'What on earth's this?' Charlie said, having abandoned his paperwork to find out what his wife was up to.

The delivery man beat a hasty retreat and Libby was left to explain things herself. 'It's nothing for you to worry about.'

'But what is it?' Charlie asked, looking the box up and down for labels. 'A dolls' house? What do you want with another dolls' house?'

Libby gulped. There was no getting out of this one. Or was there? 'It's not for me. It's for Anna,' she lied.

'Anna?' Charlie said incredulously. 'But she hates dolls' houses.'

'No, she doesn't. Not this type – it's a miniature dolls' house. She specifically asked me to look out for one for her so I did and here it is.'

'Well, that really is the limit – you getting her collecting,' Charlie said, shaking his head in amused despair.

'When are you going out today?' Libby asked, trying to sound casual about it.

Charlie held his hands up in the air. 'I can take a hint when I'm not wanted.' Half an hour later and Charlie had left. Libby had then rushed round to Anna's – after making sure she was out, of course – and had hidden the new dolls' house up in the attic which had been no mean feat but she'd struggled along knowing that she'd be in terrible trouble if she didn't.

But it wasn't just the dolls' house she had to worry about. There were several other boxes of miscellaneous things she'd managed to collect in the last couple of weeks too. As she packed them away into the loft, she tried to remember what they contained but couldn't. Obviously vital for her collections, though, she reasoned, otherwise she wouldn't have bought them. She didn't buy just anything. If she hadn't stuck packing tape down on them to prevent dust entering, she'd take a look to remind herself but it couldn't be helped now and it would be all the more exciting opening them up in the future and discovering their contents as if for the first time.

As she descended from the loft, Libby had to admit to feeling a little anxious.

Was there a limit on how much stuff you could put up there before the ceiling fell down? It was looking pretty full now and Libby knew that it was all her stuff. Anna hadn't had a single bean up there. It seemed like such a waste of good space. Well, if Anna wasn't going to fill it, Libby was. Still, as she tidied up, she couldn't shake the image of the upstairs ceiling falling down and completely burying her sister.

She shook her head. There was only one way to get rid of such awful imaginings and that was a spot of shopping before she had to pick Toby up from school and she was sure Levy's was having a *twenty-percent off day* so that made her decision even more sensible.

After Anna had returned to the bench in Cuthland Square, Meg had begun her story.

'The truth of it is, I can't remember how I came to be homeless in London. I think it must have been the usual story of me living with a family and then the family died and I was on my own again. After I got to be about eighty or ninety and deemed unfit to work, that's been the usual pattern, I'm afraid – I'll stay somewhere, they'll all die, I'll move on.

'But there's one thing I do remember. I was sitting on the steps of St Catherine's Church – it's not far from here. How I came to be there, I don't know. But it had just started to rain and the street was silver and shining like a shilling. I must have looked very odd sitting there. A little old lady with nowhere to go, surrounded by the jostle of people travelling home from work. The funny thing was, nobody stopped to ask questions. That's one of the bonuses – and penalties – about living in the city; you can be completely anonymous. Only one man stopped to ask if I was all right. He helped me up off the step, brushed down my coat and told me I should go home with him and that was that.

'His name was Albert Palmer and he was incredibly tall and thin. He reminded me of a silver birch,' Meg said with a little chuckle, 'and he had one of those twiddly moustaches. You know the sort I mean?'

Anna nodded. 'I've seen old photographs of people from that time.'

'Well, I was living in this photograph,' Meg said and she paused.

'Go on,' Anna encouraged, desperate to hear more even if it was just another of Meg's tall tales.

'Well, his house was in Bretton Place, as I said, and I managed to make it there without making too much of an exhibition of myself. I go a bit hazy after that. I think I was put straight in the bath and then to bed. I just remember feeling incredibly warm after having been cold for so long.'

'What happened then?' Anna asked as she saw Meg's vision blurring into the middle distance.

'After that? I lived with them. His wife was called Constance, I think. He always called her Connie. They had five children. Two had died before I arrived. That much I remember. They looked on me as a grandmother. That's the pattern, I've discovered. The young tend not to mind having the old around. It's a comfort, somehow. We remind them of how lucky they are not to be ancient and have creaking bones and poor responses. Of course, they don't say as much but I've seen their faces. When I move around, wincing in old-age agony, I can see it in their eyes. But I always get the last laugh, don't I?'

'What do you mean?' Anna asked.

'They always think I'm almost ready to die. *It'll come any day now*, that's what they think. Only it doesn't. They're always the first to go.'

'Oh, Meg!' Anna said, her heart breaking at the sad tone of Meg's voice.

'It's all right. Don't get gloomy on my account. Death is a fact of life and, if you're going to live as long as I have, you have to get used to it.'

'Tell me more about the Palmers,' Anna said, keen to know more.

'They were good people,' Meg said. 'He was a politician. Quite well-known in his time. Did all sorts of good deeds. Got into trouble too. Once staged a protest and got arrested. Can't remember why. It was in all the papers. Connie thought it was awful but the children thought it was brilliant. We had reporters outside the door for weeks afterwards.'

'And what happened to them?'

'Albert and Connie? They died, of course. One of their daughters never married. She stayed at home. So it was just the two of us in Bretton Place. The others all married and moved away.'

'What was the daughter like? And what happened after she died?'

'Ah, now there's a question,' Meg said. 'I dare say you remember almost everybody you've ever met in your life but, when you get to be my age, people fade. So many have been lost to me now and I feel so sad for that.'

They sat together a little while longer, Meg's story settling into Anna's mind.

'Do you want a cup of tea?' she asked at length and Meg nodded.'

They made their way to the small café in the square, choosing an inside table – the only one left. Meg ordered for them.

'I've been thinking,' Anna said when their tea arrived. 'I'm not ready to go back yet.'

'You're going to stay in London?'

'I'd like to. That is, if you'd stay with me, Meg.'

'What about William?' she asked, a puzzled expression on her face.

Anna sighed. 'I'll have to square it with him first, I suppose,' she said, chewing her lip.

'He'll worry otherwise. He's always told me to let him know where I am. He's one of life's worriers.'

'Yes, I guessed as much.'

'So, why do you want to stay?'

'To get to know you better,' Anna said, touching her hand lightly across the table.

Meg's pale eyebrows lifted a little. 'And we can't do that at Fox Hill Manor?'

'Not really. I don't think it'd be the same. William wouldn't let it be the same, would he?'

'No, I don't suppose he would,' Meg said, 'and I'd love to stay with you.'

Anna grinned. 'Would you? Would you really?'

Meg nodded. 'I would!'

'That's brilliant!'

'Provided that you ring William – right away.'

'Okay,' Anna said. 'You okay here? I'll ring him outside. I've got my mobile.'

'I'll keep your seat for you. Unless a handsome young man comes and – what is it you say these days? *Chats me up?*'

Anna laughed, leaving the café and digging in her handbag for her mobile. William was probably still in London but he'd be back at Fox Hill Manor that night and there'd be trouble if he didn't find Meg safely ensconced in her bedroom.

She got her phone out and quickly found his number. Then, turning around, she saw Meg sitting at the table nursing her cup of tea and, in that instant, she knew she couldn't speak to William. He'd want her back. He'd demand that she be brought back immediately. Anna knew that and she also knew that she wouldn't be able to do that – *couldn't* – not yet and so she put her phone back in her handbag before joining Meg again.

'All okay with William?' Meg asked as soon as Anna returned.

'Yes,' Anna said, hoping she wasn't blushing.

'Really?' Meg sounded amazed.

'Yes. Why not?'

'Oh, I'm just surprised. I thought he'd make more of a fuss, that's all.'

'I assured him you were in very good hands,' Anna said, hoping she wouldn't be struck down for such a lie.

Meg nodded and slurped the end of her tea. 'Good. I guess we're all set then.'

'Yes,' Anna said, doing her best to banish thoughts of William from her mind. She wouldn't be able to focus properly on Meg if she was anxious about William, would she? And that would never do if her story was going to be suitable for a national newspaper.

CHAPTER 20

William left things as long as he possibly could but, by mid-afternoon, he was going crazy with worry and drove directly to the local police station. It was empty but that didn't mean William got seen straight away. He waited at the reception desk and watched as a policeman fiddled with a pile of paperwork on his desk. William cleared his throat. Twice. The policeman looked up.

'Just a minute, sir, he said, his voice as infuriatingly slow as his movements.

William shuffled his feet and sighed loudly. He might have just witnessed a bank robbery for all the policeman knew.

Finally, the policeman approached William. 'How can I help you?'

'I'd like to report a missing person.'

'I see. Just let me get the form.' And off he disappeared, fiddling around with folders on the other side of the room. 'Marian's away this week,' he said, as if that explained everything. 'So we're having to look after things ourselves. Chaos it is,' he said. 'Ah, here it is.' He ambled back over to William as if there was no urgency at all. 'Right,' he said, 'can I have your name?'

'William Kitson.'

'William Kitson,' the policeman repeated. 'And the name of the missing person?'

'Meg.'

'Meg *Kitson*?'

'No, just Meg.'

The policeman looked up. 'What's her surname?'

'She doesn't have one.'

'Doesn't have one?' he said, looking puzzled. 'Is she like one of these popstars or models, then?'

William shook his head. 'No, she just doesn't have a surname.'

'*Every*body has a surname. I'll put it down as unknown with your name in brackets. Right, how old is this Meg?'

William raked a hand through his hair. These questions should have been simple enough to answer for most people but, for William, they were the most difficult. 'She's old,' he said.

'How old, *exactly?*'

'I don't know,' he said helplessly. '*Very* old.'

'Sir, that really doesn't help much. I need an exact age.'

'I don't have an exact age,' William said. 'Nobody does. Just put ninety.'

The policeman whistled. 'Missing at ninety. That puts a whole new spin on things. Is she on any form of medication?'

'Not that I'm aware of. But she's very frail.'

'Height?'

'Well, I've never actually measured her but she's tiny. About this height,' William said, holding out his hand horizontally.

The policeman nodded. 'And build?'

'Slim.'

'Hair colour and eye colour?'

'White hair, straight and shoulder-length, and pale blue eyes.'

'Any distinguishing features?'

'Such as?'

'Scars, tattoos, glasses – that kind of thing. Perhaps she was wearing something special like a ring or something.'

'Yes!' William said. 'A small square diamond ring. She always wears it – on this finger,' he said, pointing to the ring finger on his left hand.

'So, an engagement ring?'

'I suppose so.'

'And what's her relationship to you?' the policeman asked.

'She's a friend – of the family,' William added. 'She lives with me.'

The policeman raised his eyes. 'You're her carer?'

'If you want to put it like that.'

'And how long's she been missing?

'Since yesterday. I don't know the exact time. I've been away – in London – but, when I came back home, she was gone. She never goes anywhere on her own. She shouldn't even have left the house,' he said, his nerves jangling as he thought about it all again.

'Can you think of anywhere she might have gone?'

'No.'

'Anyone she might be with?'

'I've already tried that with no success.'

'So, she's not gone missing before?'

'No, not since she's been staying with me.'

'And how long is that?'

'About four years,' William said.

'Have you got a photograph of her?'

'No.'

The policeman sighed. 'So, let me get this straight. You don't know this woman's surname, you're not sure of her age or her height. You can't exactly say how long she's been missing and you've no idea where she could be?'

'That's right,' William said.

'Well, at least we've got *that* straight.'

Meg wasn't sure what she'd let herself in for saying she'd stay in London with Anna but it probably wasn't an afternoon in a library on the computer.

'What are you doing?' Meg asked.

'I've just got to check my email,' Anna said, which was true enough but she was also using the time to search the internet for Albert Palmer.

'I've never got the hang of all these things,' Meg said.

'What things?'

'Things with plugs.'

Anna grinned. 'Things with plugs make up half the world these days.'

'Didn't need plugs when I was your age.'

Anna grinned as she continued her search for Albert.

'Bingo!' she said at last.

'What is it?'

'Oh, just a message I've been waiting for,' Anna lied, her eyes scanning the page that appeared after clicking on a link.

Albert Palmer. Politician. 1839 – 1928.

'A ripe old age for those times,' Anna said under her breath.

'What's that?'

'Nothing,' Anna said, quickly reading the information. *Married to Constance nee Fielding. Five children. Only three survived into adulthood. Albert was famous for his outspokenness and could often be seen leading protests. Indeed, in 1882, he was arrested for protesting against the pollution of the city, hanging banners across Westminster reading: "The Stink Stops Here!"*

There was a link with more information about his political life but Anna didn't need to read any more. She had enough to persuade her – at long last – that Meg had been telling the truth.

She turned around in her swivel chair and looked at Meg who was sitting in a chair beside her.

'Are you working, Anna?'

'Sort of.'

'You young girls and your work,' she said shaking her head. 'You can't leave it for a minute, can you?'

'You're right. We shouldn't be sitting in a stuffy library. We should be out making the most of our time here. Come on, let's go!' And the two of them got up in a flurry of giggles and were promptly shushed by the other library users.

Once outside, Anna crooked her arm for Meg to link and that was when she caught sight of Meg's diamond ring. She'd never really looked at it properly before but it was the sweetest square diamond which looked almost misty with age as it winked at her in the spring light. It wasn't your usual sparkly stunner but it was all the more precious because of it.

'Meg, that really is a beautiful ring!'

'Oh, this old thing?' Meg said with a chuckle. 'I've had this for as long as I can remember and a little bit longer.'

Anna stared at it. 'It's very old, isn't it?'

'I should say,' Meg said.

Anna could see it was an antique and, whereas a few hours before, she might have thought that anyone could buy an antique ring, she now knew better. Meg had been wearing this ring since it had been made.

'It's lovely,' Anna said. 'Was it an engagement ring?'

'Can't remember,' Meg said.

'You don't have any other rings?'

'I think I did once. Wedding rings. But they've long gone. All lost or sold.'

'You must tell me more about your husbands, you know.'

'Must I?'

'Yes,' Anna said. 'If you'd like to, of course.'

'So, you believe me now, do you?'

Anna stopped walking and turned to face Meg. 'I believe you,' she said.

'Was that what all that library business was about?'

'Yes,' Anna said honestly.

'Good,' Meg said.

'You're pleased?' Anna said in surprise.

'Yes. I am. Now we can be completely honest with each other.'

'You mean you haven't been honest with me?'

'Oh, *I've* been honest,' Meg said, 'but I get the feeling that you haven't.'

Anna nodded and cast her eyes to the ground like a schoolgirl who'd been caught red-handed by the headmaster. 'You're right, Meg. I haven't,' she said, 'but I do believe you now.'

'So what happens now?' Meg asked.

'You tell me everything – *absolutely* everything.'

'And what are you going to do when I've told you?'

'I'm going to see who else might be interested in your story.'

'You think others might be interested?'

'Meg!' Anna laughed. 'You're sitting on the story of the century – the story of *all* centuries! *Everybody's* going to want to hear what you've got to say.'

'Really?' Meg said.

'Yes!'

Meg gave a little laugh. 'How extraordinary!'

CHAPTER 21

When William came out of the police station, he checked his phone and discovered the message he'd been so anxious to receive.

Meg's with me. Anna.

That was it. No explanation and no indication as to where they both were. Still, he breathed a sigh of relief that they were safe and together and, before texting a reply, nipped back into the police station to explain the change in circumstances.

Anna had waited and waited before texting William. She knew it was the right thing to do, of course, but she also knew that William would probably be on her case as soon as she did and, sure enough, he was.

Where are you? William.

Anna wondered if she should be honest. After all, it would be pretty hard to track them down in London, wouldn't it? But, in the end, she bottled out.

We'll be back soon. All is well. A.

She waited a moment, knowing that a reply was imminent.

I need to speak to Meg. W.

It was then that Anna switched her phone off.

'You girls today,' Meg said as she saw Anna putting her mobile away in her handbag. 'Can't leave those things alone for a moment.'

'I'm sorry, Meg. I promise you have my undivided attention now.'

They'd left the library and walked back onto a street where they were waiting for a tour bus to hop onto. Anna had decided to play now and work later. The sun was shining and London looked so invitingly beautiful that she didn't want to think about Meg's story for the time being. She was happy, for now, just to get to know Meg. The questions would wait. For now, they were two friends with the rest of the day ahead of them.

'Here's the bus,' Anna said a moment later, placing her arm around Meg's waist and leading her gently up the step. Anna had their tickets and presented them to the driver. 'Downstairs is easier,' she said.

'Oh,' Meg said, sounding disappointed. 'Can't we go upstairs?'

'If you think you can manage it?'

'I'll go first. Shove me in the back with your hands.'

'Okay,' Anna said, noticing a group of tourists had just boarded and were buying tickets so that would give her and Meg plenty of time to get upstairs before the bus moved off. 'How are you doing?' she asked a moment later.

'Nearly there – I hope!'

A rush of cool air greeted them as they came out into the open but there was a huge smile on Meg's face.

'You won't be too cold?' Anna asked. 'It's really cooled down, hasn't it?

'I have a pair of gloves in my bag,' Meg said, sitting down on a seat and opening up her voluminous handbag and fishing out a pair of bright pink gloves. 'A necessity at my age.'

'Mine too,' Anna said, producing her own pair from her pockets. Hers were scarlet and she grabbed the rail in front of their seat, her hands joining Meg's. 'Look! We clash horribly!'

Meg smiled. 'I love colour. Colours don't clash to me – they play.'

Anna grinned. She liked that. 'What do you want to see, Meg?'

'Everything! The whole city.'

Anna laughed. 'Good,' she said, patting her handbag. 'How much can you actually see now?'

Meg looked around her. 'There's a big white building over there and dark gates near to us here.'

'That's the British Museum.'

'Ah, yes. I've heard William mention it before. He often visits.'

'He's probably tried to buy their entire collection for FHM.'

Meg gave a chuckle. 'That sounds about right.'

'Can you see those people over there?' Anna said, pointing to the pavement.

'Well, they're a bit blurry.'

'They're tourists,' Anna explained, 'and they're all wearing Union Jack hats.'

The bus moved on and Meg's white hair flew back behind her. Anna had tied hers back with a slide but bright tendrils blew around her face as the bus picked up speed. She looked around for things to point out to Meg. She didn't fancy using the earphones for the bus commentary; it would be more fun to make up her own.

London for the partially sighted, she thought. Where could she and Meg go? The bus had been a good idea – she was pleased with that. She looked at Meg with her hair flying free, revelling in the full assault of the city. Car horns honked, taxis screeched and the constant buzz of London filled their ears.

'There's Big Ben!' Anna exclaimed when the tour bus entered Westminster. 'And the river. How beautiful it looks today – all sparkly and blue. And that's the London Eye – it's like a huge Ferris wheel.'

'Have you been up in it?' Meg asked.

'Yes – just once. Oh, Meg! The views are amazing. You feel so high up, it's as if you're flying over the city. Even Big Ben looks tiny from up there.'

'I wish I could see it all,' Meg said.

'Would you like to go up?'

Meg shook her head. 'I'm afraid it would be a dreadful waste on me.'

Anna felt saddened by this admission and reached out and squeezed Meg's gloved hand in hers. 'Not to worry. There's so much else we *can* do.'

And so they did.

As the bus entered Piccadilly, they hopped off. Well, not *hopped* exactly. Ladies aged three hundred and fifty-five don't usually hop. Taking Meg's arm, Anna led her into one of her favourite shops: Fortnum and Mason and they were both instantly in scent-heaven.

'I know that smell,' Meg said.

'Oh, yes!' Anna enthused. 'Forget perfume, this is the scent for me.'

The air seemed saturated with the aroma of chocolate and Anna's eyes swam as she gazed at the fabulous displays. There was every flavour imaginable from soft cream centres in peppermint, rose and violet, to champagne truffles, stem ginger, and luscious caramels. There were chocolates made from cocoa beans from Madagascar and Venezuela, there was rectangular chocolate, square chocolate, chocolate wrapped in ribbons, or piled into neat stacks. It was all too much for a sane woman to bear.

Then there were the cakes and the biscuits and the candied fruits and beautiful jars of jam in jewel-bright colours. There were tarts and bonbons, fudge and Turkish delight, hickory dickory mice tumbling in glass jars, and tiny macaroons and towering wedding cakes.

Anna always loved the ground floor with its plush red carpet and its long, elegant chandeliers. She loved the smell of coffee and the wooden display stands that looked as if they'd been confiscated from some stately home. It was shopping at its most luxurious.

'Are you up for a treat?' Anna asked.

Meg nodded. 'Go on.'

'How about afternoon tea?'

'Here?'

'No,' Anna said. 'I was thinking about The Wolseley just down the road from here. I've heard they serve the most perfect tea and cakes.'

'Sounds wonderful!'

'Let's go, then,' Anna said, suddenly feeling very excited.

It was a slow amble to The Wolseley along busy Piccadilly. Meg clung on to Anna's arm and the two of them did their best not to get squashed as they moved through the crowds.

On reaching their destination, they had a moment's wait before being led through a maze of tables to a tiny one at the far side of the room. The excited thrum of chatter filled their ears and Anna was instantly hungry as she saw plates of delicious food on the diners' tables.

'What shall we have?' Meg asked. 'Will you read the menu for me?'

Anna obliged and the two of them decided on sandwiches followed by treacle tart and camomile tea.

'Won't William be bemused when he sees this on his bill?' Meg chuckled.

'I hope we're not overdoing things,' Anna said, gasping as their sandwiches and tea arrived in two glass pots filled with bright yellow camomile heads swimming in hot water. 'Isn't that the prettiest thing?'

Meg peered at it and nodded. 'Wonderfully calming, camomile tea.'

'Just what we need after the streets of London,' Anna said, and the two of them got on with the business of eating.

It was fun being with Meg even when they weren't talking, Anna thought. She took such pleasure in everything. She sat opposite Anna, quietly nodding to herself as she ate her sandwiches with the tiniest of bites, her thin mouth smiling between mouthfuls.

Anna poured her tea out for her and she took a dainty sip, closing her eyes and inhaling deeply.

'Good?' Anna asked.

'Very,' Meg said. 'We shall come here again.'

Anna liked the sound of that. It was as if Meg was planning a bit of a holiday and that would give Anna plenty of time with her.

At last, when the treacle tart had been served and devoured, Meg leant back in her chair and gave a sigh of satisfaction.

'Meg,' Anna began, 'I know today is a sort of holiday and I shouldn't ask you any questions but–'

'I'm just too tempting a subject?' Meg suggested.

Anna gave a small smile, half amused, half shy. 'It's just that I've so much to ask you.'

'Well, I'm not likely to run off, am I? I don't think I could after all that treacle tart.'

'You don't mind, then?'

'I don't mind. Now, what did you want to know?'

That was quite a question, Anna thought. What did she want to know about a woman who'd lived through three and a half centuries?

'I guess what's been bothering me the most is actually your age. I can't get my head around the fact that anybody can be so old. I mean, people start ageing as soon as they're born, don't they? I'm only thirty-one but I'm already starting to fall apart.'

Meg gave a chuckle. 'Really?'

'Yes!' Anna said. 'My eyesight isn't as good as it used to be. I used to be able to read the smallest print in books but now I really struggle. I'll have to wear glasses soon. And bruises take an age to heal now.'

'But you're a mere baby.'

'I know! And that's what's bothering me about you. When did you start to feel old? I mean most people start to fall apart, don't they? They get arthritis or osteoporosis or cancer or have strokes or heart attacks. I don't understand how you haven't.'

Meg sat perfectly still for a while. 'I don't know if I can answer your question, Anna dear, because I don't understand it myself. I've never had an illness to worry about. I've had the usual suspects: flu, mumps, a bout of shingles and the odd patch of eczema but nothing to really worry about. What can I say? I've been incredibly lucky.'

'But don't you *feel* old?' Anna asked.

'Well, my eye-sight was probably the first thing to go and I do take a good number of naps each day and there's the constant aches and pains but, other than that, I feel absolutely fine.'

Anna shook her head. 'You're extraordinary. You really are.'

Meg shook her head. 'Not really, my dear. I just do what everybody else does – try to survive each day.'

After that, they walked to the nearest bus stop for their tour and joined it until it reached the nearest stop to Covent Garden.

'You'll love this place, Meg. Have you been here before?'

'No, I haven't but I've heard of it.'

'It used to be a proper market selling fresh fruit and vegetables to Londoners but it's just nice shops now and street entertainers.'

They walked slowly towards the main piazza of Covent Garden, Anna carefully guiding Meg so as to avoid the worst of the tourists who crowded the streets. Long before they entered the piazza, a blast from a silver trumpet sounded, making Meg jump.

'It's one of the street entertainers,' Anna explained.

'I wasn't expecting that.'

'You'll love them. Oh, look! There's a couple of jugglers. Can you see them?'

'There's something flying up into the air,' Meg said. 'I can see those.'

'Yes, it's their batons. Blue and yellow. '

Again, the trumpet blasted into life from the other side of the piazza and Meg moaned in response.

'What is it?' Anna asked, wondering, perhaps, if she was beginning to tire or if the noise and crowds of Covent Garden were too invasive.

'I think I might have lived with a musician once,' Meg said.

Anna blinked and, all of a sudden, it was too much for her. Her journalistic instinct to probe and record was too strong to ignore. 'Come on, Meg,' she said. 'Let's get back to the hotel. I've just *got* to talk to you about your past.'

William had been pacing the rooms of Fox Hill Manor for the last two hours, straightening a painting here, polishing a sword there, and generally managing to get very little work done. Cocoa and Beanie had given up shoving their wet noses into his hand in the hope of some attention and had returned to their baskets and snuggled down for a kip.

He'd tried Anna's mobile at least a dozen times since her last text and had finally given up. There was nothing he could do. He would have to wait until she came back in her own time. What was she doing, he wondered for the hundredth time? But he knew the answer to that question. She was doing exactly what she'd wanted to do since she'd first laid eyes on Meg and she'd betrayed him in order to do it.

He took his glasses off and rubbed his eyes. Anna didn't have any feelings for him at all, did she? He'd just been kidding himself. What he'd thought was a tender, loving moment between them had been absolutely nothing to her. She'd simply used him.

CHAPTER 22

Libby buzzed around the kitchen tidying things away as fast as she could.

'It's all right,' Charlie said, 'I'll do that. Why don't you get a head start on the crowds?'

'Right,' Libby said, looking at the clock and nodding. 'Thanks. If you're sure. You know the high street's a nightmare on Saturday.'

'Of course I'm sure. Where's Toby?'

'TOBY!' Libby yelled up the stairs.

A pair of small but thunderous feet tore down the stairs on the double.

'What's that?' Libby asked, seeing Toby carrying a small rucksack.

'You always get far more shopping than you can carry, Mummy.'

'Nonsense!' she said. 'We can manage perfectly well with carrier bags.'

'That's not very green, is it?' Charlie said. 'Here, take this,' he said, producing a hessian bag from underneath the sink. 'And don't buy anything that doesn't fit in here, okay?' His voice sounded teasing but Libby knew that he was being dead serious.

She rolled her eyes. 'You two seem to have it in for me this morning.'

Toby and his father exchanged a knowing look. 'Have a nice morning, you guys,' Charlie said. 'See you at lunch. No later, right?'

Grabbing Toby's hand, Libby opened the front door.

'Oh!' Charlie suddenly shouted. 'Don't forget my drill! The one I told you about. It's on special offer at Murphy's.'

'Okay, okay,' Libby said. 'I won't forget.' Then, Libby and Toby left the house.

Saturday was shopping day – not the big weekly grocery shop that Libby and Charlie did on a Monday together but the smaller, local shop when Libby took Toby to the newsagents to choose a magazine and a bar of chocolate and they would buy fresh vegetables from their local grocer for their weekend meals.

It was only a five minute walk to Elmington's high street which was a terrible temptation for someone like Libby but she managed to restrict her visits to once a week most of the time.

'Where shall we go first, Toby?' she asked, her stride long and fast.

'Newsagents!' Toby shouted, desperately trying to keep up with his mum.

'Okay,' Libby said. 'Your wish is my command.'

They walked up the road that led to the high street, joining the throng of shoppers who came into town on market day. Libby always got a buzz from market day. It was when Elmington really came alive. There were young couples walking hand in hand, parents steering children, coach loads of retired people, and farmers with dogs – it seemed to Libby that the whole world was there.

After a slow and stilted walk which would have taken two minutes on a normal day but which, on market day, took ten, they reached the newsagents where Toby rifled through the magazines. What would he choose? Football, popstars or a comic?

Libby loved watching him. His face was excited and serious at the same time. She wondered if she wore the same expression when shopping and reasoned that she probably did.

'I can't make up my mind,' he said at last. 'There's this pull-out poster in this one but this other one has more to read.'

Libby nodded, knowing well the difficulty of being selective. 'Why don't we take both then?'

'Really?' Toby said.

'Yes, really,' Libby said, delighted to be able to give such happiness with only a few pounds. 'But don't tell Daddy.'

'Two magazines!' Toby said. 'Does this mean I won't have a chocolate bar this week?'

Libby frowned. 'Of course not. You can have chocolate too. What else could you possibly eat whilst reading your magazines?'

Toby beamed as he chose a chocolate bar and took it to the till together with his magazines and was soon joined by his mother who had also chosen two magazines.

'I couldn't resist! Look – this one's got a free set of knitting needles.'

'But you don't knit, Mummy,' Toby pointed out.

'Yes but they're still free, aren't they?' she said and they shared a little chuckle before paying and leaving the shop. 'Now,' she said, 'let's do some *real* shopping.'

Levy's was Elmington's much-loved department store. Sitting at the very top of the high street and boasting views across the whole of the town, it was a favourite with shoppers. Their clothes were conservative and their handbags and shoes were horribly old-fashioned but those weren't what attracted Libby into the store. Upstairs, opposite the small café, was a long glass cabinet full of china figurines.

'Mummy,' Toby said, tugging Libby's hand as she dragged him up the stairs.

'What is it?' Libby asked, reaching the top, her eyes fixed on the cabinet.

'We haven't got the food yet.'

'Yes, yes, I know. There's plenty of time,' she said, striding towards the cabinet.

And there it was. The new *Ballet Beauties* range she'd read about in one of her collector's magazines. Libby's mouth dropped open in wonder at the slender, graceful figures depicted in pink and white, their golden hair gleaming. She didn't know much about ballet but she knew that she loved the figures. There were six in the collection and they were all too perfect for words.

'Can I help you?' a sales assistant asked, flying across the soft and soundless carpet at the first hint of a sale.

'Yes,' Libby said. 'I'm interested in the ballet figurines.'

Toby pulled at his mother's hand. 'Mummy.'

'In a minute, Toby.'

'But M*ummeeeee!*'

'Toby!' Libby yelled. 'In a *minute*.'

The sales assistant cleared her throat. 'The figures are new in this week and they've caused quite a sensation, I can tell you. Best to buy early to avoid disappointment as they're limited edition.'

'Oh, really?'

'Yes. Very collectible, these,' the sales assistant went on.

'I can see,' Libby said, suddenly worrying that they might all be sold before she had a chance to buy them herself.

She looked lovingly at the names on the information cards. Olivia. Phoebe. Anastasia. Katharine. Marianne. Freya.

'Experience the timeless beauty of ballet with these six special figurines.'

Libby nodded. That's *exactly* what she wanted to experience.

Already, they seemed like daughters to her and she knew she had to have them, had to take them home and care for them.

'I'll take them,' she said.

The shop assistant looked surprised, her eyes almost popping out of her head. '*All* of them.'

'Mummy!' Toby cried.

'Yes. No point in splitting the collection, is there? That would be so sad,' Libby said.

The shop assistant nodded in agreement. 'And you'd like to take them now?'

'Yes please. You can help me carry them, can't you?' Libby said to Toby.

'But, Mummy – Daddy said not to get anything that didn't fit into your bag.'

Libby laughed. 'Oh, he does talk some nonsense sometimes, doesn't he?'

It took a good twenty minutes before they were ready to leave the shop with their three carrier bags. Libby had a big smile on her face as she usually did after making a purchase but Toby didn't look at all happy.

Libby saw his expression and tutted. 'Toby, shopping's meant to be fun. We're having fun, okay?'

Toby nodded obediently but a smile refused to show itself.

'Well, then, shall we head home?' Libby asked, ignoring his sullen face.

'Don't forget Dad's drill,' he said.

Libby's mouth dropped open. 'Oh, drat it.' Libby looked down at her shopping bags. She really didn't want to be lumbered with another heavy bag but Charlie would definitely notice if she forgot it and then he'd be more likely to be angry about her *Ballet Beauties* if she didn't do a good job of hiding them from him first. 'Okay, then,' she agreed reluctantly. 'I guess we'd better go to Murphy's.'

Toby, she noticed, looked mildly happier.

Murphy's was one of the few kinds of shops that Libby detested. It was what she called 'a man's shop' – full of strange objects like plugs, wires and ugly tools. She shivered as she went in.

'Oh, cool!' Toby immediately said. 'Look at that!'

Before she could stop him, Toby had picked up an enormous hammer.

'Put that down!' Libby shouted. 'If you drop that, you'll break a toe – a *foot!*'

'Are you sure Daddy won't want it?' Toby asked hopefully.

'Quite sure,' Libby said.

Toby replaced the hammer.

'Now, where's this wretched drill?'

Toby pointed to something near the till and Libby rolled her eyes. There was the wretched drill. She was hoping they'd have sold out by now.

'Come on, then,' she said but Libby didn't quite make it to the drill. Something else caught her eye before she managed to walk the brief space towards the stand. It was a kettle. A bright silver and pink kettle. They already had a kettle at home, of course, but it was old and a nasty cream colour that had yellowed horribly over the years.

'I didn't know they sold kitchen things here,' she said, more to herself than to Toby. 'Look at that cute iron over there,' she said, pointing to the lime green creation. 'I didn't know irons could be so beautiful.'

Libby's eyes roamed the store with a new-found interest. Why hadn't she come in here before, she wondered? It was a whole new kind of shopping and one she hadn't thought of before. Kitchen accessories! There was even a zany ironing board with yellow legs and the cutest of covers: a sunshine yellow dotted with daisies. It was beautiful beyond words and, almost instinctively, Libby moved towards it. Yellow legs! It was inspired. It would make ironing fun. She had to have it.

'How much is the ironing board?' she asked a nearby assistant. The assistant told her and Libby took a sharp intake of breath. 'And the kettle?'

'Forty-nine pounds,' the assistant told her.

Again, Libby flinched. That was some price for a kettle. But then, Libby had a rule about such things. She thought of the figure she was willing to pay for something. For example, a cheap kettle might be about twenty pounds. Well, she didn't want a cheap kettle, did she? She wanted something special and that something special cost an extra twenty-nine pounds. So it was only twenty-nine pounds really, wasn't it? Because she'd have paid twenty pounds anyway.

'I'll take it,' she said, mentally making a note to come back for the ironing board another day.

'Mum!' Toby complained, tugging at his mum's arm again. 'We've got to get Dad's drill.'

'Oh, rats!' Libby said, knowing, immediately, that she didn't have enough money in her purse for both items. Charlie had given her cash for the drill but she'd spent the rest of her own money already and pushed her credit card to the max with the *Ballet Beauties*. Still, she might have brought a couple of cards out with her. That was one of the hazards of being a shopaholic: one always had so many pretty purses and handbags and it wasn't always easy to find your credit cards. That was one of the reasons Libby had so many.

Rifling around in her newest handbag, Libby was relieved to see one of her friendly visas. 'And I'll take that special offer drill too, please,' she said. 'I'll pay cash for the drill,' she said, knowing Charlie would check the receipt and thinking it would be easier to sneak the kettle in separately and tell him that was on special offer too. 'See, Toby?' Libby said. 'I've got Daddy's drill.'

Toby nodded but he looked far from impressed by his mum's idea of shopping.

'I'm sorry, madam,' the shop assistant interrupted, 'but your card is not working.'

'Oh, dear,' Libby said. 'That's never happened before. How strange.' She rifled in her handbag, hoping, praying to find another card.

She did.

'Ah, this one should work,' she said.

The young lady accepted it with a quick, tight smile and, a few moments later, Libby and Toby left the shop with Dad's drill and the new silver and pink kettle.

They walked home in silence together. Toby was now carrying the kettle on top of his share of the *Ballet Beauties* and Libby had taken charge of the slightly heavier drill.

'Nearly there,' she said as they walked up the path to their front door. 'Now, we've got to sneak these things in, okay?'

Toby looked at his mum, a frown wrinkling his young face.

'Don't be awkward now, Toby. You know what Daddy's like.' Libby reached for her front door key and opened the door as quietly as possible. With any luck, Charlie would be upstairs on the computer and they'd be able to hide the ballerinas before he made it downstairs.

She was in luck.

'Toby – quick *now!*' Libby said, charging into the hallway and pushing her son towards the under-stairs cupboard. It didn't take Libby long to deal with the bags but it was just as well that she was quick.

'Did you get everything you needed?' Charlie asked, coming down the stairs at a good old pace.

'Oh, yes,' Libby said, holding up the remaining bags.

'But you didn't get anything you *didn't* need?' Charlie teased her.

Libby could feel herself blushing under her husband's close scrutiny. 'I don't know what you mean?'

'Been keeping an eye on Mum, Toby?' Charlie asked.

Toby looked up at his dad but then ran into the safety of the living room before being pressed for an answer.

'He can't wait to read his magazines,' Libby said with a smile she hoped looked sincere and unflustered.

Charlie nodded. 'So what did you get us for lunch?'

Libby's mouth dropped open. 'Oh, dear,' she said. 'I quite forgot.'

'Forgot what?' Charlie asked. 'That we eat lunch on a Saturday?'

'I'm so sorry,' Libby said, making a display of checking the shopping bags in case she'd remembered the groceries after all. 'But I did get you your drill.'

'Excellent,' Charlie said. 'But that's not going to feed us, is it?'

'There's a bit of left-over shepherd's pie,' Libby said. 'And we could open a can of beans with it.'

Charlie rolled his eyes. 'Darling, sometimes, I wonder what it is you do when you go shopping,' he said, resignedly making his way to the kitchen in search of left-overs.

By Saturday afternoon at the hotel in Marble Arch, both Anna and Meg were exhausted. Meg was lying on her bed, fighting sleep, and Anna was rubbing her wrists in an attempt to relieve her RSI after a mammoth typing session. She had over eight thousand words as dictated by Meg. They'd barely stopped for air. Meg just kept on going. It was as if that trumpet player in Covent Garden had unlocked some secret door to her memories and out they flooded.

Anna looked over the notes she'd made. There were stories about at least nine different husbands, fifteen separate houses Meg could remember living in from Worcestershire to Norfolk. She even remembered as far back as her childhood, growing up on the edge of a large estate where her father worked as a stable-hand.

'What his name was, I don't know,' Meg had chuckled.

But there *were* names: Anna had a whole list of them and, just like Albert Palmer, she was going to look them up only not right away.

She scrolled down the pages on her laptop.

There were so many wonderful stories here. Meg had lived in Bath during the Regency period; she'd watched the ladies and the gentlemen crowding into the Assembly Rooms in their finery. She'd helped to look after evacuees during the Second World War. She had a dim recollection of a relative who'd died in the Great Plague of 1665. On and on it went. Story after story after story.

'Meg,' Anna said, 'we can't keep all this to ourselves, you know. We've got to share this and I think I know just the right newspaper for it too.'

But there was no answer from Meg.

Quickly, Anna got up out of her chair and rushed to the side of the bed.

'Meg?' she said, her fear obvious in her voice. '*Meg?*'

An eyelid flickered.

'Oh, *Meg!*' Anna cried. 'What a fright you gave me.'

Meg stirred, said something inaudible, and then continued her sleep, and Anna breathed a sigh of relief as she got out her mobile to call the newspaper.

CHAPTER 23

Libby was not having a good day. Firstly, one of her credit cards had been declined for an online purchase and then a set of vintage teacups had arrived with two smashed and one missing. She'd consoled herself with a trip to Elmington High Street where she bought herself the ironing board she'd seen at the weekend as well as a new set of pans. Well, Charlie wouldn't want her cooking in ugly pans, would he? That would just be unreasonable and their old pans were pretty ugly. She knew she'd made a mistake when she'd bought them last year.

She'd arranged to have her purchases delivered and had walked home unencumbered by shopping bags for possibly the first time in her life. See, she thought to herself, she didn't need to buy things all the time.

When she arrived home, she noticed something was wrong – terribly wrong. Five bin bags had been placed on the little lawn and, when she opened the front door, she could hear the sound of a vacuum cleaner coming from the living room.

Libby's heart began to race. Was Charlie home from work? And had he taken it into his head to start sorting through her things and cleaning? But, as she entered the living room, she saw that it wasn't Charlie. It was a stranger.

'Who are you?' Libby shouted above the vacuum cleaner. 'And what *on earth* do you think you're doing?'

The woman, who was in her late forties, visibly jumped at the voice and turned the vacuum off.

'What's going on?' Libby demanded.

'Mr Robertson asked me to tidy up,' she said, looking blank, and obviously still getting over her shock at being disturbed. 'Are you Mrs Robertson?'

'Yes, I'm Mrs Robertson,' Libby said, her hands on her hips, 'and I don't appreciate coming home to find a stranger in my front room!'

'I'm ever so sorry,' the woman said, 'but I was told to make a start downstairs by Mr Robertson.'

'Yes, well *Mrs* Robertson runs this house and *I* don't want you here!' Libby said, her voice wobbling audibly and her eyes threatening to fill with tears. 'Please leave.'

She watched in silence as the woman unplugged the vacuum cleaner, picked up her coat from the sofa and mumbled an apology before leaving. Libby followed her out of the front door and started rifling through the bin bags, fearful of what she might find inside them. A moment later and she had her answer. They were mostly filled with rubbish. Libby shook her head. Where had it all come from? Sure, there were a few plastic packages from purchases which hadn't quite made it to the bin but *five* bags?

She returned to the house and sank down onto the sofa in despair. How could Charlie have done this to her? Why hadn't he just told her he was unhappy with the way she ran the home? Why had he gone behind her back like this?

She spent the rest of the day doing her best to tidy around and surprised herself by filling a further three bin bags. Where had all this rubbish come from, she wondered?

By the time she went to bed, she was exhausted and fell into a deep sleep as soon as her head hit the pillow. It was an hour later when she was rudely awoken.

'Oh, Charlie!' Libby groaned. 'I was asleep!'

'Sorry,' he said, pulling the bed covers down and jumping into bed.

Libby was instantly awake as she remembered that it was this very husband who had hired a cleaner without letting her know.

'Charlie?' she said.

'I said I'm sorry. I had to work late. Didn't you get my message? I've got to sort the books out before the accountant arrives and you know how hopeless I am with figures.'

'Charlie!'

'What?'

'Why didn't you tell me you were unhappy?' Libby said.

'What?' Charlie said, sounding genuinely puzzled.

'I came home today to find a stranger in our house – throwing things out and vacuuming!'

There was a moment's silence and then Charlie spoke. 'Oh, no!' he groaned. 'That must have been Mrs Arnley from the agency. I thought she was coming next week. I'm sorry if she startled you. I was going to tell you only I got the dates confused.'

'But I don't need a cleaner!' Libby said, her voice sounding high and out of control.

'Sweetheart – I can't find anything anymore. Toby can't find anything anymore. Half the time, I can't even find Toby because he's buried under a pile of clutter,' he joked. 'Everything's always buried. It's getting impossible!'

'You're exaggerating – as always!'

Charlie sighed. 'And I'm genuinely worried about the state of the house. I moved one of those bin bags in the dining room. Lord only knows what's in it but the carpet was virtually rotting away underneath. We can't go on living like this – it's not healthy!'

'If you weren't happy with things, why didn't you say something?'

'Darling, I have – a *dozen* times! But you don't seem to hear me.'

Libby frowned in the darkness as she tried to remember Charlie pointing out that he had a problem and she couldn't, she really couldn't.

She felt him snake his arms around her and pull her close to him. 'Listen,' he said, 'I think, perhaps, you need some help.'

'I *don't* want a stranger cleaning our home, Charlie.'

'No,' he said, his voice very low, almost a whisper, 'I mean *help*. Real help.'

She pulled away from him, leaving a cold gap in the middle of the bed. 'What do you mean?'

'I mean all this buying stuff all the time – it's getting out of control, don't you think?'

'Don't you like nice things around you?' Libby asked, her voice half cry, half plea.

'Well, of course, but not quite so *much* of it,' Charlie said calmly. 'I've been thinking this through, Libby, and I don't think it's natural to want to have so much stuff. I think–' he paused, closing the space between them and stroking her long, soft hair, 'I think there's a reason behind all this. A reason you're not telling me and I think that you might need to talk it through with someone.'

One of the great mysteries of the world is why some stories grab the media's attention and some don't. There might be a story about a woman found dead in her apartment at the age of twenty-two and the world will read the article and think, how sad, but then think nothing more of it. But Meg's story wasn't one to be forgotten quite so easily.

Since getting in touch with the newspaper a friend now worked at, and having her short piece published, Anna's phone hadn't stopped ringing.

'We want to know more about Meg,' they said. 'Can you write a piece for our magazine?'

'We'd like you both to come in and talk to our listeners on the radio.'

'We simply *must* interview Meg!'

It had been a whirlwind of excitement for Anna and she'd felt spoilt for choice. For years, she'd been desperate to find a story that would make her name – to write about something that people would be passionate about – that *she* could be passionate about, and now she'd finally done it. The whole world seemed to be pounding on her door.

So why wasn't she happy? Perhaps because there was something at the back of her mind that she just couldn't shake: William. In her heart of hearts, she knew that what she was doing was going expressly against his wishes. Her dream coming true was, perhaps, William's worst nightmare. He'd kept Meg safe at Fox Hill Manor. It had been a little haven away from a world that might hurt her if they found out about her and – more to the point – Meg had sought him out. She'd chosen to live there – to hide away amongst the antiques and disappear from view. But she'd changed – Anna was sure of it. Getting Meg alone and away from William had meant that she'd opened up. She was – at last – ready to share her story.

Anna smiled. And what a story Meg had to share. If only she didn't feel as if she were betraying William's trust. That wasn't the only thing that was worrying her either. The last time she'd seen him, she'd realised that he was falling in love with her and that she was falling in love with him. How that had happened, she didn't know. She'd tried to put it to the back of her mind but it simply wasn't working.

'What a mess!' she cursed to herself. The first decent story she'd found in a long time and it had to go and be complicated by love.

Anna thought about William. She'd never met anyone like him. When she'd first been told about her assignment, she'd immediately wanted to back away from it. A collector, for goodness' sake. She detested collections of any sort and deemed all collectors eccentric, and her first meeting with William hadn't swayed her opinion. He'd seemed completely obsessed and his home had appeared strange and alienating. So what had happened? When had her feelings begun to change? It hadn't been a thunderbolt moment, that was for sure. Not like in the romantic novels she liked to read in her free time where the hero and heroine would meet and sparks flew as soon as they looked at each other. No, it hadn't been like that, had it? It seemed to Anna that it had been more like the gentle flowering of spring. You might not notice the first few blooms opening in the warmth of the new season but there comes a time when you walk out into your garden and the whole place is filled with colour.

She wondered if William was he missing her or was he just anxious for the well-being of Meg? Anna swallowed hard, wondering if she'd jeopardised her chance with William. He was one of the sweetest men she'd ever met but she hadn't bargained for romance. It would only interfere with Meg's story and she had to get on with pursuing that.

Anna nodded to herself. There was nothing more important to her than a story and, when she had hold of one, she was like a terrier with a rodent – she just wouldn't let go. There was nothing more thrilling than the feel of her fingers tap-dancing over her laptop as she got everything down into neat type. Watching the ideas form in her mind and then translate themselves onto the blank screen was one of the most magical things and she couldn't put that at risk for the chance of love, could she? Meg's story was – potentially – the biggest she'd ever tell. So, when she got a phone call to appear on the local news with Meg in a feature about old age, she leapt at it.

'We're looking at what it means to be old in today's society,' the woman's voice from London News Night told her. 'Would Meg be interested in taking part?'

'Absolutely,' Anna said, needing no time to think about it and not worrying if Meg might object. Anna was quite sure that Meg had never been on television before; it would be a brand new experience for her.

The woman gave her instructions and said that a taxi would collect and take them to the studio.

'What was that about?' Meg asked, waking up from a doze a moment later.

'We're going to be on television,' Anna announced.

'Us? Why?'

'An interview about old people,' Anna said. 'Won't that be fun?'

Meg didn't look too sure. 'What will I say?'

'They'll probably have lots of questions for you. You'll be fine. You've had plenty of practice answering questions with me, haven't you?'

'Well, I suppose I have,' Meg said, sounding unsure.

'It'll be so much fun, Meg!' Anna assured her.

'What kind of programme is it?'

'The local news. It won't take long. They're sending a car for us. We're being treated like royalty.'

'And what's William said about it?' she asked.

Anna bit her lip. Should she level with Meg and tell her that William didn't know any more than the fact Meg was with her? Or should she just keep quiet?

'He's fine,' Anna said. Well, he probably was fine so that wasn't exactly a lie, was it?

'Oh,' Meg said. 'I didn't think he liked television very much. He's always said that it's a big load of opinionated waffle and that he prefers books.'

That sounded very like William, Anna thought with a little smile. 'But *being* on television is different. He wouldn't want you to miss out on that experience,' she told Meg.

Meg still didn't look very sure. 'He's always told me not to worry.'

'But there's nothing to worry about, Meg,' Anna said, walking across the room and sitting on the edge of her bed. 'What are you worried about?'

Meg's bony hands were clutching each other in the lap and her eyes looked paler than ever. 'William always said I'd be safe at Fox Hill Manor.'

Anna was beginning to get nervous. 'And so you are.'

'But I'm not there now.'

'No. You're here with me – out in the wide world in one of the most exciting cities in the world, having a *great* time,' Anna said.

Meg was silent and then she looked at Anna, her eyes fixed on her face. 'Yes,' she said. 'You're right. It should be all right, shouldn't it?'

'Of *course* it will be,' Anna said, taking one of Meg's feather-light hands in hers and giving it a comforting squeeze. 'What could possibly go wrong?'

* * *

It wasn't until they were on the way to the studios that Anna began to worry. Everything was happening so quickly. Her short article in the paper simply entitled: *Is this the oldest woman in the world?* had obviously been read by a lot of people. Whether or not they believed Meg's story was another thing. But that didn't worry Anna. The fact was, Meg's story was being read. People could make their own minds up about it – that's what journalism was all about, wasn't it?

But what concerned Anna was that she no longer felt in control. For a few brief hours in the hotel, Meg's story had been exclusively hers. She'd been in the most privileged of positions but a story wasn't a story until it was told. She'd had to release it and now it seemed to be taking on a life of its own.

In the back of the taxi to the studios, Anna looked at Meg. She seemed happy enough. After their little chat before, Meg hadn't had any further misgivings and seemed to think that William was happy with what was happening now. So it seemed rather perverse for Anna to be anxious.

'Are you all right?' Meg asked, looking across to Anna.

'Yes,' Anna lied.

'Not nervous, are you?'

'A little,' Anna said, deciding that nerves might be a good mask for her concerns.

'I probably won't be able to see very much anyway so I've decided not to worry.'

Anna nodded. 'That sounds like a good plan to me.'

'I'm not going to think about who might watch it although it does seem a shame to think that William won't see the programme.'

Anna's eyebrows rose. As far as she was concerned, that was a definite blessing.

'So, you're going to be there with me?' Meg asked.

'Yes, of course.'

'Good,' Meg said. 'Do you think you'll be asked any questions?'

'Perhaps. Although I'm not as interesting a subject as you, am I?'

'I've been thinking,' Meg began, 'you know all sorts of things about me now but I don't know much about you.'

Anna grinned. There's not really much to know. That's why I write about other people.'

'But everyone's got a story to tell. If there's one thing I've learnt in my time here, it's that *everybody* is interesting. They might not think they are but you usually find some little hidden thought about the world that will knock you off your milking stool.'

Anna laughed. 'I'm sure you're right.'

Meg nodded. 'I like being right and I usually am, you know.' She paused. 'So, what about you?'

'What about me?' Anna asked.

'Ah, the typical response of a person who likes to know everything about everyone else but won't share a snippet of information in return.'

'But there's nothing to tell.'

'Pah! Rubbish!' Meg scoffed. 'Start at the beginning if you're stuck. You're the eldest, right? You have a sister?'

'Yes. Libby. Elizabeth. We've never ever called her that, though. It's always been Libby.'

'And she's the collector, isn't she?'

'You see – you know everything that's of any interest,' Anna said with a smile.

But Meg wasn't going to be discouraged. 'And she's married with a son, right? Have I remembered?'

'Yes.'

'And what about you? No time for husbands and children in your busy timetable?'

'Not yet, no,' Anna said honestly.

'Then there's hope?'

'Maybe. I like to think so,' Anna said, thoroughly uncomfortable at being the centre of attention and hoping Meg would soon grow bored of asking questions.

'What about your parents? Are they still alive?'

There was a pause.

'I'm sorry,' Meg suddenly said. 'I don't mean to pry.'

'Yes you do,' Anna said, giving a nervous laugh.

'All right, yes I do. But I'd really like to know more about you – if you don't mind telling me, that is.'

Anna waited a moment. 'My father's dead.'

'Oh, I'm sorry.'

'It's okay. It happened a long time ago.'

'And your mother?'

'Not dead.'

Meg looked at Anna in surprise at her strange response. 'Is that all you have to say about your mother? *Not dead*?' Meg said and there was an edge of laughter to her voice.

'For the time being, yes,' Anna said.

'I take it you're not close, then,' she said.

'That's right – not close.'

Meg shook her head. 'You play a very unfair game, Anna,' she said.

'I know,' Anna said and then, to her great relief, the taxi pulled up to the studios and Meg's brief interrogation came to an end.

CHAPTER 24

William decided that the best thing he could do whilst Meg and Anna were in hiding was to keep himself busy. He'd recently decided to turn one of the spare rooms upstairs into a library and had already started to collect old books about arts and crafts with a special emphasis on country crafts. Being William, he had already amassed an impressive number of volumes which were currently being stored in his bedroom – not an ideal solution since he had given himself the smallest room in the house.

He'd had one near-catastrophe just the other night when he'd stumbled out of bed for a glass of water and – on his return journey – had stubbed his toe on a copy of *Wood Carvings in Country Churches.* He'd very nearly spilt his glass of water over a teetering pile of precious cloth-bound books which would have been a disaster. So, in spite of not having a room in a fit state to receive shelves, he thought he'd get on with the task of making some. Physical work was a good way to take one's mind off things, he'd always found.

Just before he'd bought Fox Hill Manor, William had completed a course in woodwork. It had always been a favourite subject at school and he'd found it both straightforward and fascinating. There was something about holding a piece of warm wood in your hands and knowing that, for the next few hours, your entire attention was going to be focussed on it.

His shelves, he'd decided, were going to be as beautiful and precious as the books he was going to place on them. That had been one of the promises he'd made in buying Fox Hill Manor. Nothing ugly was to pass the threshold. Everything had to be beautiful – like the William Morris maxim he subscribed to: *"Have nothing in your house that you do not know to be useful or believe to be beautiful"*.

So, he'd work on his shelves today. Mrs Boothby was in, doing her rounds of the house and, like most men, he didn't like being around when there was a duster hovering. Instead, he took a mug of tea out to one of the workrooms he'd made in the old stable-block and settled down to a day of sawing, sanding and polishing.

It was a good plan and it almost worked. If it hadn't been for Mrs Boothby insisting that he have a proper break for lunch, William would have happily worked through the whole day, thinking of nothing but the job in front of him.

'You've got to eat,' Mrs Boothby said, ushering him into the kitchen like an errant child. 'Can't have you living on cups of tea and then passing out, can we?'

William sighed. He sometimes wondered if he could manage FHM without Mrs Boothby. She meant well, of course, but meaning well sometimes really got in the way of things.

'I've made a nice quiche and bought a French loaf and some salad.'

William nodded. Come to think of it, he was a little peckish. 'Thank you, Mrs Boothby. Whatever would I do without you?' he said kindly.

'Starve most likely,' she said. 'Now, what's happening with that lass, Anna, who was here?'

William groaned inwardly. He *knew* he should have refused lunch.

'I don't know,' he said, hoping to end the conversation right there. 'That quiche *does* look splendid.'

'Never mind about the quiche. What do you mean by *you don't know?*' Mrs Boothby said, not one to be put off the scent so easily.

'She's done her job here,' he said with a shrug. 'I guess she's doing whatever she's got to do next.'

'Oh,' Mrs Boothby said. 'Is that all?'

William took a mouthful of quiche to stall answering. 'Yes,' he said a moment later.

'Not coming back then?' she said.

'Why should she?' he asked, looking up at her.

Mrs Boothby frowned. 'But I thought you two were getting along.'

'We got along fine,' William said nonchalantly.

She sighed, folding a tea-towel in frustration. 'How often do you get a beautiful young woman knocking on your door?'

William chose not to answer.

'Not very often, I'm sure,' Mrs Boothby continued without his input. 'And I could tell.'

William stuffed a slice of tomato in to his mouth. 'What?' he said, his voice snappy and tomatoey.

'That you two – *you know* – got along.'

'Really,' William said, his voice flat and lifeless.

Mrs Boothby shook her head. 'She was bright and beautiful and, most important of all, interested in you. And she didn't seem to mind all your old things all over the house. You'd be hard pressed to find another woman like her again,' she said with a nod. 'You just think about that.'

William took a final mouthful of quiche before standing up. 'I've got to get on,' he said.

Mrs Boothby put her hands of her hips. 'You don't get ones like that knocking on your door every day,' she called after him.

No, William thought. And thank goodness for that.

Returning to his workshop, William continued where he'd left off. He tried to banish Mrs Boothby's words and he tried not to think of Anna but it was impossible. He'd managed to succeed this morning but the lunchtime interruption had knocked him sidewise and he was no longer able to concentrate on the job before him, not when the sweet face of Anna kept filling his mind.

But she wasn't sweet, he told himself. She was anything but. For all her interest in him and his collection, for her brightness and brilliance, her charm and sparkle, she was nothing more than a scheming journalist and he should never have let her into his house.

So, he'd come to a decision: he would try and forget about her. He'd made a terrible mistake. Anna didn't care about him at all. All she wanted was access to a story, and his rash display of emotions had merely embarrassed them both.

William sighed and shook his head. Him and women. It was always a disastrous combination. In the future, he would stick to antiques. It was a much safer option.

The afternoon drifted into evening with relatively few interruptions in the form of visions of Anna. He'd finished a number of shelves, was reasonably happy with his work and had decided to return to the house.

He was just pouring himself a tumbler of whisky when the phone went.

'Hello, Bro,' George's cheery voice said. 'You're never going to believe what I've just seen.'

'What?' William said, thinking his brother might have found that piece of medieval armour he'd spent a lifetime looking for.

'Anna.'

'In London? You've spoken to her?'

'No but I've seen her.'

'What do you mean?'

'Well, kind of seen her. She was on television,' George said.

'What do you mean?'

'On our local news. With some old lady with long white hair. Meg something-or-other. I didn't catch her last name.'

'Oh my god,' William said.

'That's a strange surname. Do you know her?'

'Yes – of course I know her,' William said.

'Who is she? I didn't really hear much of the story.'

William sighed. 'She's a friend.'

'I've not met her, have I?'

'No,' William said bluntly.

'I thought not. I'd remember someone like her. She had the most extraordinary eyes. They were like – I don't know – blue pearls or something. Looked like they'd seen the whole world in her time.'

Once again, William couldn't help but be impressed by George's perceptive comment.

'Who is she, Will?' he asked.

William cleared his throat but didn't reply.

'Well, it looks like the whole world's going to find out about her now,' George said.

'Why do you say that?'

'Because the TV said she was going to be interviewed on that Andre Levinson programme later in the week.'

William felt his heartbeat accelerate. 'You're kidding?'

'No. That's the one bit of the interview I did hear properly.'

'This is terrible,' William said.

'How so?'

'Because she should be *here*.'

'Where?'

'Here! With me.'

There was a moment's silence. 'I wish you'd tell me what's going on,' George said and then he paused. 'She's your big secret, isn't she?'

'What do you mean?'

'She's the thing you've been hiding all this time,' George said. 'I *knew* it! Wasn't I right? I knew you had something hidden away at that old manor of yours. It's her, isn't it? It's the old lady.'

'I haven't hidden her away,' William said.

'Rubbish! How come I've never known she was there then?'

'If it hadn't slipped your notice, we've not exactly been on friendly terms these past few years,' William pointed out.

'No. But I think I should have noticed my own brother living with a geriatric when I last visited.'

'She isn't a geriatric,' William said angrily.

'No, sorry. I didn't mean that. She sounded very articulate, actually,' George said.

'Oh, God!' William exclaimed. 'What did she say?'

'I've no idea. I told you. I missed half the interview.'

'I should never have let Anna–'

'What?' George said. 'Has she been abducted by Anna?' There was another pause.

'Look,' William said, 'I really don't know what's going on.'

'Do you want me to try and find out?'

'How?'

'Give me Anna's number and I'll have a chat.'

'She's not answering it,' William said.

'Maybe not to you but she doesn't know my number, does she?'

William paused, wondering if that might work. 'You'll try and find out where she is? And what she's doing?'

'If that's what you want me to do.'

'It is. Meg's *got* to come home, George.'

'Okay, Bro. I'll see what I can do.'

Anna was so relieved when the ordeal by television was over and they returned to their hotel. Meg had fallen asleep in the taxi home and Anna had been given time to reflect on what had just happened.

On the whole, it had gone rather well, she thought. Although the woman interviewing them had been completely misinformed and seemed to be one of the few people in the UK who hadn't heard about Meg.

'It says here that you're a hundred and fifty-five,' the interviewer had said, 'but that must be a mistake.'

'Yes, it is,' Meg had replied. 'I'm *three* hundred and fifty-five.'

The poor woman's mouth had dropped open and her eyes had glazed over in shock. She'd looked around the newsroom for help but none was forthcoming and she'd had to stumble through the rest of the piece.

But Meg had shone. She seemed to be a natural in front of the camera – perhaps because she'd been completely unaware of them. She'd talked about the changes she'd seen in medicine and healthcare, the opportunities that were open to women now which she hadn't had when she was young, the varieties of food that were now available – on and on she went, providing a unique and very articulate look at her life.

'Well – er – Meg,' the interviewer said at the end, 'that was most interesting.'

Meg had thanked her politely and then they'd been led back to the green room.

'She didn't believe me, did she?' Meg said to Anna as they left the heat and brightness of the studio.

'I think she doesn't take to anyone who steals her limelight,' Anna told her.

As soon as William had hung up from his brother, George, he'd poured himself another whisky. He wasn't in the habit of having more than one glass in the evenings but this, he reasoned, was an extenuating circumstance.

What the hell did Anna think she was doing letting Meg be interviewed on television? And what, exactly, had Meg said? William downed the tumbler of golden liquid in one and thought about pouring a third measure. That way lies doom, he thought. No, he had to keep a clear head about this because it was quite obvious that both Anna and Meg had lost theirs.

CHAPTER 25

When Anna woke the next morning, it took her a few moments to realise what was happening. It wasn't all a dream, was it? She and Meg had really appeared on television together and had been told that a call had come through from the Levinson show too for an interview later in the week. Andre Levinson, for goodness' sake. He was the biggest name in UK chat shows and he'd personally invited Meg to appear on his show.

This Meg story really was taking off big time, Anna thought, as she got out of bed and ran a shower. She'd already been asked to write several pieces about Meg for various magazines and had received innumerable phone calls from journalists asking if they could interview Meg themselves.

'Meg will only talk to me from now on,' Anna told them, feeling just a little bit smug. Of course, she hadn't actually run this by Meg – she'd be a fool to do that in case Meg said, "bring it on" in that happy-go-lucky way of hers and Anna became redundant. No, Meg was *her* story and she didn't intend handing it on to anyone else.

Once showered and dressed, Anna checked her mobile. One missed call. She checked the number but didn't recognise it although she could see it was a London number. Perhaps another cheeky journalist wanting a slice of the action?

Suddenly her mobile rang, making her jump. Maybe America had got hold of the story or some big movie producer who wanted to turn Meg's story into a blockbusting film and Anna was to write the script and the novelisation of the film and the official biography of Meg.

Anna tutted at herself. How ridiculous. It was probably just another newspaper.

But it wasn't a newspaper and it wasn't Hollywood either. It was George.

'Anna?' he said, his voice bright and loud.

'George?' Anna said in surprise.

'How are you?'

'I'm fine,' she said, instantly suspicious as to how he'd got her number and why he was calling her. 'What's up?'

'Just rang to say hello. Not seen you since that evening at Will's. You okay?'

'Yes,' she said, her eyebrows drawing together as she wondered where this conversation was going.

'Good, good,' George said casually.

'George, why are you calling? Has this got something to do with William?'

'What makes you say that? Can't a bloke just ring for a chat?'

'No, not usually,' Anna pointed out.

She heard George sigh. 'Oh, all right. You're too sharp for me. Remind me never to date a journalist.'

'You've talked to William, haven't you?'

'Yes. Last night – after I saw you on TV.'

'And you told him that?'

'Of course. I thought he'd have known about it but he hadn't a clue.'

'Is he furious?' Anna dared to ask.

'You could say that. But it's a fury born of deeply rooted anxiety about you both.'

'Yeah, right!'

'No, *really*,' George said. 'Look, I don't know what you're up to but I think you owe it to Will to tell him.'

Anna bit her lip. She knew George was right but she didn't want to admit that. 'I will,' she said. 'I've just been busy.'

'So, are you going to tell me about it?'

'About what? I thought you said you'd seen the interview?'

'Not really. Just caught the end of it and recognised you. Who's Meg?'

'She's a friend of William's.'

'That much I gathered.'

'What's he told you?' Anna asked.

'Nothing. You know what he's like. But I gather this Meg's been living at Fox Hill for some time now.'

'Yes,' Anna said. 'George, I feel a bit uneasy talking to you about all this. I mean – William–'

'Oh, don't worry about that. We're good. We actually made up.'

'Really?' Anna said.

'Yep. Got a few things straight after the funeral.'

'Oh, George! I'm so pleased.'

'Me too. Will's not a bad guy, you know.'

'I know.'

There was a pause as they both thought their separate, gentle thoughts about William.

'So are you going to tell me who this Meg is?' George continued.

'I expect you're going to read about it sooner or later,' Anna said.

'But I want to hear it from you,' George said. 'Go on, Anna. Please!'

She took a deep breath. He was a very persuasive person, this George, so she told him. She told him about the night she'd discovered Meg at Fox Hill Manor and William's strange reaction to it. She told him about the stories Meg had told her and of how she'd come to be at FHM. She told him everything she knew about Meg, her voice charged with excitement as she recalled everything. And, finally, her story came to an end.

'And you're sure Levinson's is a good idea?' George asked.

'Why not?' Anna said, immediately on the defensive.

'I think William's worried about Meg,' George said. 'I mean, I'm not convinced that she's over three hundred but she's still an old woman – by anyone's standards. Should she really be put through the ordeal of national television like that?'

'But she got so excited by the news programme – you should've seen her,' Anna said, her eyes sparkling at the memory. 'She told me she's never had so much fun and, believe me, she's had no end of fun experiences in her life.'

George sighed. 'It's just that William said she's not strong.'

'Not strong! She's got more energy than me,' Anna said with a deflecting laugh. 'She takes a fair number of naps during the day but that's normal, right? And they energise her. She's always raring to go. Really, George – you should see her.'

'I just think you should be careful,' George said.

'I am being careful,' Anna assured him. 'I adore Meg. I wouldn't do anything to harm her.'

There was a moment's silence.

'And William?' George said.

'What about William?'

'When are you going to tell him what's going on?'

'I don't know,' Anna said honestly.

'You have to call him,' George said. 'Anna? Promise me you'll call him.'

'Is that what he asked you to tell me?'

'Are you going to?'

Anna sighed. 'I'll think about it,' she said before hanging up.

But Anna didn't ring William. She thought about it but it was all too easy to put it at the back of her mind as she got swept along in the surge of interest surrounding Meg. Journalists had started camping outside the hotel in Marble Arch and the owner had made it perfectly clear that that couldn't continue so Anna decided to book somewhere else, choosing a large hotel near Cuthland Square which would surely put everyone off the trail for a while.

'There are so many people,' Meg had said as they left the hotel.

'They're all here for you, Meg. They all want to ask you questions,' Anna said as she escorted Meg to the waiting taxi.

There were photographers too, stuffing their obtrusive lenses into Anna and Meg's faces.

'This must be what it's like to be famous,' Meg laughed, ducking into the taxi.

'Yes,' Anna said, realising that it wasn't something she was that keen on pursuing. It was one thing to have your words read by the masses but quite another to be photographed on the street without your permission.

But that was just the start of things. The press soon discovered where they were hiding out and, after the Levinson show, were virtually camping out there around the clock, snapping photographs of Meg and Anna if they so much as looked out of the window.

The worst of it for Anna, though, were the stories that were being written about Meg.

'Is this *really* the world's oldest woman?' one newspaper questioned.

'What's in it for Meg?' another speculated.

'Hoax Meg makes a mint,' another said which was most unfair, Anna thought, seeing as no money had come Meg's way at all.

And everyone, it seemed, had an opinion. From doctors to politicians, celebrities to scientists, the whole nation had something to say about Meg.

'It just isn't possible,' Dr Philip Sallis said in one newspaper. 'The human body simply can't last that long.'

'I hope to get the opportunity to meet Meg,' Bishop Candy said. 'For all we know, she might well be a modern-day miracle.'

'I'd just *die* to play her in the film of her life,' model-turned-actress, Cerise, declared. 'The *younger* Meg, of course!'

But, whether they believed in Meg's story or not, the nation was enraptured.

It wasn't until Meg didn't wake up one morning that Anna realised something terrible had happened.

CHAPTER 26

'Meg?' Anna whispered as she ran towards the bed and sat down next to her. 'MEG!'

Meg didn't respond. Anna waited a moment, holding a porcelain-fine hand in hers and half-expecting to see a flutter of eyelids and Meg's pearly-blue eyes looking at her questioningly.

'What is it?' she'd say. 'Have we another interview? Are we late?'

But her eyelids didn't flutter and her beautiful eyes didn't open.

'MEG!' Anna shouted again. 'Oh, God!'

Leaping to her feet, Anna ran down to the reception. 'We need a doctor!' she yelled at the startled girl. '*Quickly!*'

There then passed the worst half hour of Anna's life as she sat with Meg in their room. It was unutterably silent and Anna wished more than anything to hear Meg's voice again – the sweet unassuming voice that could tell a thousand tales and share a wealth of knowledge and yet not expect anything in return.

'Meg? I'm here,' Anna said. It seemed such an insubstantial thing to say but Anna could think of nothing else.

The hotel manager came to see if there was anything he could do.

'You've checked for a pulse?'

'Of course,' Anna said. 'She's breathing but it seems a little erratic. She just won't wake up. I don't know what's wrong with her.'

The manager stepped forward and peered at Meg before placing a hand on her forehead. 'She feels very warm.'

'But her face is so pale,' Anna said.

'You don't think she's had a stroke, do you?'

Anna's face fell. 'How would I know? Oh, where's the doctor?'

When the doctor finally arrived, he took one look at Meg and turned as pale as her himself.

'What is it?'

'How long's she been like this?'

'I don't know,' Anna said, 'an hour? She went to bed early last night and then I couldn't wake her this morning.'

The doctor started his examination and Anna paced the room.

'Call me if I can be of any further assistance,' the hotel manager said but Anna didn't hear him. She was too anxious. What on earth would she tell William and what would he say? He would blame her, wouldn't he? And rightly so. If she hadn't taken Meg away from Fox Hill, if she hadn't subjected her to interview after interview and exhausted her with endless questions of her own, then this might not have happened. She'd be sitting happily in her room at FHM, looking out over the garden and nodding off to audio books.

'What's wrong with her, doctor?' Anna asked, unable to wait a second longer.

The doctor sighed. 'I can't seem to find anything wrong with her. She doesn't seem to have had a heart attack or a stroke. Her heart rate seems to be normal. She has a slight temperature but, without further tests, I really can't confirm anything. I suggest you take her to hospital where she can be properly assessed.'

Anna nodded.

The doctor stayed for a little longer and Anna joined him. 'Meg?' she whispered. 'Can you hear me?'

'Meg?' the doctor said. 'As in *Meg*?'

Anna nodded.

'You should have told me,' the doctor said.

'Why? What's wrong?'

'Well,' the doctor said, 'it's probably just exhaustion. I've been watching her on the television and reading all those interviews. You really should be taking better care of her. That sort of timetable's punishing enough for a youngster and Meg's no youngster.'

A thought suddenly occurred to Anna. 'Can you tell how old she is?'

The doctor's eyebrows rose. 'You mean *exactly*?'

'Well, I guess within about fifty years would be good enough,' Anna said.

He sighed. 'You don't really believe her, do you? That she's hundreds of years old?'

'Don't you?' Anna asked.

He shook his head.

'But is there a way of proving it?' Anna said.

'You mean dating her bones?' the doctor said.

'Can that be done?'

'Radio carbon-dating,' he said.

Anna's eyes widened. She hadn't thought of that before. 'We've got to do it.'

'Well, we can't actually do it until she's deceased,' the doctor said and he gave a little smile.

'Oh!' Anna said.

'It's not like dendrochronology when you drill a hole and take a sample from a tree or piece of wood to date it. You can't do that with humans.'

Anna nodded, feeling awful for having suggested it.

'But it might be an option at some point,' the doctor said in a subdued voice. 'If you really want to know, that is.'

'Want to know what?' a faint voice asked from the bed.

'MEG!' Anna shouted. 'Meg!'

'What's going on?' she asked, trying to sit up.

'You're okay,' Anna said in relief.

'Well, of *course* I'm okay. Why shouldn't I be?' she asked, her bright eyes blinking. 'Who are you?'

'I'm Doctor Hammond.'

'Anything wrong?' Meg asked.

'It appears not,' Doctor Hammond said. 'Although I must caution you against such a busy lifestyle, Meg. You've been overdoing things. Your body's exhausted.'

'I'm afraid we've got to slow down a bit,' Anna said, squeezing Meg's hand.

'Not just slow down,' Doctor Hammond said, 'but completely rest. I don't want to see any more interviews or TV appearances, do you hear? You're to stay right where you are, Meg, is that clear? I'll come back tomorrow to check up on you.'

He stood up and nodded towards Anna. 'Complete rest,' he repeated before leaving the room.

'Oh, what a bore,' Meg said as soon as the door was closed.

Anna laughed as much from relief as anything else. 'Oh, Meg! You do know how to startle a person.'

'Were you worried? I'm sorry,' she said, a little smile on her face as she tried to plump her pillows behind her.

'It's okay,' Anna said, giving her a hand. 'You're going to be all right – that's the main thing.'

'Anna?'

'Yes?' she said. 'Is there anything you want? Can I get you a glass of water or a little something to eat?'

Meg shook her head. 'No, no thank you. Just–' she paused.

'What?'

'Take me home.'

Anna's eyes narrowed. 'To Fox Hill?'

Meg nodded.

'The doctor said we shouldn't move you, Meg. You need to rest.'

Meg just stared at Anna. 'Take me home,' she said and Anna stared back at her, knowing that this was the only heartfelt request she'd ever had from Meg.

'Okay,' she said. 'I'll take you home.'

Since their departure by taxi from the hotel in Marble Arch, Anna had made arrangements for her car to be kept in the new hotel's underground car park so it was handy for a quick getaway.

'Oh, I'm such a nuisance,' Meg said as Anna loaded their bags. 'And you were really enjoying things. And I was too.'

'Don't keep apologising,' Anna told her. 'It can't be helped. I'm just glad you're okay.'

Meg eased herself down into the passenger seat and Anna got in, wondering if they'd have to drive through any hoards of photographers on the way out.

Sure enough, on leaving the hotel, they were snapped and flashed by half a dozen cameras and two very game ones even ran down the road after them.

'Will they follow us?' Meg asked.

'Not to the Cotswolds,' Anna said. 'We'll be fine once we get you home.'

The two of them settled down for the journey ahead of them. Meg closed her eyes and nodded off, leaving Anna to contemplate what lay ahead. She was going to have to face William a lot sooner than she'd imagined and she had no idea what to say to him. She rehearsed a few options in her mind.

'We've had *such* a good time!' she could say casually. 'You should've come with us!' or: 'You should take Meg to London more often. She really thrives in a big city.'

But she knew they wouldn't wash with William. She wasn't going to be able to get out of this one and, as they drove through the Oxfordshire and Wiltshire countryside and on into the Cotswolds, she became more and more nervous at the confrontation that lay ahead of her.

It was just after three in the afternoon as they entered the Elm Valley. The bluebells and the cow parsley were long over and everything felt heavy and green with the approach of summer. The sky was a dazzling blue and swallows were dancing across the fields, their long cries filling the car when Anna opened her window. As much as she'd enjoyed the excitement of the city, it felt good to be back. It wasn't just that feeling of coming home – of being intrinsically attached to what was familiar – but more a case of being so in love with a part of the world that everything else paled in comparison. The gentle curves of the hills, the emerald sloping fields, and the cottages huddling together against the elements. It was hard to imagine living anywhere else, Anna thought.

'We're nearly there, Meg,' she said as they drove through the final few villages, passing churches, golden stone walls and cottage gardens filled with roses.

Meg blinked and gave a little yawn.

'Okay?'

Meg nodded. 'I think I must have fallen asleep.'

Anna laughed. 'Not to worry.'

'I thought we'd still be getting out of London.'

'We've made good time,' Anna said and nodded as she saw the two stone posts marking the entrance to Fox Hill Manor. But, as soon as they entered the drive, they saw a dozen photographers milling about.

'Blimey!' Anna said. 'I didn't think they'd dare.' She swallowed nervously. She really hadn't imagined that anyone would be there, let alone in such numbers, and she could only imagine what was going through William's mind at this sudden invasion of his privacy.

'What is it?' Meg asked, obviously unable to see what was going on.

'There are photographers outside the house.'

Meg gasped. 'From London? They followed us?'

'No, I don't think so. They're probably from the national papers, though. With maybe a couple from local ones. I really don't know,' she said, worry etched across her face.

'Not all here for me?' Meg said in surprise.

'Well, there's no other reason for them to be here,' Anna said.

'Unless William's become famous during our absence.'

'Oh, dear,' Meg said. 'Whatever will William say?'

Anna sighed and she felt fear coursing its way through her body. 'I'm dreading finding out.'

But they didn't have long to wait. As soon as Anna was parked, William came charging out of the house, opening the passenger door. Before Anna could say a word, he'd ushered Meg into the house and slammed the door on the awaiting photographers.

Anna waited, trapped in the car as a few photographers took pictures of her. Was William coming back outside? Was she expected to just go? Ten minutes ticked by before the front door opened again and William strode towards the car. Anna got out and greeted him with a tiny smile, as if testing the waters. He didn't smile back.

'Get inside,' he told her. 'This place has become unbearable.'

'William – I–'

'Get out of here!' William shouted to the press. 'Out – NOW! This is private property!'

'How long have they been out here?' Anna asked.

'Ever since Fox Hill Manor was mentioned in the national press.'

'But I don't remember mentioning–'

'I think Meg might have let something slip,' he said as they entered the house and closed the door behind them.

'Oh!' Anna said. 'I'm sure she had no idea what would happen.'

'Of course she didn't,' William said. 'But some people should've known better. Even if Meg hadn't mentioned it, they would've found out somehow. They're not stupid, these people. If they hadn't done some quick investigating, they would've just followed you.'

'I'm so sorry,' Anna said, knowing how ineffectual the word seemed. 'Where's Meg?'

'Up in her room – where she belongs,' William said. 'What in *God's* name were you thinking of?' he suddenly yelled. 'I was worried sick. I came home after the funeral and Meg was gone. What was I meant to think?'

'William, I'm *so* sorry. I meant to call – really I did. It's just, well, we were having such a good time and we totally forgot.'

'You totally forgot that you'd run away with Meg and not left so much as a note to tell me what you were doing?'

'It was a spur of the moment decision,' Anna said.

'Rubbish! You'd been planning this for days.'

'That's not true!' Anna pleaded.

'Stop lying to me, Anna.'

'I'm not lying,' she said, desperately trying to remain calm. 'Okay, so I took advantage of you being away to come and see Meg – I admit that. But I didn't plan the trip to London. I was just going to talk to her here. We went out that first afternoon and we got on so well. I didn't want to let her go. It was selfish of me. Stupid of me. But she's the most amazing person I've ever met and I just wanted to get to know her better. You've got to realise how special she is.'

'You think I don't?' William said, his grey eyes flashing with anger.

'Of course you know that. But you've been keeping her all to yourself for years. It's not fair, William. The world should know about her.'

'Why? So they can pour ridicule on her and hound her until she's ill?'

Anna shook her head. 'No! So they can *listen* to her.'

'She doesn't need to be listened to,' William said.

'Maybe not,' Anna said. 'We don't always *need* things, do we? You don't *need* to collect antiques. I don't *need* to buy a slab of dark chocolate every Friday, but I do anyway.'

'What are you talking about?' he said, his face filled with consternation.

Anna shook her head. 'What you think Meg needs and what she might actually *enjoy* could be two very different things.'

'She needs to be kept safe,' William said. 'She looks terrible. What's wrong with her? She went straight to bed.'

'She's just tired, that's all,' Anna said, wondering if she should mention the doctor's visit. No, she thought. She was in quite enough trouble at the moment. 'London's a tiring place. It's knackered me completely.'

William glared at her and walked through to the living room. Anna followed him.

'I can't believe you just took her away like that,' he said, shaking his head.

'I didn't exactly handcuff her to me,' she said. 'She came away quite willingly.'

'But you shouldn't have let her. She's frail.'

'William! You can't keep her under lock and key for the rest of her life. She needs to be able to get out and do things.'

'Like appear on national television, you mean?'

Anna sighed. She could see she wasn't going to win this argument easily. She'd have to convince him that the trip had been for Meg's own good and then she remembered something. 'We visited some of Meg's old stomping grounds whilst we were in London. Have you heard of Bretton Place?'

William shook his head.

'There are the remains of a Georgian terrace there. The rest were bombed during the Second World War,' Anna said. 'Meg once lived there with a family called the Palmers. She told me all about them and I looked them up. They really existed!

'It wasn't your business to do that, Anna.'

Anna's eyes widened in surprise at his comment. 'Yes it was. I'm a journalist! It's absolutely my business for me to find stories and Meg wanted to tell me hers.'

William poured himself a drink from the sideboard and offered one to Anna. She shook her head.

'I really don't want you to see her again,' he said, his voice low, like a warning.

Anna looked at him but he was obviously avoiding eye contact. 'I see,' she said. 'And that's an order, is it?'

'I don't think you care much about orders, do you? I'm just telling you what I think is best for Meg.'

'Can I see her here?' she asked him.

William looked up and their eyes locked. 'I don't think that's a good idea.'

Anna didn't know what to say. They seemed all out of words.

'I'd better go, then,' she said at last in a voice as low as his.

As she left the room and entered the hallway, she half-expected that he would follow her to say something more and, indeed, she found that she was walking deliberately slowly towards the door. But he didn't follow. He didn't have anything left to say to her, did he?

Anna opened the door and was immediately besieged by photographers. As she pushed her way towards her car, she didn't realise that every single one of them managed to get a shot of a beautiful young woman with tears sparkling in her eyes.

CHAPTER 27

Anna did her best to blink the tears away as she left Fox Hill Manor behind. Turning out of the driveway, she sincerely believed that she'd never see Meg or the beautiful old house again.

Or William, she thought to herself.

Anna the Journalist had been superseded by Anna the Woman as she recalled the blank look in William's eyes as he'd told her to leave.

He didn't even say goodbye, she thought. *He must hate me. Hate me for going behind his back and hate me for the risk I took taking Meg away. And that*, she thought, *was a lot of hate.*

There was no going back now, was there? She couldn't have both the excitement of sharing Meg's story with the world and the man she loved. She'd made her decision and it had cost her dearly.

Reaching Elmington at last, Anna found the last parking space in her street and took out the suitcase she'd bought in London, noticing that Meg's case had been left in William's rush to get her into the house.

She made her way to her front door and unlocked it, pushing it open against a heap of mail and flyers. Bending down to scoop the whole lot up, Anna felt her eyes brimful of tears again.

'Stupid, *stupid* girl!' she cursed herself. 'What's wrong with you?' She put down her suitcase and threw the mail onto the kitchen table before collapsing into a chair.

How did all this happen, she thought? How had she got herself into this mess in the first place? Catching sight of the mail once again, she realised that the answer was a very mundane one: paying the bills. That's why she'd taken on the article book about William's collection. She'd needed the money. And that was one of the reasons she'd been keen to tell Meg's story too – because she'd known there'd be money in it.

Anna walked through the rooms of her house. It seemed an age since she'd been there and so much had changed in the meantime. Her collection of books from the library had remained unread and were probably long overdue now. The loaf of bread she'd bought would need to be thrown away and the stack of ironing still hadn't done itself. Life might have changed irrevocably for her but her day-to-day existence was still the same.

It was then that she caught sight of something on the stair carpet. Bending down, she picked it up. It was an earring – a single silver earring the size of a thumbnail and in the shape of a fairy. Anna frowned. It wasn't hers and there was only one person it could belong to and that was Libby. But what had Libby been doing there? Perhaps she'd caught the Meg story in the press and knew that she'd been stuck in London and had come round to check on the place. Still, if she'd done that, surely she would have thrown the mouldy old bread away and picked up the mail. Anna looked around as if for more clues but there was nothing obvious. Perhaps she should ring her sister and touch base but she was so tired after everything that had happened over the last few days that she thought she'd put it off a while.

Opening a kitchen cupboard, she found a packet of pasta and a jar of sauce. She made herself a simple ten-minute meal and ate it in front of the television, instantly wishing she hadn't turned on the local news.

'The alleged oldest person in the world returned to her home in the Cotswold's own Elm Valley today where she was seen in the company of local journalist, Anna McCall – the woman who brought Meg's story to the attention of the world. Miss McCall refused to comment on why they'd left London but there are grave concerns over the health of Meg.'

'Oh, Meg,' Anna sighed, putting down her knife and fork and staring at the image of Meg being taken into the house by William, 'I'm so sorry.'

Libby had spent the evening trying to help Toby with his English homework. He was meant to be writing a description of his house but Libby was trying to edit it.

'Don't say it's messy,' she told him crossly.

'But it is,' he said, his eyes wide and innocent.

'No it's not. It's –' Libby searched for the right word, 'eclectic.'

Toby frowned at her. 'I don't know what that means.'

'It means *interesting*.'

'Spell that for me.'

Libby did so, making sure he'd rubbed out the word *messy* first.

'What else should I put?' he asked.

'You could write about your bedroom and how nice it is.'

'But it's full of your stuff. You said you'd move those boxes,' Toby complained.

'And I will, my love. As soon as I get a chance.'

'You said that *last* week, Mummy!'

Libby sighed. She had no idea homework was so trying. 'Just write your piece, Toby,' she said, ruffling his hair. 'I've got to check up on something.'

Libby disappeared up the stairs and logged onto the computer to check her email. There was one from China Collectables which she opened straightaway.

Are you aware of our twenty percent discount if you buy three or more items by the end of June?

Libby wasn't aware and made a mental note to check out the link to their website later on.

There was also an email from The Pretty Porcelain Company telling her that her order had been dispatched. Libby bit her lip, hoping that Charlie wouldn't be around when it was delivered. That was always the chance she took with deliveries. She couldn't keep saying that they were for Anna.

And then her eye caught the email she'd been avoiding. It was from one of her credit card companies telling her that her statement was ready. *Yes*, Libby thought, *but I'm not.* Nevertheless, she followed the link and typed in her details, opening the page she'd been avoiding for at least four months.

The figure that stared back at her wasn't what she'd been expecting and she laughed. Something must be wrong. This couldn't be her account, could it? She hadn't really spent that much.

She clicked on the link to view her statement and saw the list of items purchased. Yes, that item certainly rang a bell. And that one – that was definitely hers. Oh, yes – and that one was the divine dolls from Russia. And on and on it went, with Libby acknowledging each and every item.

When she clicked back to see the total amount now due, a chill ran through her body. She really did owe that amount. And that wasn't all. This was only one credit card and she'd lost track of how many she had. They were all in different purses in different handbags. A card for every occasion. It hadn't really worried her before. It had all seemed so – easy! Buy now, pay later. Simple. But the reality was beginning to sink in and, for the first time, Libby had to admit that she was scared.

Anna was also sitting by her computer checking her emails. There wasn't really anything important. She had a reminder from Hester North at Red Moon Publications that the first draft of her piece about William and the Fox Hill Manor collection was due shortly. She'd also written a personal note.

Many congratulations on your recent success with Meg's story. We've been following it here with interest. Do you really think it's true?

Anna thought about replying, *Well, of course it's true! Do you think I'd waste my time if it wasn't?* But perhaps Hester North thought she was the kind of journalist who might enlarge on the facts in order to sell a story. That's what a lot of people were thinking, wasn't it?

Anna switched her computer off. She was too tired to make a start on Meg's story tonight. She had the beginnings of a headache which didn't surprise her so she took a couple of paracetamol with a cup of tea and was just going upstairs to run a hot bath when the telephone rang.

'Hello,' she said, closing her eyes as her headache thumped somewhere behind them.

'Anna?' a voice said. She recognised it instantly.

'William?' she felt her heart immediately begin to race as she waited for him to speak again.

'I thought you'd better know. Meg's been taken into hospital.'

CHAPTER 28

Anna didn't know what to do with herself. She'd wanted William to say more but what else had she expected?

'Meg's in hospital but I can't stop thinking about you.'

She was being ridiculous.

As soon as he'd hung up, Anna had made a dash for her handbag and car keys but had stopped when she'd reached the front door. William wouldn't want her there, would he? He hadn't said, *'Come quickly, Anna.'* He'd just told her the news – that was all. He didn't expect anything else from her – not now. But that didn't mean she shouldn't go, did it?

Anna stood for a few minutes arguing with herself. Surely she should be there for Meg and for William – whether he wanted her there or not. She should try and make him see that she cared about them both more than anything else in the world.

But it's too late for that, a little voice in her head said and she returned her keys and waited by the phone until she fell asleep.

The phone didn't ring until the next afternoon. Anna had woken up in the middle of the night to find her shoulders stiff and her neck aching from where she'd fallen asleep in a chair in the living room. She'd gone upstairs to take a quick shower, forgoing a much longed-for bath for fear of missing a phone call.

She got up early the next morning, sitting herself in front of her computer to finish her article about William's collection. It was the only thing she could do and she was determined to make it the very best thing she'd ever written. It would be her gift to William; her way of showing him how very special he was to her.

She'd waited for William to ring again but, when it had got to lunchtime and she hadn't heard anything, she'd rung the hospital herself to be told that Meg was 'stable'.

After that, she'd worked on until stopping for a quick lunch at one o'clock, continuing with her work again until late afternoon, and that's when the phone rang.

'Hello?' she said, picking it up after one ring.

'Anna? It's Charlie.'

Anna frowned at the agonised voice of her brother-in-law. 'Are you okay?'

'Yes. No. I'm not sure,' he said. Can you come over? There's something I need to talk to you about.'

'About Libby?'

'Yes.'

'Okay. I'm on my way,' Anna said, hanging up quickly and leaving the house.

She drove through Elmington with unusual speed as she tried to second guess what was worrying Charlie. Her sister had married the sweetest man in the world. He was kind and considerate and always put the needs of his wife and son before his own which was why his recent decision to strike out alone and set up his own company had worried him. Would he be able to provide for them? Anna knew that Libby put a constant strain on the family budget. Was that what he wanted to see her about? Surely he could have talked to her on the phone, though. No, it must be something more than that, Anna thought as she drove up Elmington High Street before turning off to reach her sister's house.

There was a rare car parking space opposite the house and Anna was thankful for it, leaping out and running to knock loudly on the front door.

Charlie was there almost instantly. 'Thanks for coming so quickly,' he said. 'Come in. If you can.'

Anna pushed her way into the hallway but there wasn't much room to move because it was absolutely full of boxes.

'Charlie!' Anna exclaimed. 'You didn't tell me you were moving house.'

'I wish we were,' he said and Anna immediately saw that his face was drained white.

'What on earth's the matter? What *is* all this stuff?'

Charlie cleared his throat. 'All this stuff is Libby's.'

'What do you mean?'

Charlie motioned for Anna to follow him and she soon discovered that the front room was worse than the hallway.

'Charlie, I don't understand. I know it's usually a bit chaotic in here but this is *much* worse than normal. Where's all this stuff come from?'

'Tanya – a friend of Libby's – called me yesterday in desperation and then she came round today whilst Libby was out. She didn't know what to say.

Apparently, she's been keeping all this stuff for Libby but she's moving, you see. She told me she'd phoned Libby at least three times about the stuff and that she couldn't go on hoarding it any longer. She had to hire a van to bring it all over – and a guy to load and unload it all. I paid him, of course.'

'Where had Tanya been keeping it?'

'In a spare bedroom,' Charlie said with a weary sigh.

'A very large spare bedroom, I take it?'

Charlie nodded. 'The woman's been a saint.'

'And you had no idea?'

'None at all. God, I knew Libby had a bit of a problem with collecting but I never envisaged it was on a scale like this and that she'd roped friends into keeping stuff for her.' Charlie flopped down on a small patch of sofa that wasn't yet occupied with Libby's stuff.

'But it's just so much!' Anna said.

'Tell me about it. I don't know where to start.'

'And *she* doesn't know when to *stop*,' Anna said. 'Charlie, you've been a saint too, you know, but this has got to be taken in hand and right now.'

'Don't you think I don't know that? I've talked to her – endlessly – but her collecting's like some kind of addiction. A mania. I don't know what to do, Anna.'

Anna looked around the room in horror. It was her idea of a perfect nightmare. For a moment, she couldn't help comparing it to her own neat and tidy home where there wasn't so much as a candlestick out of place and everything – *every*thing had a use and purpose.

'Have you looked at any of this stuff? I mean, what's in all these boxes?' Anna peered closer. 'These are all proper boxes too, aren't they? She must have paid for them.'

Charlie nodded. 'Knowing they were to be stored.'

Anna's fingers reached out and undid the lid of one of them and dared to peer inside. It was packed with dozens of bubble-wrapped figures. She pulled one out for inspection, gently peeling away its protective wrapping to discover a porcelain soldier. 'Oooo!' she exclaimed. 'That's quite horrible, isn't it?'

Charlie pulled a revolted face. 'She doesn't even like soldiers.'

Anna pulled out a second one. 'They're all military figures.'

'But she's a pacifist!' Charlie yelled. 'Christ! What's going on with her?'

Anna moved onto a second box. It was filled with a whole Noah's Ark of hideously painted animals. There were yellow bears and purple giraffes, green elephants and pink lions.

Charlie scratched his head. 'What could she possibly want with them?'

A third box contained a collection of glitzy tiaras, sparkling prettily in the afternoon light, and a fourth housed a vast array of miniature handbags.

'But these things are all so – impractical,' Charlie said, completely baffled by it all. 'They're not useful in any way. I mean, I could almost understand if she was putting things away for Toby's future or something but these – *these*,' he said, peering into another box which housed a collection of floral jugs, 'what could she be thinking of?'

Anna looked at him. 'I don't think it's about the things themselves anymore,' she said.

'What do you mean?' Charlie asked.

Anna took a deep breath. 'I've been reading about collecting. Since I started this article with William Kitson, it's kind of been an obsession. Anyway, I've found out that people collect for all sorts of reasons. Maybe an interest – like football – blows out of proportion and you suddenly have bedspreads, towels, curtains etc all in your club's colours; or a person buys one item – say an unusual teapot. Next thing you know, friends and family have latched onto it and, all of a sudden, everyone's buying you teapots and your house fills up.'

Charlie shook his head. 'I can assure you, I've *never* encouraged this collecting, Anna.'

'No, I know you haven't,' she said, 'but collecting just sometimes takes over. It becomes like a job or a bit like what you said – a mania.' Anna bit her lip. 'But it can also be a distraction from something else.'

'Like what?' Charlie asked in a quiet voice.

'From someone or something that the collector doesn't want to face.'

Charlie and Anna stared at one another for a long moment.

'She's not happy?' Charlie asked, his face seeming to drop before her. 'But she's never said anything. I mean, we trundle along. She supported my decision to go solo. She never said anything about that. Do you think it's worrying her – secretly?'

'Oh, Charlie,' Anna said, chewing her lip. 'I don't think this has got anything to do with you.'

'What, then?'

Anna shook her head. 'Well, I've got some ideas but I think we'd better find out for sure, don't you?'

Charlie nodded. 'If you think you can,' he said. 'I'd be very happy to try and get to the bottom of this.'

'We will. Don't worry.' Anna looked at him and her heart filled with love and sympathy for her brother-in-law who had to put up with so much and did so with such sweetness and patience. 'Is this it, then?' Anna added.

'What do you mean?' Charlie said.

'Is this what you called me for or is there some other catastrophe?'

Charlie gave a small smile. 'No, this is it.' But then his expression changed.

'What is it?'

He sighed. 'I almost forgot. I'm afraid this isn't the complete story.'

'Don't tell me there's more to come,' Anna said, envisaging a fleet of white vans full of more of her sister's rubbish.

Charlie sighed and ran a hand through his hair. 'Her friend gave me this.' He fished in his jacket pocket and pulled out a silver key.

'What's that?'

'I dread to think,' Charlie said, 'but I believe it's a key to some kind of locker.'

Anna frowned. 'Where?'

'A placed called Extrahome.'

'That's a storage place, isn't it? Out on the Bromleigh Road.'

Charlie looked at Anna. 'Her friend had a spare key. Apparently Libby's got the other.'

'And you think there's more stuff there?'

'I don't know what to think,' Charlie said hopelessly, 'but I can't imagine it's empty, can you? Not knowing Libby.'

Anna took a deep breath. 'When's she back?'

'Not until six at least. She's over at Ursula's with Toby.'

Anna looked at the clock. 'That gives us plenty of time, at least.

Do you want to take a trip out there?'

'Not really,' Charlie said, 'but I suppose we should.'

The man at the reception of Extrahome checked Charlie's key and looked at him and Anna. 'Down the corridor on the left,' he said, nodding them through.

'Number twenty-four,' Charlie said. 'I don't suppose we can shift it all to Room 101,' he said with a grin.

'Better wait and see what's in it first,' Anna said.

The place was vast with rows of white doors with neat black numbers at their centre. The floors were hard and grey and the strip lighting was harsh and unwelcoming. Anna took an instant dislike to it and hoped they'd be in and out of there as quickly as possible.

'Here,' Anna said as they reached door twenty-four at last.

Charlie gulped. 'I had hoped it would be a simple locker like at a railway station,' he said, realising that door twenty-four opened into a room.

'You can't fit much in a locker,' Anna said as Charlie opened the door. 'And maybe it's only a small room.'

They both gasped. As rooms went, it was fairly small but Libby had always had the ability to pack the smallest space with the greatest volume of stuff.

'Oh my god,' Charlie exclaimed. 'It's worse than I thought.'

Anna sighed. She'd been trying to keep calm for Charlie's sake but what she saw nearly bowled her over. Like the house they'd just left, the room was stacked with boxes but there were also carrier bags: large and small, and items placed loose around the room at intervals. One, in particular, caught Anna's eye. It was some kind of Indian totem pole. She frowned, looking around as if she might see more but was relieved to discover that there was only the one.

'At the moment,' Anna whispered.

'What?' Charlie asked.

'The totem pole. Only one.'

Charlie nodded. His face was ashen. 'My god,' he said. It was all that he could manage.

Anna was able to contain her shock slightly better than Charlie but she could barely curb her anger and frustration. Had her sister really accumulated all this stuff herself? It must have taken months if not years. And when had she found the time? Shopping – at this level – took time to say nothing of carrying it all home. Looking around the room, something occurred to Anna. She couldn't remember exactly when it had been but it wasn't long ago. They'd been sitting in Libby's kitchen together, chatting over a cup of tea when, suddenly, the cooker alarm clock went off.

'Cooking something nice?' Anna had asked.

'Oh, no,' Libby had said. 'I've got to place a bid on this fabulous handbag online.' And off she'd disappeared to the computer upstairs. Anna had a feeling that a good proportion of her sister's collection had been bought over the internet. How much easier it was than scouring shops. How quick too. It was just so easy to press a few buttons and part with your money.

Charlie was bending over some of the boxes and trying to see their contents and Anna decided to do the same.

'Some of this stuff's never even been opened. Look,' she said a moment later, pointing to one corner of the room where a stack of boxed dolls stood.

'Maybe she's collecting them for the future? You know when boxed items increase in value,' Charlie said with optimism.

Anna gazed wide-eyed at her brother-in-law. 'You don't honestly believe that, do you?'

Charlie sighed. 'I suppose not.'

Anna crouched down and looked inside a particularly large box. 'Curtains,' she said. 'Stacks of curtains.'

'But we've got curtains,' Charlie said, bemused.

It was then that Anna spotted another carrier bag filled with envelopes. 'What's in here?' She opened the bag and took out a handful. 'Oh, no,' she said.

'What are they?' Charlie asked, taking a step forward.

Anna had already taken two letters out from their envelopes. Only they weren't letters – they were bills. 'I'm afraid they're credit card statements,' she said.

'Give them here,' Charlie said. Anna handed over the two statements and Charlie sucked his teeth when he saw them. 'Anna!' he exclaimed. 'These are for thousands of pounds.'

Anna nodded. 'And the bag's full of them.'

'Does that mean they've not been paid? Why's she keeping them here?'

Anna sighed. She could see exactly why Libby was keeping the bills under lock and key: because she didn't want Charlie seeing them.

Pure anger coursed through Anna. She knew Libby and Charlie had a huge mortgage to pay and that Charlie's new business had meant taking out a crippling loan. The last thing they needed at the moment was more debt. Anna looked around the room, trying to estimate what everything might be worth but it was impossible to know.

They left Extrahome half an hour later, having given the storage room a thorough going over for more bills.

Charlie's face was completely white.

'It'll be all right,' Anna said.

'How? *How's* it going to be all right?'

Anna placed a hand on his shoulder. 'We'll talk to her – *both* of us. She's got to listen. This can't go on.'

'But there's thousands of pounds worth of stuff, Anna.'

'I know. But we'll find a way to sort it out.'

Reaching home, they parked the car and walked up the path to the house.

Charlie opened the front door.

'Toby!' he exclaimed, seeing his son sitting on the one seat in the living room that wasn't covered in boxes. 'You're home,' he said, unnecessarily. 'What's the matter?'

Anna frowned for it was obvious that her nephew had been crying. 'Toby?' she said, crouching down beside him. 'What is it? Where's Mummy?'

Toby sniffed loudly. 'Mummy left.'

'When?' Charlie asked.

Toby shrugged. 'We got home and then she left.'

Anna looked at Charlie. 'It's all the boxes,' she said. 'I think she must have guessed what's happened.'

'Toby,' Charlie said, kneeling down beside his son, 'where's Mummy gone? Did she say anything?'

Toby's eyes filled with tears but he didn't answer his father. Instead, he slipped off the sofa and, tripping over a huge carrier bag full of sequinned cushions, ran out of the room and up the stairs to his bedroom.

CHAPTER 29

'She's gone. Just upped and left, Anna,' Charlie said, pacing the room as much as he could with the boxes crowded around him.

'Okay, don't panic,' Anna said, instantly panicking. 'Have you any idea where she might be?'

'No, I – er – *no*!'

'Think, Charlie. There must be somewhere. A friend's house. Somewhere nearby. She didn't take her car, did she?'

'No. Her car's here.'

'So she must've walked.'

'But she might have called a taxi. She could be anywhere – miles away by now!'

'Keep it together, Charlie. Come on. *Think!*'

'Okay, okay,' he said, taking a deep breath in an attempt to calm himself.

Anna heard him sigh. 'Is there *any*where you can think of?' she asked.

'Just one place, really. She has a friend called Cat.'

'Okay,' Anna said. 'And where's she?'

Charlie told Anna the address. 'I should go too,' he said.

'Don't be silly. You stay here with Toby, okay? I'll call you as soon as I have any news.'

Charlie nodded. 'I can't believe this is happening. What on earth's got into her?'

'We'll find out, okay?' Anna said.

'And then there's all those things at yours too.'

'What do you mean?'

'The things she takes round to yours. I know she's doing it. She pretended that this doll's house was for you but I knew it wasn't.'

Anna frowned. 'There isn't anything at mine.'

'Are you sure?'

Anna gasped. 'The earring!' she said. 'Libby was round mine whilst I was in London.'

Charlie looked puzzled.

'Look, we'll have to check that out another time. I'll get round to this Cat's place first, okay?'

'Call me as soon as you know anything, won't you?'

'Of course,' she said and then she did something she hadn't done since the day of her sister's wedding – she embraced Charlie, giving him a big kiss on his cheek. 'It'll be all right,' she told him. 'I promise.'

He nodded solemnly and she left the house and got in her car. She was worried. Libby had never behaved like this before. It just wasn't like her to walk out on her family.

Looking at the address Charlie had given her, Anna hoped with all her heart that her sister was there.

As she drove across town, she couldn't help wondering what might be hiding in her loft at home. Was it as full as that storage room, she wondered? How hadn't anyone realised before how out of control things had got? As soon as she asked the question, she realised what the answer was: everyone was wrapped up in their own little worlds with their own problems. She had been so focussed on Meg over the last few days that nothing else had existed – not William and certainly not Libby. Just as Charlie must have been so busy at work. That was life, wasn't it? Nobody was to blame but it meant that situations like these were allowed to escalate and she felt truly awful that Libby hadn't had the support she'd obviously needed.

'But she has now,' Anna told herself.

Finding Cat's house, Anna parked in the driveway and rang the bell. It didn't take long for the door to be answered and, as soon as Anna saw Cat, she knew that her sister was there.

'Is Libby here?' she asked, knowing the question was unnecessary.

Cat looked a little anxious but then nodded. 'You'd better come in,' she said, leading Anna into a long hallway. 'She's upstairs. She asked me not to call anyone but I've been beside myself, really. She won't talk to me. She just locked herself in our bedroom. I keep knocking and checking up on her and I can hear her crying but she insists she's okay. What on earth's going on? Has something happened with Charlie?'

Anna shook her head. 'No. Nothing like that. She's just got herself into a state.'

Cat looked annoyed that Anna wasn't confiding in her. 'Is it about her collecting?'

Anna was a little taken aback. She hadn't known Cat knew about her sister's habit but, then again, she was a good friend.

'Yes,' Anna said. 'It is.'

'I thought it might be. She's got some of her boxes round here and asked me if I'd take some more just last week but the spare room's full as it is. I felt awful saying no but we'll be needing that room soon. Terry's mum's coming down to stay and that'll be her bedroom.'

Anna nodded. 'Is there much stuff in there?'

'You can have a look if you want,' Cat said, leading the way upstairs to the spare room.

It was pretty much the scene Anna expected: a room stacked with neat packing boxes. She didn't even want to look inside them.

'They've got to go,' Cat said. 'I've told her.'

'We'll deal with it,' Anna said. 'I promise. Is Libby in there?' Anna asked, nodding towards the bedroom door which was closed.

Cat nodded. 'Can I get you a tea or coffee?'

'No thanks,' Anna said, shaking her head.

'I'll leave you to it, then,' Cat said. 'I hope you have better luck than me.' She retreated back down the stairs, leaving Anna with a little privacy.

Taking a deep breath, Anna knocked on the bedroom door. 'Libby?' She paused. 'It's me, Anna. Are you okay?' She waited a moment. 'I've just been speaking to Charlie. He's really worried about you. He's desperate for you to come home. And Toby too. He wants to see his mummy. Libby?' Anna bit her lip. Was her sister really in there at all? 'Let me in, Lib.' She knocked lightly on the door again.

Finally, after what seemed an eternity to Anna, she heard a lock slide. She pushed the door open and walked inside. Libby was standing by the window, her back to the room.

'Libby? Are you okay?'

Libby didn't reply but gave a little shrug.

'Look at me,' Anna said.

Libby turned around and Anna saw that her face was red and tear-stained.

'Libby!' Anna cried. 'Look at the state of you!' In a few brief steps, Anna was by her side, hugging her in a tight embrace and Libby was sobbing, great wracking sobs that wrenched Anna's heart.

'I've m-made such a t-terrible mess,' Libby stammered between sobs. 'Oh, Anna! I don't know what to do.'

Anna let her cry. There was no point trying to sort things out until she'd calmed down. Instead, she stroked her hair and hugged her close as an avalanche of pain flowed freely from her.

'It's all right,' Anna said soothingly. 'We'll sort it out. There's nothing that can't be sorted.'

Libby pulled away a little and Anna found a tissue for her from her pocket and watched as Libby trumpeted into it.

'Let's sit down,' Anna said, ushering her towards the window seat which overlooked the street.

'I don't know where to begin,' Libby said after a few moments. 'It's all so huge.'

'How long have you known you were in trouble?' Anna asked quietly.

Libby shrugged. 'I don't know,' she said. 'I guess a while now. But I've tried to forget about it. It's been too awful to think about.'

Anna swallowed hard, wondering how her sister would react to her confession. 'We found your bills,' she said.

'What?'

'In the storage place,' Anna said.

Libby hid her face in her hands.

'It's all right,' Anna assured her.

'How can it be?'

'Because we know what we're up against now.'

'But they're not the only ones,' Libby told her, her eyes like huge wounds in her reddened face.

'I know,' Anna said.

'Oh, god! I feel so ashamed. 'Did Charlie see them?'

Anna nodded. 'Yes.'

'What did he say?'

'Not much. He was just worried.'

'About paying everything?'

'Well, yes, but he's mostly worried about you,' Anna said.

'He must hate me,' Libby cried.

'He's never said that, has he?'

Libby blew her nose. 'No,' she admitted. 'But I could see it in his eyes the other day when I got a delivery.'

'That wasn't hate,' Anna said. 'That was worry. He's so worried about you. And Toby is too. And me!'

Libby shook her head. 'I've let you all down. I'm *so* stupid. I don't deserve any of you.'

'Don't say that,' Anna said, hugging her again.

'But it's true.'

'Look, all this has just got a bit out of hand, that's all. It's not the end of the world,' Anna said. 'We can get through this.'

They sat in silence for a moment. Libby was the first to speak.

'I'm afraid I've been hiding stuff in your loft too.'

'I thought you might've been. You dropped an earring on the stairs.'

'Tinkerbell?'

Anna nodded. 'Safe and sound on my dressing table.'

'Oh, thank goodness,' Libby set. 'She's a limited edition.'

Anna's eyebrows rose at the phrase and Libby instantly bit her lip.

'We've got to sort things out,' Anna said.

'What do you mean?'

Anna sighed. 'You know what I mean.'

Libby looked momentarily perplexed but then she seemed to understand.

'It's not just you, you know.' Anna cast her eyes to the floor. 'It's had the most awful effect on me too.'

'How? I don't understand, Anna.'

'Mum,' Anna said simply.

Libby frowned. 'Go on.'

'Ever since I took on this book about the Fox Hill collection, I've been reading a lot about collections and collectors too.' Anna paused. 'And I think I know why this collecting of yours has got out of control. Just think about it. When did you start collecting?'

Libby looked a little puzzled. 'Ages ago,' she said.

Anna nodded. 'When you were about seven or eight, wasn't it?'

'Yes,' Libby said. 'So what does that prove?'

'It was when we were all together – as a family,' Anna said. 'A *proper* family before Dad died and Mum went off the rails completely.'

'What are you getting at?' Libby asked with a frown.

'You felt safe then. Collecting was a joy. It was something you did when you were happy,' Anna said. 'And perhaps that's why you're collecting now – to make yourself feel safe. It reminds you of those times.'

Libby blew her nose again and looked at Anna. 'I've never really thought about my collecting. Not really. Not until the last few days,' she said. 'But then I got all these bills at once. It seemed to be raining statements and I was looking at all the items on the bills and wondering how on earth I'd managed to buy so much. Oh, Anna!'

'Don't worry,' Anna said, placing her hand on her sister's.

Libby shook her head and Anna thought she was going to cry again but she didn't. 'I began to wonder why I was doing it,' she said. 'Why did I have this need to keep on buying and buying? And the things I was buying – things I'll probably never even look at again, let alone use.' She gave a huge sigh.

'We did come across some rather odd things in the storage locker,' Anna said, daring a little smile.

Libby gave a weak smile back. 'Don't tell me. I don't want to think about it.'

They were quiet and the gentle tick of a bedside clock was the only sound in the room.

'I've done something awful,' Anna said at last, feeling the time was right for her own confession. 'I knew at the time that it was wrong but there was a part of me that wasn't listening.'

'What is it?' Libby asked, concern in her voice.

'You know this article I'm writing?'

'Of course – about William Kitson and his collection.'

Anna nodded. 'I kind of got sidetracked by another story.'

'You mean, one that's nothing to do with William?'

'Well, it's very much to do with William, I'm afraid.'

Libby waited for more. 'What's the story, Anna?' she asked after a moment.

'There's someone living with him,' Anna said at last.

'With William?' Libby said in surprise. 'But I thought he was a confirmed old bachelor.'

'Oh, he is. But there's an old lady at Fox Hill. Really old. She says she's the oldest woman in the world and you should hear the stories she has to tell. She's amazing, Libby. You'd love her.'

'Wow,' Libby said. 'She sounds wonderful. I had no idea there was anyone living with him but why's that a problem for you?'

'William didn't want me to write about her,' Anna explained. 'He didn't even want me to talk to her but I went behind his back. You know what I'm like when I get wind of a story?'

Libby nodded. 'Oh, yes.'

'Well, William was away for a couple of nights. I'd left the manor by then but I went over there again to see Meg and, well, to cut a long story short, I ended up taking Meg to London and we kind of got a lot of publicity.'

Libby frowned. 'In the papers, you mean?'

'And on TV. I'm surprised you've not seen anything about it.'

'We don't get a newspaper,' Libby said. 'And the only TV we watch is for Toby and, well, the shopping channels.'

'Anyway,' Anna continued, tying her hands in knots in her lap, 'everyone's fascinated by Meg. She's turned into a bit of a superstar and the press are hanging around the manor now. William's furious.'

'But what's wrong with that?' Libby asked, cocking her head to one side. 'She's obviously led an interesting life.'

'Yes, she has but William insisted that I wasn't to write about it.'

'But he doesn't control what you can and can't write,' Libby pointed out, instantly backing up her sister's point of view.

'I know he can't but that's not the point really.'

'Then what *is* the point? Why shouldn't you have written about her?'

Anna stared into space for what seemed like an eternity. 'It's just – well – I've been thinking about why I wrote the story in the first place and I don't like what I've come up with.'

'What is it?' Libby said gently.

'Why would I go against William's wishes like that when I knew it was wrong? When I knew I loved him.'

'Anna!'

'I know,' Anna said with a sigh. 'I've managed to go and fall in love, haven't I?'

'But that's wonderful!' Libby said and her face broke into a smile. 'Does he feel the same way?'

Anna shrugged. 'I think he did – once upon a time before I went and shouted Meg's story from the rooftops.'

'But you're a journalist. That's your job,' Libby said.

'I don't think that's why I did it.'

'Then *why*?'

Anna looked down at her hands. 'I think I'm still trying to impress Mum.'

Libby's mouth dropped open. 'Really?'

Anna nodded. 'I wanted to do something that would make her take notice of me.'

'But why?'

'I don't know! I mean, we haven't spoken for years. Why can't I just accept that she doesn't care? It's ridiculous, isn't it? I'm a grown woman and I'm still reaching out to this person who really doesn't want anything to do with us.'

Libby rested her head on her sister's shoulder. 'It isn't just you,' she said. 'We've both made mistakes – both of us seem to have chosen destructive ways of dealing with it.'

'But *why?*'

'Why?' Libby said. 'Because she's our mother and I guess we haven't taken easily to being ignored. But – and I know this is going to sound so like a self-help manual – I guess we have to confront our past if we're to have a happy future.'

'But it makes me so angry when I think about it,' Anna said. 'What she did to us. How could she just leave like that after Dad died? She didn't say a word. No note, no call – nothing! And I know we were both old enough to take care of ourselves but it just seemed such a heartless thing to do.'

Libby raised her head. 'I know,' she said. 'I don't think I'll ever understand how she could have done that. But we mustn't continue being angry. We've got to get on with our own lives now. I've got a wonderful husband and son and you've got your sparkling career as a renowned journalist.'

Anna looked at Libby. 'You sound so wonderfully in control.'

'Do I? Well, that's the first time in a long while.' Libby reached out and squeezed her hand and Anna instantly felt tears welling up.

'What a mess,' Anna whispered.

'Yes,' Libby said, 'but at least it's a mess we're in together. You know, Charlie said I needed help.'

'What do you mean?'

'The other night, he told me he knew something was wrong – deep down wrong, you know?'

Anna nodded.

'And he said he thought I should talk to someone about it – someone who could help.'

'You mean like a psychologist?' Anna said.

'I guess,' Libby said.

'Well, I don't suppose it would do any harm,' she said. 'I could even come with you.'

'Really? You'd do that for me?'

Anna smiled. 'I think it's something we could probably both benefit from,' she said, taking her sister's hands and squeezing them encouragingly.

Libby nodded. 'I hadn't realised how much our past had affected us both until this moment – not truly, anyway.'

'I know,' Anna said. 'I think you tend to bury these things deep within you but they find a way of coming out, don't they? In confusing and destructive ways that you often can't control.' She smiled lightly. 'But we're taking control now, aren't we?'

'Yes,' Libby said.

'Together.'

'Together,' Libby agreed, resting her forehead against her sister's.

Anna blinked her tears away before giving a great sigh. 'Now, we've got to get you home,' Anna said. 'Charlie and Toby will be worrying.' She stood up from the bed and waited for Libby.

'I'm scared,' Libby said suddenly.

'What of?'

'Of facing Charlie.'

Anna's face creased into sympathy. 'Libby! That man adores you. If you'd chopped his garden shed up for fuel, he'd still adore you.'

'But all that money–'

'Will be paid. I promise,' Anna said. 'I've got the most amazing idea.'

'You have?'

Anna nodded.

'What?'

'Wait and see.'

'Oh, Anna!'

'I've got to talk to William first. And, if *I* can do that then *you* can jolly well talk to Charlie,' she said. 'Come on. Let's get you home.'

CHAPTER 30

Anna was both looking forward to and dreading speaking to William. She was desperate for news about Meg and she was longing to hear William's voice again.

'Even if it's full of condemnation,' she said to herself. She spent the whole morning pacing up and down before picking the phone up and ringing.

'Hello,' a female voice said. 'Fox Hill Manor.'

'Oh, Mrs Boothby!'

'Anna?'

'Yes. How are you?'

'Very well, my dear. How are you?'

'Okay.'

Mrs Boothby sighed. 'I've given that William a good telling off, you know. You should be here. You two youngsters! I don't know. Can't you both tell when you're right for each other?'

Anna was so surprised by this declaration that she didn't know what to say. 'Mrs Boothby!'

'I could see, you know. And now he's gone and scared you off, hasn't he? So stuck in his ways, that one, but I've given him a piece of my mind – that I have! And now all this worry with Meg.'

'Is she okay?' Anna asked.

'She's still in hospital. Stable but needing constant care.'

'I wasn't ever sure how much you knew about her,' Anna said.

'Well, it was kind of William's secret. He never told me the full story, you understand.'

'But why not? I really can't make him out at all sometimes,' Anna said.

'You know our William,' she said and Anna couldn't help smiling at her phrase *our William*. 'Always full of secrets, isn't he? Always wanting to protect people.'

'Yes,' Anna said. 'As I've found to my cost.'

'Now, don't you go taking any notice of anything he's said.'

'But not taking any notice of what he's said is what's got me into trouble with him,' Anna said helplessly.

Mrs Boothby tutted. 'And you want to speak to him now?'

'Is he at home?'

'He is. He's in that confounded stable of his banging bits of wood together. Do you mind waiting?'

'No. I'll wait, Anna said and heard Mrs Boothby putting the phone down. She imagined her walking down the corridor and out the great wooden door at the side of the house, down the golden steps worn with age and out into the stable-block.

She waited, worrying in case the next voice she heard was Mrs Boothby's again. 'I'm sorry,' she'd say, 'but he doesn't want to speak to you.'

Anna wasn't sure what she'd do then. But Mrs Boothby didn't return to the phone and the next voice she heard was William's.

'Anna?'

'Yes,' Anna said and then blanked. She felt completely unable to utter another word because so many of them were tumbling around her head.

'What is it? Are you okay?'

The kindness of his question gave her the prod she needed. 'Yes,' she said, 'well, no. I need your help.'

'My help?'

'Yes. Can I come over?'

There was a pause and Anna groaned inwardly as she imagined him going over the excuses he could use to put her off.

'Of course,' he said and Anna breathed a sigh of relief.

'Thank you.'

'It'll have to be right away. I'm going to visit Meg later.'

'Is she okay? Mrs Boothby said she was still stable.'

'She's got a bit of colour back in her cheeks but the doctors aren't letting her come home yet and she's driving them nuts.'

'I can imagine,' Anna said, relief surging through her. 'I'd love to see her.'

'That wouldn't be a good idea,' William said quickly and Anna felt instantly reprimanded. 'She's not to have too many visitors,' he added.

'But you'll send her my love, won't you?' she asked.

'I will. See you soon, then.'

'I'll leave right away. Thank you, William,' she said.

'You're welcome.'

Anna hung up and breathed a sigh of relief. The ice had been broken but it remained to be seen if it would thaw completely.

She tried not to think much about what lay ahead of her as she drove out into the Elm Valley once more. She was doing this for her sister – that was all. And yet, as she drove the car around the familiar bends in the country roads, she held on to the hope that there might be some kind words between her and William. Meg was stable; no harm had come to her. But would William ever forgive her for what she'd done?

She thought about the kisses they'd shared. How tender and passionate it had been. How adoring William had been – and how amorous! Anna blushed as she thought about it. Had he really been able to push that aside and move on?

Before she knew it, she was through the golden pillars of Fox Hill Manor. The photographers and journalists had long gone and the hills and valley looked so peaceful today and Anna half-wished that she could take off into them, striding across their green expanses and losing herself in the beech woods. It would be easy enough to do. Easy but wrong. So she parked her car and made her way to the side door.

Mrs Boothby was the one to answer.

'Why, Anna! Come in,' she chimed. 'How lovely to have you back at Fox Hill.'

'I'm not staying, I'm afraid. Just popping in.'

'Oh,' Mrs Boothby said, looking slightly crestfallen. 'Well, let me get you a cup of tea to begin with. William's in the living room. He's expecting you and I've told him to be nice to you.'

Anna blushed and followed Mrs Boothby down the wood-panelled hallway. Anna's eyes caught sight of the familiar objects. It was good to see them again. There was the suit of armour Meg had hidden behind and there were the crossed swords and the old longcase clocks. And, as she looked at the front door, she saw the spot where she and William had first kissed.

'Anna's here,' Mrs Boothby said, bringing her back to the present as they entered the living room. William stood up, placing a book on the coffee table in front of him. *Curious Corners of Country Houses.* Anna couldn't help but smile. It was a typical William-type title.

'Hello,' Anna said.

'Hello,' William replied. Neither of them smiled.

'Tea?' Mrs Boothby said with a sigh. 'And perhaps some biscuits.'

William nodded and Anna turned to watch her leave, half-wishing she'd stay with them and warm the room with her presence.

'Have a seat,' William said, as politely and coolly as if he were interviewing her for a job.

Anna sat down and William took his place once more on the sofa opposite her. He was wearing a cream and brown checked shirt, a tweed waistcoat and matching jacket and his hair was as dishevelled as ever and Anna couldn't help but want to reach out and run her fingers through it.

'Any more news about Meg?' she asked.

'No. I'll see her later today,' he said.

'Yes,' Anna said. 'Send her my love.'

'I said I would,' William said and Anna flinched at his words. It was as if he was saying, *Don't waste my time repeating things.* 'You said you needed my help.'

'Yes,' Anna said, deciding it was best to get on with things. 'It's about my sister – Libby.'

'The collector?'

'Yes. She's in trouble.'

William frowned at the news. 'What's the matter?'

'She's not just been collecting, I'm afraid. She's been buying en masse,' Anna said. 'Her husband, Charlie, called me. He'd known for a while that something was wrong but he hadn't realised the extent of the problem. It seems she's let things get totally out of control. There are masses of things she's kept round friends' houses – mine too – I had no idea but she's been using my loft as storage, and she's hired a place to store things too – Charlie and I went to see it and it's chock full of stuff.'

'What sort of stuff?'

Anna sighed. 'Everything you can think of. Dolls, totem poles, plates, figurines, hats – *every*thing!'

'All new?'

'I'd say most of it was. A lot are still in the original packing boxes from the manufacturer. I think she's also bought a lot second-hand but I don't think there are any real antiques. It's not the same sort of collection as here. I don't think any of it's going to be worth anything in the future and – in the meantime – she's got herself into the most appalling debt. She didn't tell me how much or how many credit cards she has but we're easily talking about thousands of pounds.'

It was at that moment that Mrs Boothby came in with the tea things, laying down the floral-patterned tray with teapot, cups and saucers, milk and sugar and a plate of lemon and ginger biscuits.

'You two getting on all right?' she asked, as if they were a pair of warring children and she the parent.

'Everything's fine, Mrs Boothby,' William said calmly.

'I'm very pleased to hear it.'

They waited until she'd left the room and then William sat forward and poured the tea.

'I'm very sorry to hear that Libby's in such trouble. I'd be very happy to help in any way I can. Did you have anything particular in mind?'

'Well,' Anna said, 'I was thinking about that auction we went to. They had so many things for sale and I thought it could work really well for Libby. It would be a fast way of getting some money back for her.' She waited for William's thoughts.

'I can see that might work,' he said at length, passing Anna a teacup.

'But?' Anna said. She could definitely hear a 'but' forming on William's lips.

'You say a lot of Libby's things are brand new.'

'Yes. I think they must be.'

'Then she'd be best to return as much stuff as she possibly can. I'm guessing there won't be a problem with that. There's usually a returns policy. She'll just have to pay the postage but she'll be better off doing that than risking a loss at auction.'

Anna nodded. That made sense. Why hadn't she thought about that before? 'Thank you,' she said. 'I guess we'll be spending the next few days at the post office counter, then.'

'I really think that's the quickest way to get as much of the lost money back as possible.'

'And the auction?' Anna asked. 'Can you help?'

'Leave that with me,' William said. 'I think we'll manage something.' With that, he got to his feet. Anna put down her half-finished tea. This obviously wasn't going to be the cosy little chat she'd hoped for. It was a business-only meeting.

'And you'll let me know?' she said.

'Of course,' he said.

'And about Meg too?'

'Yes,' he said flatly.

Anna looked at him. His grey eyes looked tired and had lost a little of their brightness. She desperately wanted to reach out to him but her arms were stiff and she feared his rejection if she moved towards him.

'I'll see you to your car,' he said and Anna could bear it no more. It was time to leave.

She walked the length of the hallway again, searching desperately for something else to say – some magic words that would make everything all right again but nothing came to her and they'd reached the door.

'William?' she said as he opened the door for her. 'William, I–'

'I know,' he interrupted. 'Send Meg your love.'

Anna nodded in defeat. She wasn't about to say that at all.

CHAPTER 31

The next few days flew by in a whirl of packing tape and postage labels as everybody got to work on Libby's collection. They started with the things at home and managed to clear enough space so that the whole family could sit down at once. It was a small miracle.

It was lucky that Charlie had a van because they needed it for the endless trips to the post office. The assistant there was getting accustomed to their visits and had started playing a game of guessing what was inside each of the parcels.

'Another china doll, perhaps?' she asked one morning.

'Not this time,' Libby said. 'It's a miniature sewing machine. Doesn't work or anything. Don't know why I bought it.'

'A moment of madness, perhaps? We all have them,' the assistant said.

'Unfortunately, I seem to have more than my fair share,' Libby told her with a little blush.

When Charlie wasn't at work and Toby was at home from school, they both joined in.

'Where shall I put this, Mummy?' Toby asked, holding a brass bedpan in the air.

'In that huge box marked auction,' Libby told him.

'Will it sell for lots and lots?' he asked, his eyes wide with excitement having seen one too many TV shows in which contestants often hit the jackpot in the sales room.

'More than the twenty pounds I paid for it, I hope,' Libby said.

And on it went with the four of them sifting through heaps of stuff and sorting out the returns from the auction pile.

'The sooner we can pay these credit cards off, the better,' Charlie said.

Anna nodded. 'We'll have to see which is the most desperate. Check the interest rate you're paying on them. We'll prioritise once we know the figures,' she said.

Libby sat back on her heels from where she was sorting through a bag of multi-coloured scarves. 'I don't deserve you two,' she said in a voice that sounded like it might crack at any moment.

'Nonsense,' Anna said, determined to keep things upbeat. 'Now pass me that hideous pink and green scarf. That's going straight in the auction pile.'

Once the house was sorted, they moved on Cat's house and then on to the storage facility.

'If we manage to empty it, we can close it down and save money there too,' Anna said. But it wasn't as easy as that. There was just so much stuff. It took days to clear it and, when they had, they'd filled the house once again.

'Oh, dear!' Libby said. 'There really seems to be no end to it.'

'We mustn't forget Anna's loft too,' Charlie said.

'But where are we going to put all the things for auction?' Libby asked.

'I'll find out,' Anna said, knowing that she'd have to ring William and, because she didn't want to prolong the anxiety, she did it straight away.

'I'm glad you called,' he said when he answered the phone.

Anna's heart lifted a little. 'You are?'

'Yes,' he said. 'I've got it all arranged. We're going to hold the auction right here at FHM.'

'Really?'

'Yes. I thought the courtyard would be a good venue.'

'Well, as long as the weather holds. But I thought you didn't like crowds of people at the manor,' Anna said, surprised by his suggestion.

'I was thinking that we've been in the press so much that people would flock from all over the place to take part in an auction here. It'll be good for Libby's sales,' he said and she could hear the smile in his voice.

Anna was touched that he'd do that for her sister. 'I don't know what to say. It's extraordinarily kind of you.'

'Not at all. Anything to help a fellow collector. There might even be one or two items fitting for the Fox Hill collection.'

That made Anna laugh. 'I somehow doubt it.'

'I'm trying to arrange the auction for the weekend. How would that suit you all? Saturday afternoon. They're going to advertise it in the local papers and the radio and I'm pulling a few strings with an auctioneer friend of mine.'

'That sounds really great,' Anna said.

'And can you get the goods over here?'

'That's actually why I was ringing you. We have so much here, we don't know what to do with it all,' Anna confessed.

'I'll send a van over – would tomorrow be okay?'

'Yes!' Anna said. 'I didn't know you had a van.'

'I haven't but I know a man who has, and I've roped in an old pal who owes me a favour. He'll be on hand for the day if people need help carrying things back to their cars. I'm opening up one of the fields for parking and we're hiring benches and auction paddles and Mrs Boothby's going to be our sales assistant.'

'And Meg?' Anna asked. 'Will she be able to attend?'

'She'll still be in hospital.'

'She's no worse, is she?' Anna asked. 'William?'

'She sleeps a lot,' he said vaguely.

'What have the doctors said?' Anna pressed.

'That she's very old.'

'They've given her an actual age?'

'No. Just warned me not to expect miracles.'

'Oh, William!'

'But she's coming home,' William added, and there was sudden determination in his voice. 'I'll bring her back here. This is where she belongs. I can't bear for her to be any place else.'

There was a pause. 'I miss her so much,' Anna said and realised that tears were threatening to spill. She quickly blinked them away.

'So do I,' William said. 'I've never met anyone like her.' And, with that, he hung up the phone.

William was as good as his word and, the next day, the van arrived for Libby's things. Charlie, Libby and Anna had spent all night sorting through the remaining items and the van was soon full of bags and boxes to be taken to Fox Hill Manor for the auction.

'I can't believe this is really happening,' Libby said. 'It's quite exciting, isn't it?'

'As long as you don't bid for all your own things,' Charlie said with a naughty smile.

Libby play-thumped him but she had to admit that he had a good point. Auctions were rather addictive, weren't they? It would be very easy to be caught up by it all and end up bidding on the very items you were meant to be selling.

'We'll have to arrange it so that you're banned from bidding,' Anna said.

Libby pouted but then grinned. 'I promise I won't bid. As long as you let me keep my original doll's house and those two sun hats. And the china vase shaped like a pineapple.'

'Libby!' Anna warned.

Libby held her hands up in defeat.

Anna and Libby drove out to Fox Hill Manor behind the van.

'I feel so awful about all this,' Libby said. 'All the trouble I've caused everyone.'

'Nonsense. We're all having a ball,' Anna said, grinning at Libby.

Libby didn't seem too sure about that and rolled her eyes. 'And I've been such a rotten sister too. I can't believe I've missed your amazing Meg story in the press. And I've no idea what's going on with you and William. Have you made up?'

'Not exactly,' Anna said. 'He's talking to me, which is a start, I suppose.'

'But you've not leapt into bed together yet?'

'Libby!' Anna said, shocked.

'Well, I want to know!'

'All right then. No. We've most certainly not leapt into bed together.'

'What a shame. I bet he's got a fabulous old four-poster somewhere too. It would be so romantic!'

'Oh, Libby!'

'And he's very cute. Charming too,' Libby said.

Anna looked at Libby, a puzzled expression on her face. 'You've met him?'

'Yes. Didn't I say? He came round when you'd gone AWOL. He was so worried about you. It was really sweet.'

'Not worried about *me*, I fear,' Anna said.

'Yes, I think he was.'

'No,' Anna said. 'Now Charlie – *he* was worried about you. No ulterior motives there.'

'I know,' Libby said. 'I'm very lucky, aren't I?'

'Yes, you are. Most of us only ever dream of finding such a man.'

'But you *have* found one.'

'Have I?' Anna asked.

'Of course you have. You just need to get things sorted out, that's all,' Libby said.

Anna pouted. 'I'm not sure they ever will be. I messed up big time.'

'*You* messed up big time!' Libby laughed. 'Look at me and what I did. If I can find a man to forgive me that, then your man can jolly well forgive you.' Libby sighed. 'I just hope I can get most of these things sold. There's time for Charlie to walk out on me yet.'

'He won't walk out on you,' Anna said. 'Charlie is forever.'

Libby smiled a great warm smile and her eyes pricked with tears. 'Thanks for everything you've done for us,' she said to Anna. 'For me.'

Anna glanced at her sister and her heart filled with love. 'It's been my pleasure,' she said, knowing that Libby was referring to the session they'd recently had with a psychologist. She really felt that sharing their memories of their past together was bringing them closer as well as settling issues that the two sisters had done their best to bury at their cost.

Anna shuddered as she thought back to the days after their father had died. Their mother had been cold and distant, unable to communicate with her daughters so each one of them had been locked into a world of isolated pain, totally unable to reach each other. And then she'd left. Anna had just started her first job as a young reporter on a local paper and Libby was finishing sixth-form. They'd both come home one day to find their mother gone and the next thing they knew, their family home had been put up for sale.

They'd never heard from her again but had made their way through life still carrying the scars of that strange and cruel departure and they hadn't realised how much it had affected them until Libby's breakdown but, talking it all through now, things were beginning to make sense to Anna. She'd had been right all along – Libby's collection had just been a way of masking her pain from all those years ago and buying herself things and surrounding herself with beautiful objects had been a kind of comfort blanket – a very expensive comfort blanket. She'd remembered those early days of collecting when she'd been a little girl and how it had brought focus to her life and had been a safe and healthy thing to do but it had escalated into something dangerous and destructive.

And what about herself? Anna's own destructive behaviour had come from her unhealthy obsession with her work and the wondering if her mother would see the pieces she had written and if they would prompt her to get into contact with her daughters again. She never had, of course, but Anna kept pushing anyway. That's why she'd risked so much with the Meg story – because it was so huge. Her mother was bound to hear about it, wasn't she?

'And I've lost William because of it,' she whispered to herself.

'What's that?' Libby asked.

Anna shook her head. 'Nothing,' she said, putting all thoughts of the past out of her mind for now. 'Just wait until you see this place,' she added, turning into the driveway of Fox Hill Manor just behind the van. 'You're going to love it.'

Libby did. She *wowed* and *goshed* most appreciatively. 'Now I can see why you want to make things work with William.'

'Libby! What a thing to say.'

'I'm just teasing. Still, it's some house, isn't it?'

'And I very much doubt there's room for me in it. He's got it packed with his collection.'

'He'll make room,' Libby said.

Anna parked the car and they were both walking towards the house when William appeared to greet them, Cocoa and Beanie dancing in a mad furry frenzy at the feet of the visitors.

'Libby!' William said, leaning forward and kissing her cheeks. 'Lovely to see you again.'

'And you too,' Libby said, returning his kisses. 'Thank you so much for all this.'

'It's my pleasure.' He then turned towards Anna, leaning forward and kissing her cheeks. It was the first physical contact they'd had since they'd kissed in the hallway and Anna's skin tingled as he touched her. 'Anna,' he said simply.

'Hello,' she said, their eyes meeting briefly before William pulled away and clapped his hands together.

'Right,' he said, 'let's get to work.'

There was then a period of several hours when everyone pitched in with unpacking and sorting the items into lots. William cast his eye over each piece, carefully assessing its worth.

'What's the verdict?' Libby asked him after he'd seen virtually everything.

'Well,' William said, scratching his head, 'you'll only get a fraction of what you paid for most of the items. I'm afraid the majority of the collection isn't really up to much – not in terms of accumulating value over time, I mean. But there are some nice pieces.'

'Okay,' Libby said.

'Most of the items will have to be sold as individual lots but there are some quite nice collections too. The animal ornaments, for example, and some of the dolls. They're perennial favourites of collectors and you should get a fair price for them.'

'Well that sounds promising,' Libby said. 'And you are taking a fair cut, aren't you? I don't want anyone to be out of pocket for all the trouble you're going to.'

'I wouldn't hear of it,' William said. 'But Mrs Boothby is arranging tours of the gardens at a small fee. Refreshments too. All proceeds will go towards restoring the wing upstairs. I must say, I'm rather looking forward to it all,' he told her.

'So am I,' Libby said.

The two of them smiled at each other and Anna couldn't help but feel a little left out.

Finally, the day of the auction dawned and a clear, speedwell-blue sky meant that everyone sighed with relief. Although the publicity circus which had surrounded Meg had died down, it had made it easy for William to get lots of attention for the auction and, by the time it was due to start, it was standing room only in the courtyard of Fox Hill Manor.

Anna, Libby, Charlie and Toby all arrived with plenty of time to spare and William was there to greet them along with Mrs Boothby and his auctioneer friend, Roger Bergman.

'I never thought there'd be so many people!' Libby said. 'I hope they won't be disappointed when they discover it's not proper antiques.'

William shook his head. 'Everyone knows what to expect and I'm sure we'll be successful.'

He led them to a bench from where they could see all the action and they watched as people got themselves comfortable and Roger took his place on the homemade platform at the front of the crowd. A microphone had been rigged up and, once that was operational after several ear-piercing screeches, the auction was under way.

Anna watched, her eyes wide as she took in the enormity of her sister's collection for the last time. There went the miniature hat collection and the *Romance of Steam* china plates and the *Dawn Chorus* teapots. Anna glanced at Libby to see how she was coping. She had grabbed hold of Charlie's hand and was squeezing the life out of it as she saw her colourful collection leaving forever.

'I rather like those teapots,' Toby said.

'Why didn't you say something? I would have bought them for you,' Libby said and she was absolutely serious.

Charlie raised his eyebrows. 'Libby?'

She sighed and nodded. 'I know,' she said.

'I didn't *want* them, Mummy,' Toby said. 'I've got everything I want.'

Libby cupped his face in her hands and kissed his cheeks. 'You darling boy!'

'Aw, Mum!'

Anna watched with a grin and then stood up. 'I'm just going to have a word with Mrs Boothby,' she told Libby. 'See if she needs any help with anything.'

'Okay,' Libby said.

Anna made her way out of the courtyard, squeezing through the crowds as best as she could.

'Hello, my dear!' Mrs Boothby said as Anna approached. She was standing at the back of the crowd wearing a pretty little sun hat with a green ribbon around it. 'Seen anything you like?'

'I'm afraid not,' Anna said, 'but I'm not really here to buy anything.'

'I'm hoping to make a bid on the china dogs later. My sister adores anything like that. You off somewhere?' she asked. 'Not staying for tea and scones at half-time?

'I'm afraid I've got to run,' Anna said.

'What a shame. Will you be back for the end?'

'I expect so but don't wait for me,' Anna told her.

Mrs Boothby nodded absent-mindedly as another lot came up under the hammer and Anna made her escape.

She felt awful. She hadn't been going to offer her help to Mrs Boothby at all and she probably wouldn't be back for the end of the auction either.

She was going to visit Meg.

CHAPTER 32

Anna wasn't sure what Meg was able to eat and she certainly wouldn't be able to read magazines so she stopped off at a florists and chose a beautiful bunch of delicate freesias. Their scent was delicious and their colours reminded Anna of a summer sunset. They were perfect.

Ten minutes later, she entered the hospital and went up to reception. 'I'm here to see a patient,' she announced.

'What name, please?'

'Meg.'

'And the surname?'

Anna bit her lip. 'She doesn't actually have one.'

The receptionist frowned. 'No surname? Are you sure? Everyone needs to be registered properly.

Anna thought quickly. 'Try Kitson. Meg Kitson.'

The receptionist tapped the name into her computer. 'Ah, here we are. You want ward six. Take the lift over there. It's on the third floor, right out of the lift.'

'Thank you,' Anna said, and followed her instructions, exiting the lift on the third floor.

The enormous windows provided an impressive view across the Cotswold landscape and Anna hope that Meg could make some of it out from her bed.

At the ward's reception, Anna was pointed in the right direction for Meg and found her in a room with three other beds. She was by the window on the left-hand side.

'Meg!' Anna said in a half gasp, half shout.

'Anna?' Meg's voice croaked. 'Is that you?'

'Yes,' Anna said, pulling the visitor's chair up next to the bed and taking Meg's hand in hers. 'You're so cold. Don't they keep you warm in here?'

'They try to but I'm a hopeless case, I'm afraid,' she said, a sweet smile crossing her pale face.

Anna opened her handbag and brought out the scarlet gloves she kept in there. 'Remember these?' she said, handing them to Meg.

'From our trip to London?' she said.

'Yes. Here,' Anna said, helping her to put them on and watching as Meg rubbed her hands together in delight.

'They're so soft,' she said, closing her eyes and sighing.

'They'll keep you warm.'

'And what will you do?' she asked in concern.

'Believe it or not, it's actually warming up out there today. William's holding an auction in the courtyard of the manor and nobody's even shivering. Can you believe it? I think summer's here at last.'

'Why aren't you there?' Meg asked.

'Because I'm here,' Anna said.

'Ah,' Meg said knowingly. 'A secret visit whilst nobody's looking?'

Anna smiled at her astuteness. 'You could say that.'

'He told you not to visit me, didn't he?' Meg said, suddenly looking displeased. 'He *is* a silly man sometimes.'

'No,' Anna said in his defence. 'He just cares about you – that's all.'

'But I wanted to see you!' Meg said defiantly. 'It shouldn't be up to William whom I can see.'

'Really? You wanted to see me?'

'Of course,' Meg said. 'Why do you sound so surprised? I got your card but that just isn't the same at all, is it? I wanted to *see* you.'

'Because I thought I'd caused you enough trouble already.'

'Nonsense. I loved every minute of it.'

Anna let out a sigh. 'I'm so relieved to hear you say that. I've been so worried about you.'

It was Meg's turn to give a squeeze of comfort. 'I'm an old woman, Anna, dear. I'm bound to tire every now and again. I just overdid things, that's all. Nothing to worry about.'

Anna watched as Meg closed her eyes. It gave her a chance to really look at Meg properly and she didn't like what she saw. Her face was completely drained of colour and she looked so fragile.

'What a sleepy head I'm turning into,' Meg said, her pearly-blue eyes opening again.

'And here I am bothering you.'

'You're no bother,' Meg said. 'You shouldn't keep thinking that you are.'

'Still, I guess I should get going,' Anna said.

'Before you're missed?'

'Something like that,' Anna said with a laugh.

'What will you say if you *have* been missed? Meg asked.

'The truth,' Anna said. 'I shall tell the truth.'

'Won't you get into trouble?'

'I expect so but I don't care.'

They looked at each other, their smiles locked together.

'Will you come again?' Meg asked.

'Of course I will but I'm expecting you'll be back at Fox Hill before I have a chance to visit here again.'

Meg didn't say anything.

'Won't you?' Anna added.

Meg sighed. 'Oh, I expect so,' she said.

'Of *course* you will. Now,' Anna said, getting up from her chair, 'I'd better let you get some rest.'

'Anna?' Meg said, grabbing her hand in her newly gloved one as she moved away.

'Yes?'

'Thank you for coming. I've so enjoyed our time together. All of it. Every minute.'

'Me too, Meg. And there'll be lots more to come too. I'll make sure of that.'

But Meg had closed her eyes again and Anna took a last look at her still wearing the scarlet gloves before quietly leaving the ward. She looked peaceful there, bathed in the light from the window and Anna only wished that she could spend more time with her.

William was the first to notice that Anna was missing. The auction had ended with a roaring round of applause and a dozen photographers had descended to take pictures of him with Libby.

'How's Meg, Mr Kitson?' a man from the back of the group yelled.

'She's stable,' William said, looking around for Anna's face as the crowds ebbed away from the courtyard.

'When will she be coming home?'

'We don't know yet,' William said, and then he suddenly realised where Anna was. 'With Meg!'

'What's that?' Libby asked.

'Where's your sister?'

'She's gone to help Mrs Boothby,' Libby told him.

William pushed his way through the photographers. Gone to help Mrs Boothby indeed. He didn't believe that for a single moment and, sure enough, when he found Mrs Boothby, Anna wasn't anywhere to be seen.

Anna had meant to go straight back to the manor but, for some reason, she passed the entrance and kept on driving. She wound down her window and inhaled the sweet air, full of the promise of summer. The light was dazzlingly bright and there was a soft breeze that made the trees dance and shimmer.

She wasn't sure where she was heading until she saw it: Chambers Cross – the place where she'd taken Meg on the day they'd headed to London. Parking her car, she walked through the long grasses to the lichen-covered bench where she and Meg had sat. How long ago that day seemed now, she thought. That was the last time Meg had been truly anonymous, wasn't it?

Anna looked out across the great expanse of the Elm Valley. There was the spire of St George's in Elmington and there was the curving road that had brought her here. She looked across at the fields and the tiny farmsteads to where the first poppies were opening and thought of Meg remembering the A E Housman poem.

'And since to look at things in bloom, Fifty springs are little room.'

For some reason, the words seemed particularly poignant today.

'I wish you were here, Meg,' Anna whispered into the wind. She didn't feel the bench belonged to her alone anymore and she felt strange sitting there on her own and so returned to her car and drove back along the lanes to Fox Hill Manor.

She was genuinely surprised to see that the courtyard was completely empty when she got back. The benches and auctioneer's podium were still in place but there wasn't a single soul present. Until–

'William,' she said, suddenly seeing him walking towards her. His expression looked dark and troubled and Anna immediately knew that she was in trouble.

'Okay,' Anna said, holding her hands up, 'I know what you're going to say. I should have told you where I was going but I thought you'd tell me not to and I had to see Meg. I've waited so long. You don't blame me, do you?'

There was a pause and then William spoke.

'Anna – Meg's dead.'

Anna face froze in agony. 'What do you mean?'

'She died. About half an hour ago. I've just taken the call from the hospital.' His face was ash-white and his eyes sparkled with unshed tears from behind his glasses.

Anna shook her head. 'No,' she said. 'That can't be right. I just saw her. I was with her!'

William nodded. 'I know. They told me.' He placed a hand on her shoulder.

'I was *there*,' Anna said, her voice sounding far away. 'How can she be dead?' She shook his hand from her shoulder and moved away from him.

'Anna–'

'I shouldn't have left. I should've been there with her. Why did I leave?'

'You mustn't blame yourself.'

'But you do, don't you?' Anna said. '*You* blame me – for everything. For taking her away from here and telling the whole world her story. *You* blame me!'

'I didn't say that.'

Anna's mind was whirling crazily. 'And you're right. It's my fault that she's dead. If I hadn't taken her to London, she'd be alive today – safe here.'

'We don't know that,' William said, taking a step towards Anna but she moved away again. 'She was old. It was going to happen one day.'

'No! It *shouldn't* have happened. Meg was meant to live, don't you see? She had so much more to give. She can't be dead. She *can't!*'

'Anna–'

Anna turned to look at him, her vision blurred by tears. She didn't know what to do and barely saw William coming towards her again nor felt his arms around her, holding her tightly as she cried.

She had no idea how long they stood like that, bound together by their grief, tears taking the place of words.

'Meg!' Anna called out at one point.

'Shush,' William said. 'She's at rest now. She's at rest.'

Anna pushed away from William and looked up at him. She didn't want to be there. She didn't want him to see the appalling guilt she felt. She needed to get away and so she ran to her car, starting the engine before William had a chance to stop her.

'Anna!' he called after her but she didn't stop to listen to him. Whatever he had to say could make no difference to her now because she felt as if she was directly responsible for the death of the sweetest person she'd ever known.

CHAPTER 33

A funeral in June was one of the cruellest things anyone could ever have to face. When there were lambs in the field and the whole of the natural world was blooming and blossoming, it seemed so cruel to have to say goodbye to a friend.

Anna was still completely shaken by Meg's death. At first, she had gone into some kind of shock. She'd spent days wandering around her house, too numb to do anything but cry. Then the anger had set in both with herself and with Meg.

'Why did you have to die, Meg? You weren't meant to die. You've lived this long – why go now? I wasn't ready to say goodbye – not yet!'

Both William and Mrs Boothby had left messages about the funeral.

'You will come, won't you?' Mrs Boothby had said. 'We so want to see you.'

Anna hadn't rung back.

The funeral was taking place at St Mark's church in the village of Fox Hill. Anna had been invited to join William and Mrs Boothby to leave with the hearse from the house but she couldn't bear the thought of that and so arrived directly at the church once the rest of the guests had arrived, taking a seat at the back.

She couldn't help thinking that there were a lot of people there considering Meg had known so few in recent years. But the inevitable publicity had meant a huge turnout which included the press who at least had the decency to remain in the churchyard.

Despite the warmth of the June morning, the church was bone-chillingly cold and Anna's hands were soon drained of their warmth. Looking down at them, she remembered her gloved hand holding Meg's on the London bus tour and when she'd left her dear friend wearing her scarlet gloves in the hospital. A sad smile crossed her face. She would never hold those frail old hands again, would she?

Her eyes filled with tears. She'd only known Meg a few short weeks and yet she'd left such an impression on her. She had been like no other person Anna had ever known and she wasn't ready to lose her.

She looked around at the other people in the church. They were chatting away and nodding to each other as if this was some kind of social club instead of a funeral. They hadn't known Meg, had they? Perhaps they'd read about her in the papers and thought it would be fun to go to a celebrity funeral. They might even get in the papers themselves. Anna's eyes flashed daggers at them and yet she knew that she was the main reason they were there today. If it hadn't been for her, Meg's story would still be a well-kept secret. She couldn't blame these people for being there; she'd wilfully encouraged their curiosity.

But how she wished she hadn't. William had been right. Meg had been too frail to cope with the excitement and attention.

Anna felt her eyes fill with tears again and then realised everyone was standing up. The coffin had arrived. It was tiny – more like a child's than a woman's but there were four strong pallbearers to take its weight and William and Mrs Boothby followed behind. Anna watched, wondering if William would see her and half hoping, half dreading that he would but his eyes were fixed on the floor and she watched as he slowly marched to the front of the church.

There followed a half hour of hymns and readings and then something unexpected happened: William got up and stood in the pulpit.

'Meg left me a short letter,' he announced to the congregation. 'One of the nurses at the hospital wrote it for her and I'd like to read it now.' He reached in his pocket and found the piece of paper which he slowly unfolded before clearing his throat and reading Meg's words.

'I hate funerals and goodness knows I've been to more than my fair share of them. When you live to be as old as me, you learn that funerals shouldn't be places of sadness. They should be places of celebration. Life is a gift and yet so many of us rush through it, taking it for granted. We don't stop and just sit and look at the view.'

Anna gasped, wondering if Meg had been thinking about their special seat up at Chamber's Cross.

'And we should. We should all make time to just be. Now, that's not easy in today's society. Life has a way of sucking up time like one of them vacuum cleaners.'

There was a little round of laughter in the church at that line.

'But you shouldn't allow it to do that. It's up to you to claim it back and that's what I want you to remember about me,' William continued, reading Meg's words and then he paused, briefly looking up at the congregation before him. Anna's breath caught in her throat. Would he see her? But he didn't and his eyes slid back down to the piece of paper before him.

'Don't remember me because I was a certain age. What does that mean, anyway? Remember me because I loved my life. I did my best to live it to the full and to have new experiences and meet different people, and some of my friends helped me to do that right up until the very end and I want to thank them for that. I also want to share a favourite poem of mine.'

William then read out the A E Housman poem, *Loveliest of trees, the cherry now.*

When he came to the end, he wasn't the only one in the church with tears in his eyes.

Anna stayed until the coffin had been carried outside for its journey to the crematorium. Mrs Boothby had let Anna know that Meg had left instructions to be cremated and scattered in the Elm Valley but Anna didn't feel up to taking part in the service. As she walked out into the graveyard, a number of photographers jostled forward.

'Anna!'

'Over here, love!'

'Just one more.'

Anna did her best to hide her face but it was then that she saw William.

'Anna?' he called but she didn't want to talk to him and left the churchyard quickly, getting into her car and driving round the country lanes at a lethal speed.

She didn't want to go home yet – couldn't stand the thought of being enclosed by those silent walls. Instead, she headed to Chamber's Cross and the seat she now thought of as Meg's. Parking her car, she got out and walked away from the road. Her eyes were blurred by tears and she could barely see the few feet in front of her let alone the view across the valley but at least she was alone. There was nobody here to blame her.

Except herself.

She let the tears flow freely down her cheeks as she cursed herself again and again. What had she done? What right had she to do that to Meg?

She thought of Meg's last words to her:

'I've so enjoyed our time together. All of it. Every minute.'

Had she? Had she truly? Or was that just something to say to assuage Anna's guilt? She'd never know now.

'Oh, Meg! I'm sorry. I'm so sorry,' she whispered.

She wasn't sure how long she'd sat there but, all of a sudden, she realised how cold she was. She'd left her jacket in the car and the thin sleeves of her dark dress were no warmth in the breeze which had picked up since she'd arrived.

She was just getting up from the bench when a voice called her name.

'Anna!'

She turned around and came face to face with William. 'What are you doing here?'

'I called after you at the church. Why didn't you come and talk to me?'

She looked at him, all emotion draining away from her. 'What's there to say?' she said hopelessly.

'What do you mean? We have *everything* to say to each other.'

Anna shook her head.

'I followed you here. You were driving like a mad woman and I was worried sick about you. What have you been doing with yourself? Hiding away and not answering your phone.'

'Leave me alone.'

'I won't leave you alone,' he said, clasping her arm with his hand. She felt its warmth through the thin fabric of her sleeve. 'And you look so pale.'

She tried to hide her face from him but his other hand reached out and cupped it. 'Anna!'

She looked up at him. His eyes were bright. 'You're pale too,' she said in a whisper.

'I'm always pale. It comes from spending an unnatural amount of time indoors with antiques,' he said with an attempt at a smile but he couldn't raise one from her.

'I'm not coming back. Please don't make me. I don't think I could bear to see her coffin again,' Anna said, shaking off his hands and moving away from him.

'That's not why I came after you.'

'Then why?'

William sighed. 'Because I'm worried about you.'

'No you're not.'

William frowned. 'Why do you keep contradicting me? I'm not lying to you. I don't go driving after mad women and telling them lies when I should be attending a cremation.'

They stared at each other, the breeze ruffling William's hair and blowing Anna's across her face.

'I wanted to give you this,' he said at last. 'It's a letter – from Meg. The nurse wrote it for her.'

'For me?' Anna's mouth went dry with anticipation. Meg had left her a letter.

'Go on,' William said, 'read it.'

Anna's desperate fingers reached out and she unfolded the sheet of paper. 'You've read it?'

William nodded.

Anna took a deep breath and read the letter.

My dear Anna – how hard it is for me to say goodbye. You've been such a good friend to me and my last days with you were amongst the very best of my life. Wasn't it an adventure? If only I had more time to remember it but I don't. I feel that my time here is done now but I so want to leave something behind – my story. Will you write it for me? You said you would. It would be my way of living just a little longer and I know you'll do a splendid job of it.

Take care of yourself, my dear, and take care of William. He needs the love of a good woman and I've never found better than you.

Meg.

Anna read the letter through again before folding it in half and clasping it to her chest.

'She doesn't blame me,' Anna said.

'Of course she doesn't. Nobody does,' William said.

'But I thought you did.'

William sighed. 'I did at first. I was furious with you. But that fury was born out of fear for Meg. When I realised she'd had such a great time with you, it was impossible to stay angry.'

'But you still hate me for all the trouble I've caused.'

'What on earth do you mean? I've never hated you! I couldn't possibly hate you,' William said. 'I *love* you.'

Anna looked at him, her eyes shimmering with tears. 'What?'

'I love you,' William repeated. 'What? You don't believe me? You want me to shout it out across the whole valley? I LOVE YOU!'

A sudden laugh exploded from Anna. 'William!'

'I LOVE Y-O-U!' William grinned, his pale face lighting up for the first time in weeks. 'Don't tell me you didn't know!'

'But I thought I'd ruined any chance of anything happening between us' she said, her eyes crinkling as she tried to comprehend what was happening.

William shook his head. 'You're joking! How could you think that?'

Anna's mouth dropped open. 'Because you shouted at me and kept me at arm's length and didn't let me see Meg–'

'Oh, God! You must have hated me!'

Anna bit her lip. This seemed like the time for confessions. 'No,' she said, 'I never hated you. 'I think I loved you too.'

William's eyes widened. 'Why didn't you say something?'

'Why didn't *you* say something?' she said.

'Because you seemed more interested in Meg than me!' William said. 'I couldn't compete with her even after that rather wonderful kiss.'

'I'm sorry,' Anna said. 'I'm so sorry. I've never behaved so badly in my life. It's just – Meg–'

'I know,' William said, 'we'll never meet anyone like her again, will we?'

Anna shook her head. 'I miss her so much.'

'Me too,' William said. 'But she wants you to write her book.' He paused. 'That was the last thing she said to me.'

'Was it?'

'Well, that and something else.'

'What?' Anna asked, noticing that William was blushing.

'She put it in your letter too,' he said. 'She told me that I needed the love of a good woman.'

Anna looked down at the ground. 'Well, that rules me out of things.'

William stepped forward. 'But Meg said you were *my* good woman.'

'But I don't feel like a good woman.'

'No? You look pretty good to me,' William said. 'Apart from all that mascara down your face and those teary cheeks.'

Anna quickly wiped her face with the back of her hand.

'Here,' William said, 'let me.' And he took her face in his hands and kissed it all over. 'I've missed you,' he whispered. 'When you left Fox Hill, I wandered around like a lost thing.'

'You did?'

'Yes. I couldn't think of anything but you. Ever since you arrived with your funny little notepad and your endless questions. I've never felt this way before.

You know,' he said, 'you're the first woman to make me forget about my collection.'

Anna looked up at him, perplexed. 'What do you mean?'

'I totally forgot about an auction the other week. Missed out on a medieval sword I've been after for years!'

'But how's that my fault?'

'Because I was thinking about you,' he said.

'You see,' Anna said, 'I'm no good for you.'

'But you *are*!' William said. 'You make me feel – *real*!' He was smiling again.

'But your collection–'

'Is just a collection. I love it, of course,' William said, 'but I'm not *in* love with it.'

Anna looked up at him and their eyes locked together. 'You're in love with me?'

'Yes! How many times do I have to tell you?'

'Once more would be nice,' Anna said, a little smile tickling the edges of her mouth.

'Anna McCall, I'm in love with you!' he said, eyes bright, his hair blowing in every direction at once.

'Then I guess it's all right to say that I'm in love with you too,' Anna said, her hair whipping across her face. William brushed it away and bent down to kiss her. His lips were warm and Anna forgot all about being cold as his arms folded around her.

When they parted, she looked up at him. 'Aren't you going to be late?'

He looked at his watch. 'You're right. I'd better get going. I'll see you later, won't I?' He started to make his way back to his car.

'William?'

'Yes?'

'I want to come with you.'

'But I thought you said you didn't want to.'

Anna took a deep breath. 'I should be there – for Meg. And for you.'

'Are you sure?'

Anna nodded and gave a small smile, knowing that she could face anything with William by her side.

They headed back to their cars but, before getting in, they took one last look at the view. The wind was dropping now and the sun was peeping out from behind a huge white cloud, turning the valley golden-green.

'You brought Meg up here, didn't you?' William asked.

'Yes,' Anna said with a sigh.

'Did she like it?'

'She loved it. It's why I came here today. I feel close to her here.'

They looked at each other and they both knew what they were thinking.

'She'd want to be here, wouldn't she?' William said.

Anna nodded. 'I think so.'

William gave a little smile and then the two of them drove back into the heart of the Elm Valley, secure in the knowledge that it would always be their home and happy now that it would be Meg's too.

ABOUT THE AUTHOR

Victoria Connelly was brought up in Norfolk and studied English literature at Worcester University before becoming a teacher. After getting married in a medieval castle in the Yorkshire Dales and living in London for eleven years, she moved to rural Suffolk where she lives with her artist husband and a mad Springer spaniel and ex-battery hens.

Her first novel, *Flights of Angels*, was published in Germany and made into a film. Victoria and her husband flew out to Berlin to see it being filmed and got to be extras in it. Several of her novels have been Kindle bestsellers.

To hear about future releases sign up for Victoria's newsletter at: victoriaconnelly.com/newsletter

Or, visit her website: victoriaconnelly.com

She's also on Facebook and Twitter @VictoriaDarcy

ALSO BY VICTORIA CONNELLY

Austen Addicts Series
A Weekend with Mr Darcy
The Perfect Hero
published in the US as Dreaming of Mr Darcy
Mr Darcy Forever
Christmas with Mr Darcy
Happy Birthday, Mr Darcy
At Home with Mr Darcy

Other Fiction
A Summer to Remember
Wish You Were Here
The Runaway Actress
Molly's Millions
Flights of Angels
Irresistible You
Three Graces
It's Magic (A compilation volume: Flights of Angels, Irresistible You and Three Graces)
Christmas at the Cove
A Dog Called Hope

Short Story Collections
One Perfect Week and other stories
The Retreat and other stories
Postcard from Venice and other stories

Non-fiction
Escape to Mulberry Cottage
A Year at Mulberry Cottage

Children's Adventure
Secret Pyramid

Printed in Great Britain
by Amazon.co.uk, Ltd.,
Marston Gate.